TOO SMART T(

by

Tom Bryson

A Matt Proctor novel

Published by TJB E-BOOKS on Lulu

ISBN: 978-1-4477-2660-9

You can visit the author's website at:
www.tombrysonwriter.co.uk

For Jane

I would like to thank friends and fellow members of those writing communities I have had the privilege of belonging to, who have supported and encouraged me in my writing. You know who you are.

My sincere thanks to former West Midlands Police Detective Chief Inspector Robin Hancox for his generous time and advice on police homicide investigations (Any 'procedural' flaws in the novel are solely the author's and artistic licence!)

A contribution from the sales of this novel goes to Rotary International's PolioPlus campaign for the eradication of polio worldwide.

Prologue

A good night for killing.

The Man watched the young university student hurry up steep concrete steps in the city centre square, late for his bus. Up past the rain-soaked statue of a huge nude woman sitting cross-legged in icy water. Birmingham's 'Floozie in the Jacuzzi'.

The swirl from a water fountain hit The Man's face; he sweated even though it was a bitterly cold, wet November night. Standing with majesty overlooking the square, an austere statue of Queen Victoria peered down, dripping disapproval.

He watched the student. He remembered Iraq. That was his first time. Been here before.

A couple of young women sprinted to the Town Hall entrance late for a concert, their heels piston tapping on glistening paving blocks. Rain whipped their faces. The front of house attendant ushered them through, darted a quick look around the square. He slammed shut the door; the show about to commence.

The Man lowered his head, dropped his shoulders in a slouch.

He knew the time was near. Too wild a night for strollers. This was the feeling. This was right. He had stalked Dominic Masters for weeks. A creature of habit was Masters, from Uni to the cyber café off Corporation Street, then along Colmore Row past the Council House heading for the bus stop on Broad Street. Number 226 - the ten past seven. Tonight Dominic Masters would not be boarding the bus. Tonight he'd die.

Adrenalin surged through The Man's veins. He would do it, he would; tonight. Soon, soon, very soon. In a public place, not skulking in a back alley, but in the open like a true warrior. This was what the feeling was like in the game. Only this was for real. A rush, a blast of power; just as it was those times in Iraq. They were real; perfect garrottings - whether the victim was an Iraqi civilian or a Sunni militant didn't matter. Sergeant McCartney gave him a right bollocking afterwards - didn't like that. But it was Job Done. Another kill. That was when he'd got the taste.

Later, yet another kill. He recalled squaddies shouting, screaming across the desert, calling for medics. He hadn't moved, didn't want to. Remained still, watching, features immobile, listening, smelling, then sucking in hot air, feeling his lungs expand, holding in the air, his chest about to explode. He wanted to raise his arm in celebration, like a rabid football fanatic among fellow devotees celebrating a goal. But it wasn't a moment to share. No, a private moment, his secret, and his triumph. Something to savour alone, the way he preferred things.

He had moved across the desert mound to get the right line of fire - the line that brought McCartney squarely in his sight. Gunfire and rockets blasting all around. He hated that bastard - telling him what to do, rollicking him. Humiliating him in front of other squaddies - he was not to be scorned, he knew the day would come, the opportunity present itself and, sure enough, 'dut dut dut' from the semi-automatic rifle. Right between the eyes. Skull shattered. Gone. Dead. McCartney no more. Friendly fire...ho ho ho...

McCartney's body was soon recovered by medics, dragged away. The Man waited until they were clear, crawled to the site of the kill. Scooped brain tissue blown from the shattered skull into his hands, looked around, nobody watching; raised his hands to his mouth. He was intelligent, had read about it, and knew the score. Martin wrote to him, explained how it worked, he'd studied all that kuru stuff. Clever kid Martin, a good clansman. Not like Dominic Masters, an enemy clansman - his next victim.

Now in the centre of the second city on a brass monkey's winter night he was about to relive those moments in Iraq. No problem; this time he would take out a new kind of enemy - a cyber enemy.

A young couple scurried up New Street, eating steaming hot dogs, their heads nuzzled together against the freezing rain, the smell of scorched fried onions whisked away into the night. Sheets of rain-laden wind howled about them, drove the pair for shelter in The Pizza Factory doorway.

On the steps by the fountain, a trio of young girls tugged their jacket hoods tighter and scurried off along Colmore Row. Outside the front doors of the Victorian City Council house, a drunk puked up six pints of Foster's lager. Across the square, the magnificently restored Town Hall flaunted its multi million pounds makeover; squared up to the deafening elements.

The Man felt good. This was what it was all about. He rubbed his hands down his trousers to dry the sweat, closed his eyes to savour the moment, the thrill of it all. He put his hand into his overcoat pocket and felt for the plaited wire. Rabbit snares - as a boy he would watch rabbits wriggle in pain after a night tangled in a snare. He would linger, flat on his belly, watch the stupid animals twist and turn for ages, watch the wire cut deeper and deeper into fur and flesh, watch and grin until the suffering ended, the creature collapsed, became still. At the instant of death he felt euphoric; the end, the moment, the beautiful moment of death. Then anger; the moment gone. But he knew there would be another time. Another snare, another kill.

He gripped the wire, pulled himself to his full height, and looked around - at the puking drunk; the young couple eating hot dogs as they sheltered in the shop doorway in New Street, glimpsed in snatches through the blustery rain, snogging between bites of hot dog. Some loud-mouthed guys shoved and pushed each other as they ran up the steps in Chamberlain Square, past the Central Library heading for the bridge over Paradise Circus into Broad Street's clubland. He smiled, checked himself and stopped; attract no attention, be invisible, be quick. His eyes stung, his ears blasted by the stinging wind.

The Uni student, Dominic Masters, was just six feet away, moving fast. Skinny, wispy hair on his chin, rain smeared glasses.

The Man removed the wire and held an end in each hand. Look, check, nobody watching - he stepped up past the big reclining nude statue. Be quick. A heavy squall of rain deepened the gloom, made the night darker. He ran from behind; threw the wire around Master's neck. With his strong, fleshy hands, he pulled the wire tight. Tighter and tighter. He heard a rabbit-like squeal. Masters struggled, froze, fought again, weakened, became still, still and limp. In an act of care, The Man lowered the sagging body down onto the stone steps.

Nobody looking; the drunk held a hand against the Council House wall to steady himself, swayed, lost his balance and fell over. Across the square The Town Hall doors remained shut, the entertainment begun.

He drew a big breath, savoured the moment, loved it, just loved it. Power. He pocketed the wire. Now for the sacred moment. But quickly. He dragged the battery-powered drill from a deep pocket inside his long overcoat. He forced the one-inch diameter, carbide tipped hole cutter bit hard against Master's forehead; hit the trigger, dug deep.

Chapter 1

Detective Chief Inspector Matt Proctor looked up yet again from his computer screen willing the phone to ring. He hated 'paperwork'; wanted a reason to get out of the office. But he was behind with reports, as his boss Chief Superintendent Emma O'Rourke was quick enough to remind him. Proctor liked results; Emma liked everything done by the book.

'All our villains having a day off?' Proctor said.

DS Stevie Cole sat opposite snorted, 'Don't you believe it, Action Man.'

Proctor tapped in another sentence, dragged his hand through his thick black hair - greying at the temples - wondered if he dared follow his daughter Sarah's advice. He hadn't seen her much since his divorce, but felt elated every time she did come round to see him. He thought about what she'd said.

'Try some gel, dad, it's cool.'

At forty-one, he wasn't sure it was the right time to start using hair gel. He glanced around at his colleagues, smiled, and imagined their comments.

'Something amusing you, Chief Inspector?'

Proctor leaned back in his chair, 'What do you think of men's hair gel, Emma?'

O'Rourke compressed her lips, 'That is a matter on which I don't have an opinion.'

A voice piped up from across the office, 'All depends where you put it.' DS Stevie Cole grinned at Proctor.

O'Rourke rolled her eyes, 'Matt, I need to have a word, can you come through please?'

Proctor dragged in a long breath; he wanted to finish this shit now he'd started. He saved his report and pulled his long legs from under the desk. How long would she take?

As he followed O'Rourke's squat figure into her office he heard laughter from behind and turned to see DS Cole toss his head from side to side and tug at his hair, a gesture picked up straight away by several others. O'Rourke looked straight ahead but gave a slight shake of her head while Proctor stuck his hand behind his neck and gestured a two-finger salute. Bloody well have you, Coley, he thought.

'I've been looking at your caseload.' O'Rourke stared at her computer screen as she spoke, 'I think you need to do some reprioritising.'

'What did you have in mind?'

'We need to do more on drug crimes.'

'Yes, we probably do.' He thought about his unfinished reports. Come on, come on.

'So - I suggest you put your category C homicide on the back burner for the time being. I've got these files for you to look at and liaise with the drug squad.'

Proctor grabbed the files and flicked through them, 'Why are drugs moving up the agenda, Emma?'

'We want a clean city, Matt. You know that?'

Proctor tapped a file with his finger, 'I thought dealers - especially big time operators - were our priority.' He turned a page for O'Rourke to see, 'I mean Baz Manning - he uses and does a bit of dealing on the side. Hardly Mr Big.'

'We need to make an impact on numbers - fast. You're not the only one having work reassigned.'

'Class C drug dealing?' Proctor held up the files, 'Above domestic homicide? Above knife crime?'

O'Rourke shrugged, 'Senior management edict. Ours is not to reason why...'

Through the glass partition walls, Proctor could see a commotion and hear raised voices. His pulse quickened as DS Cole hurried over. Irritated, O'Rourke looked up as Stevie Cole's knock preceded his head popping around the door.

'Sorry to interrupt, boss. Uniformed just reported nasty homicide in Victoria Square - outside the Council House.'

Proctor looked out to where Inspector Azzra Mukherjee held up a phone. He gave her a nod.

Cole said, 'Azzra's got uniformed on hold.' He grimaced, 'Press already there. Some big 'do' on at the Council House tonight.'

'Shit,' O'Rourke scowled.

'What 'do' is that?' Proctor said.

'Announcing a major piece of news,' she said.

'Oh, yes. Reducing the Council taxes then?'

O'Rourke remained tight lipped, 'An election launch. Our esteemed police authority chairman is to stand as the next MP.'

'I see,' said Proctor getting to his feet.

'I haven't finished yet.'

'Councillor Bullivant standing on a platform of reducing drugs crime in the city by any chance?'

O'Rourke blanked Proctor, 'You'd better get over there.'

He moved fast towards the door; she pointed to the files lying on the desk. 'Don't forget those.'

Proctor grabbed the files and crashed them down on his desk in the general office. He took the phone held by Azzra and listened as the police sergeant at the other end described the incident. He interrupted him, 'Have you secured the scene, Sergeant Harris?'

'Yes sir, tape cordon in place. I'm attending with PC Dear.'

'Good, I'm on my way. Doctor?'

'Police surgeon on his way, sir. Doctor Mackenzie. Bit of a crowd gathering. Press boys too. Filthy night out here, sir.'

'I'll raise SOCOs. But scene needs protecting right away. Be careful - no contamination.'

Alongside him, DS Cole smiled and shook his head. 'All CSI's now, sir.'

'You watch too many American cop shows.'

Proctor looked across his desk and returned Azzra's concentrated stare. She was putting on her jacket even before he spoke. Just been working in his team a couple of months having been fast tracked from uniformed and the more he saw of her the more he liked. He shouted, 'Stevie - get SOCOs to scene. Azzra - with me.'

Chapter 2

The young uniformed officer's tense expression turned to relief as Proctor strode towards him accompanied by Azzra and DS Cole. An ambulance's flashing blue lights flickered through the slashing rain and sparkled the wet block paving.

'Everything under control, constable?' Proctor glanced at his watch.

The officer frowned at the growing crowd of onlookers under umbrellas, 'Think so, sir.'

The body of a young man lay face down, head on one side, arms straight alongside the torso. A pool of sticky blood darkened the wet ground around his head and shoulders.

An attending paramedic shook his head, 'Nothing we can do here?' He pointed at an open wound in the centre of the man's forehead. 'I think you've got a right weirdo on the loose.'

A young man and woman nearby huddled together shivering under a flimsy umbrella. Stood next to them a uniformed council security man added in a self important voice, 'I phoned emergency services when this young lad here ran in telling us he'd found someone with his throat cut - looks to me like he was throttled - and shot. You can tell by the...' Proctor gave him a withering glance and he shut up.

Proctor said, 'You two were the first to reach the body?' Both indicated yes. The young woman said, 'I think I saw someone...thing...by the fountain.'

15

The security man jabbed a thumb in the direction of the council house. 'All hell's broken loose inside. Big nobs everywhere.' He pulled up his lower lip, 'These two a bit shook up both of 'em. Likely first time they've seen anything...'

Proctor interrupted, 'Azzra take them both inside - they look frozen - and have a quick word. I'll join you soon. Get the medics' and security people's details too, will you?' He wiped driving rain from his face with the back of his hand and pointing to the Council House entrance said to the security man, 'You too.'

Azzra touched the girl's arm and said, 'What's your name?'

'Joanne.'

'Right, Joanne. We'll see if we can get you a hot coffee.'

'You'll be lucky,' the security man snorted. 'Vending machine's packed up.'

Azzra guided Joanne and her boyfriend away. 'Please follow me,' she said and strode out leading the paramedic and a reluctant security officer towards the building.

Proctor spoke to the constable, 'What's your name?'

'Constable Dear, sir' quickly adding, 'Tim.'

'Good job so far, Tim. Sergeant Harris phoned in, where is he?'

'Ah...inside, sir.'

'Try to keep the zoo watchers at bay, will you?' The young PC appeared pleased to have a task, 'Yes, sir,' he said and moved off.

'Right, Stevie, let's have a look then?' Proctor opened his portable bag and donned a protective white suit, overshoes and gloves. DS Cole said, 'Come on, boss. Wait for SOCOs?'

'Let's go, Stevie. Right?' Cole did not hear it as a question.

'Pro tem you're crime scene manager until Eric Cantwell gets here - we'll need to set up a HOLMES team for this. Sort roles back in the station.' He studied the victim for a few seconds then said, 'Put a chaser on Doc Mackenzie. Sooner he gets here the better.' Cole got on his mobile phone keeping a wary eye on his boss as he punched in Mac's number.

Proctor reached into the back pocket of the victim's jeans and slid out a battered cloth wallet. He opened it; Block Busters video/DVD hire card, City of Birmingham library card, Aston University student union card, a few receipts, a bus ticket, a Centro student rail and bus travel card, a handwritten list of websites, two five pound notes, a fold out pocket containing several pound coins and loose change, a well used crumpled handkerchief. He glanced over at PC Dear busy moving people back and removed the websites list, inserted it into a small plastic evidence bag that he sealed and folded inside his notebook. Cole watched him and shook his head while he checked Doc Mackenzie's whereabouts.

Proctor slipped the wallet back into the dead man's back pocket minus the list. He stood up and entered the name on the railcard into his notebook; 'Dominic Masters'.

Red spots and blotches speckled the young man's pasty face and a deep gash of torn flesh encircled his neck where the garrotte had cut through. Kneeling down Proctor peered at the hole in the centre of his head. He whistled and thought how you could put your thumb in it. Yet there was no tissue on the ground, no exit wound for a bullet. He stood up noting the faded denims, a tear across the left knee, grey tee-shirt darkened halfway down his back and chest by the congealing blood, black zip up fleece, scuffed trainers with the laces undone. A pair of rimless thick-lensed glasses clung to one ear. His fleece had ridden up revealing thin, pale arms and wrists. Proctor pursed his lips when he noted the needle marks and faded slash-marked scar tissue. He stepped back under the 'Police Do Not Cross' tape and removed his protective suit and overshoes and gloves and returned them to his bag.

He left Cole at the scene and walked towards the Council House as a team of white suited scene of crime officers arrived with a folded tent. The remains of a spewed up hot dog lay in a pool of water by the Council House wall, parts of sausage still recognisable. Proctor wiped a drip from the end of his nose and thought how much he would prefer to be out on the golf course on a summer's day with his old friend and mentor Ron Kydd, choosing whether to hit a chip and run shot with a seven iron or play a subtle wedge. Or enjoying a fine meal with friends, chatting, putting the world to rights all washed down with a bottle of best French Merlot. But this was what he did; murder and mayhem were his stock in trade. This was what got him out of bed in the morning. And he loved it.

Inside the council house, the pale-faced young man and his girlfriend clung to each other by the reception desk alongside Sergeant Harris. Azzra was nearby taking details from the security man and the paramedic.

The Sergeant produced a notebook that Proctor ignored, shaking his head. 'Too cold for you outside, was it? Go and give young Tim a hand.' Harris glowered and sloped out into the wet night.

Azzra said, 'I think we've done with the paramedic and security?'

Proctor said, 'Yes, thanks for now.' He signalled to the paramedic, 'I think you can get back to work, thanks again.'

The security officer stayed put. 'And you,' Proctor said. He looked disconsolate as he ambled towards the reception desk.

Proctor took the names and contact details of the young couple. 'So - Terry, Joanne, you two were the first to see the body?'

The young man swallowed hard as he spoke, his hand covering his mouth. 'Thought maybe he was a drunk, druggie, or something at first then I saw all the...' He waved his arm towards the dead body sprawled outside where SOCOs were erecting a white tented cover. The girl sniffed and wiped her eyes, 'It was horrible, really horrible.'

'I know, I know.' Proctor said. 'Now, Terry, Joanne just take your time over this. Think back over the few minutes before you approached the body. Don't rush. Try to remember what was happening and who was about. Will you do that?'

They looked uncertain; Proctor spoke in a quiet voice, 'Okay, Terry, let's start with you.' He seemed tongue-tied so Proctor said, 'Joanne thinks she saw someone near the fountain. What about you?'

He thought for a moment, 'No, no, can't remember seeing anyone.' Proctor waited. 'Hang on, yes, maybe there was a guy come to think about it.'

'Can you describe him?'

'Hard to say, wasn't really looking. Atrocious weather.'

'Try. Young, old? Tall, short? Jacket, overcoat? Hood, beanie?'

'Kind of...heavy, you know?'

'Fat?'

'No, not fat, more meaty like. Tallish, maybe six feet.'

'Hair colour? Headgear?'

'No, no, can't say.'

'Can you remember anything he wore?'

'Not sure, no - he kind of slouched, you know, head down.'

Proctor asked a few more questions. 'Thanks Terry, you've been a big help. We'll chat with you again but don't worry.'

He turned to the girl, Joanne, asked her to tell him what she saw.

They had travelled into Birmingham New Street station by train from Stourbridge and walked up New Street planning to have a coffee in MacDonald's before going to see a play at The Door in The Rep. A heavy squall of rain made them take shelter at the top of New Street in the Pizza Factory doorway. When they climbed the steps leading to Victoria Square, they saw the prone body. They approached tentatively but as soon as they saw the pool of blood around the man's neck Terry ran into the council house and alerted a security officer who phoned 999. The security man returned and felt for a pulse, said he was dead. He stayed by the body with Terry and Joanne as a few passers-by hurried on without showing much interest.

'And you and the security officer stayed there until Sergeant Harris and PC Dear arrived?'

'Yes, yes, that's it.'

Proctor recalled Sergeant Harris's phone conversation and wondered how long he had waited before seeking the shelter of the council house and leaving the young couple outside to freeze. He hated timeservers.

Joanne was more observant than her boyfriend. She mentioned seeing two young women running towards the Town Hall. She remembered the sound of their heels and noticed one wore red shoes and the other green.

'I love shoes, you see. I always notice what shoes people are wearing.' Proctor smiled as she glanced down at his feet, 'You see I love buying new shoes.' She also talked about a drunken guy puking by the Council House and pointed, 'Look, he's still out there.'

Proctor moved to get a better view out from the doorway and watched the man struggle to his feet, prop both hands against the building; thought 'Not going to get much from him.' He said, 'You said you think you saw a figure near the fountain, right?' She gulped and struggled to speak.

'It's all right, Joanne, take your time.' She shivered in her skimpy mauve top and short cream skirt with a wide white belt tightened around her slim waist. He caught a whiff of strong scent.

Not for the first time he wondered why girls wore so little on the coldest of nights. He remembered the pitying look Sarah once gave him when he had said as much as she got ready for a night on the town.

Proctor's phone rang. He checked to see who was calling. 'Azzra, I'll take this call, you carry on here.' He moved outside towards the crime scene.

'What have you got, Matt?' Emma O'Rourke sounded uptight.

'Prima facie homicide. Young man called Dominic Masters according to his wallet.'

'Christ, Matt, you been rifling around before the SOCOs have done their searches.'

'Cordon in place. I was suited, Emma, but we need to move fast.'

'Listen, Matt, what we need to do is secure and preserve the scene. Then the SOCOs do their work. You know how fussy CPS is these days over cross contamination. Why on earth do you think we have procedures?'

Proctor held the phone away from his ear and counted one-two-three. She said, 'The press will have a field day. They must think it's murder by appointment. TV boys will be there in no time for the big show.' A heavy sigh travelled down the line as O'Rourke exhaled, 'Police chairman will be there in a few minutes. You're Senior Investigating Officer from now.'

'I assumed that.'

'You've got Inspector Mukherjee with you, right?'

'Yes, and Stevie Cole's here too. I'll make Azzra my deputy and Stevie office manager.'

'Shall you indeed?'

'Def a HOLMES job.

'You think we've got infinite resources?'

'Is there a problem?'

21

O'Rourke was quiet for a few seconds then said, 'You deal with the media. Bare facts, Matt, got it? Any sign of dignitaries yet?'

Proctor looked across the square. A black Bentley slid to a stop outside the Council House, met by a town hall official who whipped open the car doors. From the rear door a small, sharp-suited man emerged who shot past the official, ignoring his outstretched hand. Proctor said, 'I think your man's arrived.'

'My man? What are you talking about?'

'Mr Gerald Bullivant, CBE, Chairman of the West Midlands Police Authority, prospective parliamentary candidate for Birmingham Central, moral guardian of the city's deprived and disadvantaged...'

'Proctor, watch it! I'm getting over there.'

'Thanks Emma...' The call cut off before he finished speaking. Proctor stared at his phone; since her husband ran off with their cat's young female vet over a year ago, she was like an assassin hunting down a quarry. He wondered how the cat was getting on.

He pocketed his mobile and watched the police authority chairman stride towards the busy crime scene. The now tented scene and surrounding area teemed with crime scene investigators. A photographer took shots from all angles while another filmed the scene and victim. Proctor gestured over one of the white suited figures who was directing others.

'Eric, how are you? You can take over as Crime scene manager from Stevie?' Proctor smiled at him. Their past paths were strewn with differences but he respected the man's ability. Eric Cantwell was good - but his scenes he protected with the tenacity of an old-fashioned park keeper keeping visitors off the grass. Moreover, his doggedness and caution wore thin Proctor's patience.

'Yes, and listen, Matt, I don't want any of your lot touching anything until we're done, right?'

'Of course. We'll talk about what you've got when you're ready.' So territorial; he thought; Eric, you would be ace in a land grab, lighten up, it's all yours.

Cantwell's job, as Crime Scene manager was to preserve and secure the scene, avoid contamination and ensure a thorough and disciplined approach to evidence gathering. That was the theory - people like Proctor made Cantwell's job hard work.

Stevie Cole appeared at Proctor's side. Proctor said with Cantwell listening, 'No one - and I mean no one - goes across that line without Eric's approval, got it?'

'Yes, sir,' Cole said.

Cantwell crossed his arms and spread his legs, a determined look in his eyes.

'I'm sure we all abide by the rules. Don't we, sir?' Cole said.

'That's it. No shitting on the scene.'

'Of course,' Cole said.

Eric Cantwell looked far from convinced.

'Good evening.' A dapper little man dressed in black evening suit, dark blue bow tie and shining hand stitched leather shoes approached Proctor. He frowned and his head darted this way and that like a wary bird. Our beloved chairman, Proctor thought, here comes trouble. A black suited young man held a large umbrella to protect him from the rain.

'You in charge?' Bullivant looked up at Proctor, 'I want this lot cleared out of the way. You know who I am?'

'Good evening, Chairman. I'm Chief Inspector Proctor, Senior Investigating Officer. We have an apparent homicide sir.'

'Who is it?'

'Forensic team have just started their work so we have yet to identify the victim. Of course before we can release that we will need to inform next-of-kin.'

'Right, right...' he indicated the tent. 'I want to have a look.' The Police Authority Chairman reached for the tape and straight away Eric Cantwell planted a restraining arm on his shoulder.

'I'm sorry, sir, but that's not possible.'

The chairman stared at Cantwell's arm, swallowed several times and glowered, his face flushed.

Proctor intervened, 'I'm sure you'll appreciate that this is a crime scene, sir. It's critical that forensic evidence is protected, I'm sure you understand.'

'What did you say your name was again?'

'Proctor, sir. DCI Proctor.'

'Right, Proctor.' He waved his hand towards the tented area, the investigators and photographers. 'Can we get rid of...all this as soon as possible?' He spoke to the suited umbrella carrier attending him, 'Get the press people inside and away from all this crap.' He looked around again at the massing crowd, photographers, and journalists. He whispered through clenched teeth, 'Listen, Proctor, I want this paraphernalia cleared out of the way asap. Got it?'

'We'll do our best, sir.'

'Good, good, carry on then.'

'Thank you, sir.'

A reporter pushed through the thickening crowd and stuck a recorder in Councillor Bullivant's face, 'Will you be campaigning in the election on making the city a safer place to live in, Chairman?'

Let the circus begin, Proctor thought.

Bullivant forced a smile and stormed off followed by his stumbling umbrella man and a couple more suits clutching mobile phones like comfort blankets. He held a fixed smile to the photographers' flashing cameras as he bustled past them into the Council House.

Proctor exchanged a glance with Cole who cocked an eyebrow; he checked his watch as Bullivant and his entourage disappeared inside then scrutinised the square, looking for a figure, that solitary observing individual trying to be invisible. Certain murder perpetrators had that need - to see the results of their mayhem; satisfy the demands of twisted egos. Nobody stood out for him.

He stepped back into the Council House and suppressed a smile when the security officer he had spoken with earlier leaped up and gave a military style salute. Frantic local government officials ran back and forth across the tiled reception area shouting into mobile phones. They reminded Proctor of traders on the City floor and were most likely doing jobs about as useful.

He located Azzra comforting Joanne and a bewildered looking Terry. Her genuine empathy for the distressed couple struck Proctor but he was disconcerted to find himself staring too long at her strong profile and large brown eyes. He coughed and said, 'Emma's coming over, I'm going to watch out for her. When you've finished here, join me at the scene.' He looked out for Cole but couldn't see him; he tapped a number into his phone.

'Stevie? Where are you?'

'Colmore Row - by St. Pauls.'

'You're not going religious on me, are you?'

'You could do with someone praying for you. I'm with Doc Mackenzie. Will I bring him round to you?'

'Yes, do that.'

Azzra came alongside him. She said, 'I've done with the young lovers.'

Proctor raised a thumb and spoke into the phone, 'No, listen Stevie, tell the Doc to come on his own. I have some websites I want you to look at right away back at the station. And a name, Dominic Masters.'

'You're joking, boss, where...'

'Later. I'm making you my office manager. Set up an incident room in the station. Anyway, you know you're a geek - you'll love it. Now - take a note of these websites.'

'Oh, shit.'

Azzra smiled as Proctor relayed the website addresses from the list inside his notebook. 'That'll make his day,' she said.

'And you're deputy SIO.'

'Thanks, Matt. That's made my day.' She took a deep breath, 'I won't let you down.'

'I know you won't.'

Doc Mackenzie emerged white suited from the tent and joined Proctor and Azzra. His drooping moustache, straight out of a Victorian melodrama exaggerated his doleful face. Although away from Glasgow for the best part of forty years, his glottal stops were as strong as ever, 'Nasty one here, Matt.'

'What do you reckon, wire?'

'Aye. The perp was a big strong guy. Used a lot of force to cut in that deep.'

'And the wound on the victim's forehead.'

'I'll need to get him on the table to check that out.' He stared for several seconds into the murky night, 'You know, it looks like the bastard's removed a solid core of the poor sod's brain.' He pushed his hands against his back and rocked sideways, 'I'm getting too old for this game.'

'You've always been old, Mac.'

'Aye - and you've always been ugly.'

'Touché.'

'Marks on his arms?'

Mackenzie blew out his cheeks, 'Recent drug user. Looks like he was into self-harm when younger.'

'Was in a bit of a mess then.'

'Last mess he'll get into.' He wiped the back of his hand over his moustache, 'You've got one evil bastard out there, Matt. Guessing - but I think this smacks of some ritualistic thing.'

Proctor looked across Victoria Square at a camera wielding young woman in tight jeans and a long flapping coat accompanied by what he took for a schoolboy in a beanie struggling with a boom mike.

'Looks as if the Midlands Today team have arrived. Must put on my best TV manner.'

'Once this gets out you'll need it.'

'That's the spirit, Mac. Cheer me up.'

Azzra smiled, 'What? Going on TV without hair gel?' Doc Mackenzie looked puzzled.

Proctor mouthed 'Bollocks' and stepped out towards the camera crew.

Chapter 3

Tower cranes loomed over Birmingham's Lancaster Circus, their long jibs swung across the dual carriageway like giant insects' proboscises; the ground below Proctor's feet vibrated from juddering pile drivers. It never ends, he thought, no sooner is one edifice built than the developers start another. How many office blocks does the world need anyway?

He made his way to Brasshouse Lane police station and entered the forbidding Victorian era building. His footsteps echoed along the tiled corridor where the young receptionist Martha gave him a broad smile and waved calling, 'Morning, Mr Proctor.' He acknowledged her, smelt the odour of recent paint on the green glossed brick walls; good use being made of police overtime savings there then, God save us from the accountants. He asked if DCI Romney was in. She pulled a face and put her finger in her mouth, said, 'Yes, and he's in a mood - again.' Seemed DCI Romney still suffered from both halitosis and a dearth of goodwill.

Proctor wanted to look in on Tony Romney and take a long shot on Dominic Masters' murder. Romney had been in the Drugs squad a long time and although Proctor did not like the man - they had clashed in the past and if Proctor cut corners, Romney demolished buildings. He was also not averse to fitting up someone if it served his cause. But he had a shedload of contacts accumulated over the years - dealers, users, pimps and pros.

28

Proctor thought he might have heard of Masters, know something that wasn't official, not on the databases.

He was about to enter Romney's office when he heard raised voices. He hesitated and waited outside the just open door.

'I told you he was a prat.' Romney's guttural Black Country accent spat out the words. A short silence. 'Well, ain't he?' More statement than question.

'Yeah, yeah, course he is.' Detective Constable Alan Carpenter talked like a follower; sycophancy his second nature. Proctor also heard fear in his voice.

'We need to get him sorted, mate, right?'

'Right, Tony, def.'

Romney lowered his voice and Proctor got closer to the door. 'I mean, we got a good thing going here. Don't want it ruined, do we?' Another short silence. Proctor hopped back as he heard a fist hammer the desk. 'I said do we?'

'Of course not, Tony, I mean...'

'Hassan's a weak livered shite. He needs a kick up the arse, right?'

'Right, Tony, too right.'

'How much he owes us?'

'How much?'

'Yeah, how fucking much?'

'A couple of grand.'

'Fix a meet. If he wants us to keep shtum, the good dentist needs to cough up.'

Proctor stepped away from the doorway. Hassan, who was Hassan? A distant memory stirred - what was it? Tax dodge or money laundering investigation, something like that. Worked as a dentist. Investigation never got anywhere though. Everyone associated with him clammed up. Suspected drugs dealing though.

But Romney and Carpenter - owed by Hassan? Shit - backhanders?

Proctor threw open the door. Carpenter stared at him wide-eyed, opened and closed his mouth a couple of times.

Across the desk, Romney leaped up, both fists knuckling the desktop.

'Just a couple of grand. Not worth the bother, lads, eh?' Proctor leaned across the desk towards Romney, lowered his voice, 'You still get teeth trouble, Tony?'

Romney pulled his stocky body upright, smiled at Proctor. 'What the hell are you talking about?'

'I'm talking about that well known dentist - and dealer Rajinder Hassan.' He smiled at Romney then spun to Carpenter, 'Need any gold fillings done, Alan?'

Carpenter's colour drained from his face as his eyes darted between Proctor and Romney.

Romney slid around the desk, got close to Proctor, his florid face riddled with small blue veins. He extended a finger and prodded Proctor several times in the chest, 'You mind what you're saying, Matt. Feelings run deep in this station. Wouldn't want to get unpopular, would you?'

Proctor fought not to step back from the smell of bad breath, 'Listen Tony - you too Alan. I just caught a snippet. I don't want to know anymore. So, here's the deal. Jack it in. Like now!'

'Are you threatening, Matt?'

'No, I'm not threatening. Offering a lifeline. Jack it in.'

Carpenter stuttered, 'It's…it's no big deal, Matt. Small time…

'Shut it!' Romney glowered at Carpenter who licked his lips. He spoke softly to Proctor, 'We're a close-knit family in here, Matt. Right?'

'Right, good and bad in families.'

Romney's flushed face reddened deeper; he lunged at Proctor and caught him by the collar, his fleshy hand in a tight grip, 'Don't take me on. I mean police family. We're good.'

Proctor took hold of Romney' closed fist and forced it back into his face. 'That's what I think too. I don't want to push this up the line.'

Romney let go, he extended his hands wide, 'Listen Matt, I think you've got the wrong end of the stick here.'

'Now you're taking the piss.' Proctor pointed his finger at him, 'You heard what I said. Believe me.' He looked from one to the other, turned and left the room.

The gloss painted corridor smelt sicklier than ever, as if an outbreak of Romney's halitosis was spreading throughout the building. Martha glanced up at Proctor as he stormed past then buried her head in her computer screen. Proctor thought he'd truly screwed up any chance of getting a lead from Romney on Master's murder.

Romney sat at his desk, drummed the surface with two fingers while Carpenter paced around chewing his knuckles. Romney leapt to his feet, his voice was contained when he spoke, 'Alan, call Hassan, tell him to keep his head down. If anyone contacts him, he says nothing. And go bring in that little toerag Baz Manning. I want to speak to him.'

'What do you want with Baz, Tony?'

'I want to frighten the shit out of Baz - and stuff Proctor.'

Chapter 4

At home, Matt Proctor viewed the BBC rolling news on television, a plate of scrambled eggs on his lap. He poured a glass of Chilean Merlot. More conflict in the Middle East, an earthquake somewhere south of Tokyo, unemployment at home still rising and yet more economic gloom and doom. He turned on the Sky TV guide - the Villa match was on live starting at eight o'clock. He switched channels; his chocolate Labrador Barney, lolling on a rug stirred, went back to sleep.

His mobile phone rang; he placed his plate on the coffee table and opened the phone, his daughter Sarah was calling.

'Hi Sarah, how are you?'

'Hi Dad, I'm good.'

Proctor waited and her silence spoke to him, he asked, 'Are you okay, love?'

'Yes, yes...'

'But?'

'Dad, can I come home?' Her voice broke and she blurted out her words, 'I want to come back to live with you. Mum's okay but...it's not the same...as home. They both mean well but I feel like a stranger here. Oh, dad, I'm sorry I said some horrible things but I felt terrible when you two split '

'Wait, wait, slow down love, it's all right. It's all right.'

'Can I though? Can I move back in?'

'Of course you can, no problem. Have you spoken to your mum about this yet?'

'Yes, I have.'

'And?'

'Well…she doesn't like it.'

'I'll speak with her then. Now are you sure this is what you want?'

'Yes, I'm sure.'

Proctor wanted to reach down the phone line and hold his eighteen-year-old daughter in his arms. Sure, she was a grown adult but she was still that vulnerable little girl of his. He wished he had kept closer contact since his split with Hannah but believed she had settled in with her mum and the damned car salesman. He bit his tongue.

'When? When can I move back?'

'Straightaway, if that's what you want, Sarah. You know you're always welcome here.'

'Thanks dad, oh, thanks. I love you. It'll be nice, we can have Christmas together.' She hesitated, 'Have you heard from Chris recently?'

Proctor stiffened. His son Chris had taken the break-up between Hannah and him even harder than Sarah.

'Not for a while. I plan to give him a bell.'

'Good. I think you should.'

'You've spoken with him?'

'Yes, we…we've both been a bit stupid…over you and mum.'

'Well, it wasn't easy…for you both.'

'Nor you. We were being selfish. Only thinking about how we felt.'

Proctor rubbed his forehead with his free hand, 'I'll call Chris - tonight. Soon as we're finished.'

'Christmas will be good. I know Chris wants to come down from Uni to see you then. Is that all right?'

'Of course. Yes, that'd be great. Thanks for suggesting it. Oh, by the way Barney misses you - and I love you too.'

'Oh, Barney, I do want to see him. And dad?'

'Yes?'

'There's someone I'd like you to meet.'

'Oh, right, who's that?'

'Phil, someone I've met, I'm going out with him.'

A brief pang of regret struck Proctor but he rallied and said, 'That's good, I'm pleased you've met someone, bring him round.'

'You'll be kind, dad, and no police third degree.'

'No third degree.'

'You're sure it'll be alright?'

'Of course, let's get you back home. I'll clean up your room.'

'Home - that sounds good.'

'Fine - I can pick you up with your things.'

'That'd be great. I can bring some stuff in the Smart.'

'You won't get a quarter of what you have in that.'

She laughed then looked serious. 'I hope you'll like Phil - he works for a steel firm - Hall's, he's a driver there.' She added, 'But he wants to set up on his own soon.'

'Good, good. I look forward to meeting him.' Proctor's heart sank; an image flashed into his mind of a little girl running around a garden with her arms outstretched, angled to right and left, her laughter mixed with her droning aeroplane engine noises.

'Goodnight. And dad, cousin Katie sends her regards.'

'Right, tell her thanks and give her my love. I miss seeing her around - and you.'

'Thanks. She's got a job now. Dead handy. Same firm as Phil, they're expanding. Katie's really thrilled.' Sarah hesitated, 'She's been a good friend.'

Proctor felt he had just been kicked in the balls, 'I'm very pleased to hear that.'

'Right. Good night then, dad.'

'Good night Sarah.'

He closed his phone. Does every dad think there is not a man in the world good enough for his little girl? Get a grip; she is eighteen years of age, a grown up. Still my little girl though. And what was that with Katie. My niece is the one who gives Sarah support when her dad can't make the effort.

He got up and tipped the remains of the scrambled egg into the waste bin. He poured himself a second glass of Merlot and watched Sky Sports. Villa playing Manchester United - he watched for ten minutes but even dazzling football failed to hold his interest. He got halfway down the wine glass when he slammed it down, recorked the bottle and put it in the drinks cabinet. He struggled upstairs with the vacuum cleaner and began cleaning Sarah's room. In a corner of her empty wardrobe, he came across a well-worn stuffed rabbit. He sat on the edge of the bed and stroked his finger along the rabbit's nose, sat there for some time flicking the rabbit's ear, stroking its nose and thinking.

Chapter 5

Proctor paced back and forth across the office of Chief Superintendent Emma O'Rourke's nervous secretary, moving from her desk to a window overlooking the city centre and back again. He hated waiting. For anything: trains, planes, restaurant meals, even others' unfinished sentences.

Julie Anderson tensed as she watched him, working on her PC. Proctor gave her a thin smile and walked back again to look out on the heaving commuter traffic heading home to the suburbs of the city and its wider hinterland - the leafy shire counties of Worcestershire, Warwickshire, Staffordshire and Shropshire, the urban sprawl of the Black Country conurbation. He glanced at his watch for the twentieth time in the past half hour. He hated waiting when work needed doing. This evening he had planned to hold a briefing meeting to review priorities and progress of his team's caseload - the Masters' case needed a fresh impetus. He also had reports to catch up on following the purge on overtime initiated by the new Police Finance Officer. But since O'Rourke's call he'd postponed those jobs and now felt pissed off. What was keeping her anyway? Be here at five o'clock his voice message said; it was now five thirty. He opened his mobile and played the message yet again. 'Matt, Emma here. I need to have an urgent word with you. Straight away please. My office.' A pause, 'Matt, when I say straight away, I mean like now.'

At the sound of her boss's recorded voice, Julie's head popped up like a dog startled from sleep, then her eyes dropped as she resumed her key stroking with more vigour than ever.

'Where is she, Julie?' Proctor's question was more rhetorical than directed at her but Julie felt obliged to say something.

'I'm sure she won't be long now.' Her reassurance carried no conviction.

Proctor heaved a sigh and picked up a copy of the Birmingham Evening Mail just delivered to the office. The lead story was that the Police Authority Chairman Councillor Gerald Bullivant was to stand as the local Party candidate in the forthcoming by-election following the sudden death of the well loved Birmingham born and bred MP Stan Binnion. Elsewhere the paper reported more congestion problems on Spaghetti Junction, a row over the allocation of school places in the city, a confrontation between Right wing extremists and Muslim groups and questions about the lack of progress into the gruesome murder of young Dominic Masters. The latter report included in italics in a note of press incredulity - *on the very steps of Victoria Square outside the City Council House!* Was that what O'Rourke was chasing? It was Proctor's case, he was SIO, and he was responsible for solving the crime.

He turned to the inside page and snorted, causing Julie to glance up at him again. He read about a major new initiative to tackle drug crimes and abuse and 'make the city a clean and fit place for the people of Birmingham to live in'.

'Just before the election, no surprise there then.'

'Pardon?'

'Nothing, Julie, talking to myself.'

Her phone rang and she listened for a time, replaced the receiver and said, 'That was CS O'Rourke. ACC Merritt has moved the meeting to his office. She says can you go there straight away and join them.'

Proctor blinked a couple of times. Merritt? Nobody had said anything about a meeting with the ACC.

Proctor frowned when he reached the door to Assistant Chief Constable Jonathan Merritt's office. His summons had perplexed and unnerved him. Even more so when he saw the closed door. Normally if Merrit expected someone he left his door open in that kind of 'Come on in, we're all friends here' style of informality that he fostered. Proctor liked Merritt, he was easy going without the brusque superciliousness of the old school or the smarmy chumminess of the new breed that got up his nose; university entrant officers wet behind the ears haring along the fast track. He felt the bile rise in his stomach, the sort of moment he used to experience when, in uniform, he wielded a door ram in a house raid not knowing what might be on the other side.

He entered the anteroom where Merritt's secretary indicated the entrance to his office. Proctor rapped on the dark solid oak door and pulled back his shoulders. A familiar thought visited him - this was one more of those times when he wished he were taller than his five feet eleven. He had always targeted the magic six feet. There was a short pause then Merritt's clear, well-enunciated voice. 'Come in.'

Merrit was not alone. Emma O'Rourke sat to the side of the desk. Behind Merritt, a tall man stood staring out the window.

Merritt sat behind a light coloured beech desk devoid of paper as usual; his computer terminal tilted at forty-five degrees, an angle poise lamp on his desk shone a beam of light across the keyboard. He stood up and indicated a chair positioned in front of his desk.

'Please take a seat, Matt.'

'Thank you, sir.' Proctor sat down, letting his solid frame sink into the chair, his chin pushed forward. He crossed his legs and flicked at a speck of imaginary dust on his jacket sleeve.

The other man in the room still gazed out the window. They were on the seventh floor of the multi story police headquarters building that looked down on Colmore Circus in the heart of Birmingham. A train's brakes screeched across the Queensway Ringway from Snow Hill railway station opposite. Emma O'Rourke sat still, her hands folded across her lap. She gave the briefest of nods to Proctor.

Merrit sat down. He rubbed a hand across his eyes, coughed and looked in the direction of the tall, silver haired man with both hands shoved in the trouser pockets of his dark grey suit, a manila folder tucked under his arm.

'This is Chief Superintendent Carson of the Independent Police Complaints Commission.' Carson turned, glanced at Proctor and resumed looking out the window.

Merrit coughed again and Proctor felt a chill in his back. He watched Merritt with unblinking eyes.

'I'll come straight to the point, Matt. This is extremely difficult for me, but there have been…allegations made against you.' He looked round at Carson as if seeking affirmation.

'What allegations…sir?' Proctor fought to keep still, not to leap to his feet and bang his fists on Merritt's desk.

The ACC gestured towards Carson, 'Chief Superintendent?'

Carson walked to the desk, opened his folder, and removed a single sheet of A4 paper.

'Chief Inspector Proctor. This is a matter of professional standards. Here is a copy of a statement from a known drugs dealer in the city. Two experienced officers of this police service corroborate it. The upshot is that we have to investigate allegations that you have been taking bribes and turning a blind eye on Class A drug dealing activities. I have no need to stress the seriousness of these allegations.'

Proctor's anger boiled over as he took in Carson's words. He leapt to his feet. 'I've never heard such bollocks in my life.' He leaned down towards Merritt. 'Jon, what the hell's this all about?'

Merritt appeared wounded and held out his hands palms facing upwards.

Carson waved the sheet of paper in his hand. 'I think, Detective Chief Inspector, this calls for some formality. And decorum. Please sit down.'

Proctor clenched his teeth and slowly resumed his seat.

Carson said, 'Sir?'

Merritt said, 'Go on.'

'This is something we must follow up, DCI Proctor. It is most serious. I think your ACC needs to tell you what happens next.'

Proctor's anger erupted again. He jumped to his feet and leaned on the desk with both hands. 'What happens next is that someone tells me just what these so-called allegations are, who is making them and I'll rip them to shreds.' Merrit winced not missing the ambiguity. The colour drained from Emma O'Rourke's face.

Proctor ran his hands through his hair. He lowered his voice and spoke in measured tones. 'Jon, tell me. You've known me in this force for over twenty years. You know this is all bollocks.'

Merritt leaned back in his chair and weariness crept into his voice. 'Take it easy, Matt. You know the form. I hate this sort of thing but we have to take it forward. We must go into it. Sit down, please.'

Proctor swung towards Carson. 'All right then. I want chapter and verse. I'll show you what kind of bullshit this is. I'm not wearing it, I'm telling you.'

Carson walked over to Proctor and faced him, holding his single sheet of paper, a slight smile crossing his face. 'You may wish to know that The Chief Constable is aware of this interview. He also knows your record, Chief Inspector. A loyal officer; worked up through the ranks from uniformed PC. A good record as a detective officer too.'

'Stop being patronising,' Proctor glowered at Carson.

Merrit threw a disapproving glance at Carson. He held up both hands. 'Matt, please, this isn't easy for any of us. As Chief Superintendent Carson says, the Chief...knows your record of accomplishment and is keen to see...a resolution. We're dealing with...allegations related to drug dealing...which at this moment in time is the last...'

Carson cut across Merritt, 'Sir, we agreed to adhere to procedure.'

'What resolution? What allegations? I've told you, Jon, I'm not taking this lying down. It's bollocks and I'll fight it all way. You know what I think of drug dealers, toerags, scum of the earth, they ruin young lives.' He reached across the desk. 'Here, let me see this statement, who's behind it?'

Carson jumped back, clutching the paper but not before Proctor glimpsed a name emboldened at the top of the statement - Barry (Baz) Manning. As Proctor and Carson tugged, the document ripped.

'Calm down, Matt, please.' Merrit was on his feet, he drew a deep breath. 'Listen, Matt, and understand this is for the best. The Chief doesn't want a big public shout here. There is a parliamentary by-election coming up and the Police Authority needs bad publicity - drugs related bad publicity - right now like a sweaty armpit. You know the Authority Chairman is standing as the new parliamentary candidate...'

'Sir, please! Strict procedure.' Again Carson intervened.

Merritt's voice grew taut. 'Here's the deal Matt. We can do this the easy way or the hard way. The hard way - a formal

41

investigation, disciplinary hearing.' He paused, 'Perhaps criminal charges. The easy way - your slate remains clean...'

'Sir, I must protest. This is not what we agreed...' Carson was red-faced and a vein pulsed in his neck.

'I know, I know...Matt, we need your co-operation, and we need you...off the radar for a time. It's important, Matt. I can't spell out in detail precisely what's happening.' He drew a deep breath, 'It's better you don't know. I need you to make an act of faith. To believe me. To believe in me.' He looked over at Carson who was stony faced and in a sulk.

Carson opened his folder, put away the torn statement and removed a sheet of paper that he handed to Merritt who laid it on the desk with precision, then swivelled it through a hundred and eighty degrees for Proctor to read.

'This is what we'll say in public if asked, but it's for internal consumption in the main. A question of you taking some time off - rest and relaxation, necessary to deal with work related stress.' He held up his hands, 'Personal circumstances. Just stick to that story, best keep quiet with colleagues. Believe me, it's for the best, Matt, you'll see.'

Proctor read the document. 'You want to send me on gardening leave. But you won't tell me why.'

'Matt,' Merritt leaned across the desk. 'Trust me – it's better that you don't know.'

Emma O'Rourke stirred in her chair. She hadn't said a word. Carson closed his file and clamped it under his arm. ACC Merritt stood up. Interview over.

Proctor leaned back against the wall outside police headquarters. Traffic darted up Snow Hill Queensway, past the striking Wesleyan office tower block on Colmore Circus, swinging round into The Priory towards Old Square and Corporation Street.

Drivers with people to meet, destinations, jobs to go to, trysts to keep. He closed his eyes and thought about his next move. His anger over his interview with Merritt, Carson and O'Rourke still raged. He had yelled some more before leaving the office but he could see from their eyes there was no shaking them.

Merritt's parting shot did not help either, 'Get your personal stuff out from your desk and locker, Matt. We'll manage the news, as I say, it's for internal consumption. You know, a matter of R and R.'

Part of him wanted to confide in someone, another part wanted to clam up. Make the whole nightmare go away. Sure, he would share all this with his old friend and confidante Ron Kydd, but then they were like soul mates. Once this was something he would have talked over with Hannah but that time was well past. How much should he tell Azzra? Or Stevie Cole? Doc McKenzie he had worked with for many years; their banter might be superficial but underneath there was mutual respect. And what about Sarah and Chris? He rubbed his head.

Azzra. He wanted to believe she would have faith in him, but it wasn't just that.

When he walked into the office to clear his desk, he felt the silence drop like a fire blanket snuffing out a blaze. He had brought in a couple of large plastic boxes and tipped stuff into them from his desk drawers. He left his desktop untouched. Someone would have to pick up.

Stevie Cole and Azzra came straight to him. He could tell from the expressions on their faces that the grapevine was working overtime. Doc McKenzie and Eric Cantwell stood a little way back, talking in quiet tones. Mac raised a hand in the air and Proctor gave him a brief acknowledgment while Cantwell wouldn't catch his eye. A team of civilian staff members and indexers pretended to work as normal, trying not to look nosey. One or two could not resist a glance towards him, unable to hide their pitying looks.

Cole asked, 'Anything we can do, say, Matt?'

He hated the way his mouth dried up and his eyes dampened. Azzra touched his arm. She looked across to O'Rourke's empty office.

'Emma made a short announcement. Said you were taking a - how did she put it - a bit of a sabbatical, wouldn't be away for long?' Her question hung in the air. He stopped what he was doing and looked around - all eyes were now on him, faces expectant.

'She's right. I won't.' He looked up and raised his voice, made it strong. 'Listen, I'll fill you all in later. Thanks.' He strode off.

Azzra caught up with him, 'You know you have friends here, Matt, don't you?'

'Yes, thanks.' He lifted the plastic boxes, 'Don't worry, I'll be back?'

Cole smiled, 'Course you will, Arnie's very own words. See you later, Terminator.'

Proctor laughed for the first time in twenty-four hours.

'Here, I'll give you a hand,' Cole said, picking up one of the boxes.

'Phone me, will you?' Azzra spoke with determination.

Proctor grabbed the second box and strode out of the office followed by Stevie Cole.

Chapter 6

It was that time of the afternoon in Temple Street West in the centre of Birmingham. The Old Joint Stock bar still had the remnants of lunchtime city finance diners dragging out their business meetings, the suits forcing loud laughs, mobile phones red hot, ill-considered text messages sent that would later prove to have been not imprudent but downright rash.

Matt Proctor watched his whisky on the rocks swirl around the glass, the amber liquid nudging the ice cubes in a quiet tinkling circle. It was becoming a familiar tune, a well known picture. At least he didn't have to face Hannah anymore - that would have really driven him up the wall. 'Gardening leave! What do you mean gardening leave? What have you done?' And on and on. He wondered what she was doing now. A car salesman. Of all the people to run off with - a sodding car salesman. Still, inevitable, their parting of the ways, they'd grown away from one another what with his long working hours and a progressive and mutual tediousness with each other. Was it them falling out of love or him falling into love with his work that in the end liberated both? Missed my son and daughter - missed Chris and Sarah - great to have Sarah back home again. Must try harder there - and speak with Chris at Uni more often. Shite, getting maudlin again.

Proctor looked up from the rectangular island bar in the centre of the old Victorian building, once a bank, looked up to the domed skylight in the cavernous ceiling, with busts of historical figures mounted high up on ledges. For a few seconds he felt the breath of ghosts of times past.

He held up his glass to the barman for another scotch. He was unaware of someone pulling a stool alongside until an extended hand touched his sleeve.

'I'll see to that, my old friend.'

He would recognise that voice anywhere, 'Ron, what're you doing here?'

'Wish you'd phoned.'

The rebuke stung Proctor. He studied his old mentor and long time friend, heavier jowls now but still radiating that glint from his frosty blue eyes, his steel coloured hair cut short and as always the snappy dresser; tweed jacket and light pink shirt with cream bow tie. 'Yes, sorry. How are you, Ron?'

'Leading the life of Riley. You can't beat early retirement to engender good fortune and contentment, Matt.'

'Some are born to retire; others have retirement thrust upon them.' The bitterness transmitted in Proctor's voice. 'Paraphrasing Churchill.'

'Aptly expressed. I surmised you would select this elevating establishment for a glass of nectar.' He looked Proctor up and down for a few seconds. 'Been a while, Matt. Too long in fact.'

'True. Our old watering hole, eh, Ron. Usual?'

'Absolutely right. We've celebrated great victories and drowned mutual sorrows here over the years. Shipmates, what? Listen, my good friend, after I heard about your situation I made a few calls.'

'My situation - well and truly shafted.'

'Bad whispers on the ground. I thought you'd engage in the battle, Matt. Not like you to retreat from a fight. Gardening leave my posterior!'

Proctor held up his glass and swallowed a deep draught. 'Yes, you may well be right there. Let's say...the odds weren't looking good.' He put his empty whisky glass on the bar and signalled the barman. 'Same again, please. Two.'

'What's it all about?'

'I've been well stitched up. A little snout called Baz Manning fingered me.' Proctor laughed, 'Claims I overlooked his dealing - for a "consideration" '.

'What excruciating shite,' Ron said. 'Manning, Manning...I've got him. Small time druggie, deals in the Perry Barr, Newtown and Aston areas, isn't that correct?'

'You've got him. Barry fucking Manning.'

'Yes, I can see how he would stoop to such a primordial act.' Ron tapped his glass, took a sip and said, 'I mean, he's a bloody Bluenose.'

Proctor had to laugh. He watched the barman push his drained whisky glass against the optic, 'Got to be more to it, Ron. Manning's a front for something else - got to be.'

'Bluenoses! Always the hallmark of deceivers and malcontents.' Ron snapped his fingers and got the attention of the barman, pointed to Matt's glass under the optic and raising his eyebrows mouthed the word, 'Doubles.' The barman acknowledged the order.

'They must know you'd never connive with a little tyke like Manning. And his word against yours? No way.'

Proctor frowned as the barman placed the drinks on the bar. He grabbed his glass and took a swig, 'Cheers, Ron.'

'Incredible. Why, Matt, you're a popular officer, everyone knows you're straight as a die.'

'I think it's called getting your retaliation in first. I can't be sure.'

'Whose retaliation?'

'DCI Tony Romney, and his poodle Alan Carpenter…maybe?'

'You had something malodorous on them?'

'And they knew it.'

'Why didn't you shop them?'

'Good question. I dunno - thought I was doing them a favour, keep my powder dry? Fancy another after these?' Proctor picked up the refilled double and drained the glass.

'You are an unusual cop, Matt?'

'How do you mean?'

'See the best in people.' Ron tweaked his bow tie, looked at Proctor's empty glass. 'Go easy, Matt, eh.' He touched his sleeve. 'I'll tell you what. I'm parked round the corner. What if I chauffeur you to your domicile? And listen, we're good friends, are we not?'

A rush of warmth filled Proctor's throat.

'Since I heard - and I'll tell you that the Dream Factory is rife with rumour, my good friend; I've been… pondering.'

'And when ex-petty officer, ex-legal executive and ex-superintendent Ron Kydd gets pondering the world had better watch out.'

'That's more the spirit, Matt. Listen, my good friend - I have a proposition for you.'

'Must be my lucky day then.'

'By the way, stop me if I've told you but talking about lucky days; when I first got Petty Officer rank, we had this able seaman who was a gay wrestler…'

Proctor had heard the story many times before but he stayed quiet because he knew how much Ron revelled in the telling of it.

Proctor entered the Security Industry Authority website on the internet. In the background he half listened to the TV news and glimpsed Barney scrabbling with his bedding in the living room trying to get more comfortable. Proctor had listened to Ron Kydd's 'proposition' without much enthusiasm but as he reflected on their conversation Ron's parting words kept returning to him. 'You need to work, Matt. Need a reason to arise from slumber in the morning and…'

'I know, get me out of bed.'

'Quite. Gardening leave. You wouldn't make a gardener in a millennium.'

The information on the website did not add much to what he already knew but it confirmed what Ron had said. If he wanted to come into the business with Ron, he would not need to go through a lot of bureaucracy. Ron was dead right.

'Come in and join me as a 'security consultant', and straight away you're up and running.' Ron had a contract lined up that Proctor could start at once. Hall's Steel Stockholders needed to review its overall security after a series of break-ins and a suspicion by the insurers that the thefts might well be inside jobs. 'Anyway, think it over, Matt and let me know.'

Following a spate of too much drinking in the Old Joint Stock, Proctor did not feel too bothered. Having wandered the streets of the Newtown and Aston areas of Birmingham trying in vain to pick up leads on Baz Manning who seemed to have disappeared into the ether like a virus-stricken computer file, reality hit home. He realised that Ron was right. He did need to work, to get some structure back into his life. He had suffered a few hangovers more than was good for him - drinking alone in The Old Joint Stock was getting to be too much of a habit.

He scanned the legislation on the Private Security Industry Act to get up to speed. Security was a significant industry and the legislation aimed to put it on a more professional footing; weed out the criminality and corruption that bedevilled it. With his background, not least as a crime prevention officer in the past he could contribute. This was a worthwhile career and if matters came to the worst, he could be part of a successful and profitable business. Perhaps he had to move on; the truth was life was unfair - sometimes you had to take injustice as one of life's throws; an unfortunate hit on the chin that could put you down but not out. Stitched up, yes. Surely there was life beyond the police service. Maybe Ron was right - his 'proposition' began to look more attractive.

Proctor swallowed a deep mouthful of air. Did he in truth want to work as a 'security consultant'? Installing CCTV surveillance? Training club doormen - 'bouncers'! He leaned back in his chair and the upbeat moment drained away as he thought once more about his 'gardening leave' interview.

He balled his fist and hammered the desktop sending his keyboard bouncing into the air. He sat still for several minutes, then got his phone out and called Ron Kydd. Then he called Azzra Mukherjee.

'Come on, Barney, let's go get some fresh air.' The dog shot to its feet, tail wagging, tongue hanging out.

Chapter 7

Detective Inspector Azzra Mukherjee made up in front of the large mirror on her bathroom wall. Her modern apartment in Gas Street basin in the city centre was spacious - and pricey; a stone's throw from the National Indoor Arena and Symphony Hall. Transformed from a derelict relic of the Victorian age to a dynamic upmarket residential development, the entire area felt smart and upbeat reflecting the second city's self-belief, vibrancy and newfound confidence.

Built on former industrial land it represented the new inner city landscape; populated by young professionals, well educated, money to burn - but with the pall of the credit crunch bearing down on them like a storm cloud. Can't believe everything you see on television though, she thought. Too much doom and gloom - media scaremongering. It was getting her mum down that was for sure. Mishi - thrown out of Uganda by Idi Amin and his fellow thugs, along with her husband, Mohammed - she now lived on her nerves. Had done so on and off since that fateful day in 1972 when they both arrived in England with one suitcase and the clothes they wore on their backs.

Azzra enjoyed her lifestyle, a far cry from her origins in a terraced house in Aston. For her this was now home. She wished her two brothers could see the world through her eyes; not the mad visioning of some of their fanatical friends. She narrowed her eyes when she thought of her brothers, Ali and Sanjay - especially Ali. She concentrated on the mirror. Not wanted in Uganda, not wanted in England they said - her younger brothers felt the alienation. Yet like her, they were born in England. She worried about them.

She was not vain but believed in true police style that seeing the 'evidence' before your eyes after a shower left no room for self-deception. So she made a point of looking at herself in the mirror, and being self-critical. As soon as a few extra pounds appeared, say, after a three day eating binge at the end of the month of Ramadan - or following a tough case involving long hours, poor eating habits and broken sleep; Azzra made adjustments. Her Islamic parents had taught her and her brothers will power. She looked good and that was how she was determined to stay. The thirties were critical years, she was in the middle of them; let yourself go then, and there was no way back. Must play more squash at the police recreational centre.

She liked men and she knew she needed to look good for the kind of men she wanted to come after her; the kind she went after. Nobody regular in her life at present, her last relationship had ended in acrimony and she was going through one of her careful phases, a 'picky' time. She did have a recent regret. When she first heard about Matt Proctor's split with his wife Hannah, no sisterly sympathy had stirred in her, no, more a matter of 'Get in there, girl'. But she hadn't and now this. Matt out on his ear. She stared into the mirror and became aware she was chewing her lip.

What was that stuff with Matt back in the station all about? All so hush-hush. Cliques in corners talking in whispers, colleagues tight-lipped and sombre faced. She did not understand but a worm niggled in the back of her head; gnawed over a snippet of one end of a phone conversation. Chief Superintendent Emma O'Rourke's conversation with - was it 'Tony'? She said, 'Tony, we must keep a lid on it.' Should she have said something, asked a question? Spoken with Matt? She hated being the fresh member of the team, as if she had just joined a new school and was the odd one out. Needed to feel accepted.

Thinking back six months to when she transferred to the West Midlands police, Matt Proctor was one of the few senior officers who had taken time to help her feel at ease. However, she hadn't got to know him well; they had only worked together for a short time on the same cases. A few times they shared a canteen coffee or chatted around the office cooler; she had felt his friendship, his warmth.

So when his call came last night, she was pleased. Not sure how she might help but she would try. Yet...something cautioned her; she had heard the whispers; a 'bent' cop, backhanders, that was the story doing the rounds. She had stumbled on a couple of colleagues talking, Eric Cantwell was one; he'd said, 'Proctor's ringing around, and stirring the shit. He's bad news, keep well away.' When she stepped within earshot, they turned silent, edged away.

Her career was important to her. One thing she had learned in policing was to suspect the worst in people - but her parents had taught her in life to be open to the best. She needed to be sure about Matt

She glanced at her watch - they were to meet in a wine bar in the City centre, seven o'clock. She dressed with care and looked sideways into the mirror, gave a final brush to her jet black hair, felt along her flat stomach, adjusted her silver drop ear rings, slid her hands down the sides of a tight black dress and moistened her lips a dark red gloss.

Proctor rotated the stem of his wine glass; the red Chilean Cabernet Sauvignon glinted with ruby cassis and black cherries, hints of mocha and dark chocolate shone through the glass. He smiled as he sipped and recalled the story behind the delicious wine. How more than one hundred years ago Don Melchor de Concha y Toro, an early Spanish vintner in Chile reserved for himself a batch of his finest wines. But some of the locals shared the good Don's tastes and were minded to help themselves. So the Don, good Catholic that he was, spread the word that his special cellar of fine wines was lived in by the Devil himself. The frightened peasants soon left the Don Melchor's Cellar of the Devil well alone. If only Brum's villain's could be scared off with as little ease.

Proctor hoped Azzra would share his taste for Casillero del Diablo. He stared into the glass, watched the red wine swirl, glycerine cling to the sidewalls; a whirlpool, he was slipping into a whirlpool.

The subtle lighting in the wine bar combined pink and blue colours merging to furnish a cool yet balmy atmosphere. Drinkers and diners - and a few lost souls - sat at tables or on high stools at the bars. A couple with their heads close together in a dimly lit corner looked apprehensive and glanced around a lot. French sounding music drifted around the poster-clad walls, floated over the black and white tiled floor. Proctor studied a picture of two girls wreathed in red garlands that echoed Monet's impressionist Poppy Fields. He sipped his wine and glanced at his watch. Yes, very romantic. And just seven o'clock in the evening.

Azzra stepped into the bistro wearing a tailored black dress set off with silver jewellery. She carried a clutch bag and wore matching high-heeled shoes.

Proctor's mouth dropped as he rose to greet her but she was already striding towards his table. Her jet-black hair bobbed over her shoulders, a slow smile crossed her face. Proctor realised it was the first time he had seen her out of uniform. She approached and he kissed her cheek. Her perfume was subtle and took him into summer garden territory. He pulled back a chair for her; she stayed on her feet watching him, a slight smile showing.

He stared at her for a few seconds until she gave a short laugh and said, 'I'm pleased to see you again, Matt, but I'm wondering if you've lost your tongue.'

'Azzra, great to see you. And thanks...' he rubbed a hand down his shirt. 'At times like this, well...'

'I know.' She indicated the bottle of wine and said, 'I'm quite partial to Chilean, you know.'

'Sorry, good, good.' He poured her a glass of wine and she sat down and took a drink. 'I hope you're feeling hungry. Good reputation here.'

'Thanks, yes, I'm looking forward to it.'

'Good, good.'

They sipped the wine and chatted about police service office trivia, a slight knock she'd had with her car, his daughter Sarah's obsession with computer games and Aston Villa's consistent inconsistency.

'I don't want to sound grumpy but sometimes I'd prefer Sarah got out more.'

'Give her space. She sounds feisty to me.'

A waiter came and handed them the menus. As they studied the choices Proctor said not looking up, 'I don't know how much more you've heard about my - departure?'

'No detail, just what Emma told us. A lot of whispers though.'

'Some will tell you I'm the pits.'

'I wouldn't be here if I thought that. I want to help - if I can.'

'Thanks. Much appreciated.' He put down the menu, 'I need to know a young guy's whereabouts, Barry - Baz Manning.'

Azzra fingered her wine glass. She spoke with a soft but serious tone, 'You followed a lead there - in the Masters' murder.'

Proctor said, 'Yes. Yes, I did.' She kept staring at him. 'Listen,' he said. 'I owe it to you to let you know just what happened. I suppose it's got out anyway - even if the top brass want things kept low key.'

'Have you...told Hannah?'

'No, no, we're separated now...'

'Oh. So...she hasn't heard the rumours?'

He stifled a short laugh, 'I guess if Hannah did hear she wouldn't blink an eye. She and I - well, we're history. No, it's my kids I'm concerned about. My sister too - Penny, we're very close, twins in fact. I'd hate for any of them to think I was - well, a bent copper.' He looked away and placed both hands around the glass. 'I still wonder if I should have stayed and... bastards.' Proctor looked down at the table. He picked up his head. Pathetic.

Azzra reached out her hand and covered his. 'Take it easy, Matt.'

Proctor took a deep breath. Right, go for it. In a rush, he ran through his meeting in ACC Merritt's office. Carson's threats about what would happen if he did not cooperate, the Chief Cop's concern about shit flying around that might taint him, the Police Authority and its chairman. And how having a former chairman as a Member of Parliament would do everyone's reputation a power of good; a few years down the line perhaps a nomination for the Honours List. There was a lot at stake.

'If you...' Azzra stopped and rephrased what she was about to say. 'Because you're innocent, might it have been better to let it all go through process?'

Proctor snorted, 'Let justice take its course, truth will out, that sort of bullshit?'

Azzra flushed and looked away; she drank some wine. She held out her glass, 'May I have some more please?'

Proctor refilled both glasses. 'I'm sorry Azzra, feel a bit touchy about it all. Kind of think I took the silver dollar.'

'They put a knife to your throat. So, where does Baz Manning come into it?'

'Before I ...left, I asked Stevie Cole to do some digging.'

Azzra put her hands to her head.

'I know, I know.' Proctor lowered his voice. 'Baz Manning has been dealing Class A drugs for years in Newtown and Aston. He was left alone because Tony Romney used him as a snout - got a lot of good info that led to a number of dealers being put away. But no big fish. Barry gave Romney names. But Romney went for the small fry...'

'Got paid off by the big fish?'

'Right. Including a dealer feeding a lot of stuff into the club scene. Doing a lot of damage.'

'But why did Romney set you up?'

'I sleepwalked into it. I'd had my suspicions a while back. I was on a case, money laundering and reviewing our computer logs I came across a file note of Romney's that mentioned Baz Manning and a meet with a man called Hassan. It didn't seem important at the time. But later I was trawling for something else and came back to it. Romney had deleted the entry. I made my first mistake then.'

'You told him you'd spotted the deletion?'

Azzra's penetrating brown eyes bored into his. He felt unsettled. 'Right, right. I challenged Romney, wanted to know what he was playing at. He went ballistic.' Proctor said, 'I backed off.'

'Hardly your style?'

'I was younger, Romney was the more senior officer at the time.'

'You said your first mistake?'

Proctor picked up the glass and examined the deep colour of the wine. 'Loyalty - it gets you nowhere.' He did not notice the shadow pass across Azzra's eyes. 'I fell over Romney and Carpenter having a row when I went to see if they had anything on Masters. Hassan's name came up again. They were still at it, taking backhanders to keep their eyes shut to his dealing. I'm sure there are others as well.'

'You threatened him - them?'

'You got it. But I thought I was doing them a favour - being one of the fraternity.'

'You tried to warn them off. So you gave them time to marshal their 'defence', concoct a story?' She shook her head.

Proctor leaned back and stared up at the ceiling. He was quiet for a short time. 'I'll tell you something, Azzra. I'm going to clear my name. I need to do that for myself as much as for anyone else. I know I'll become a pariah once the rumour mill gets in full swing. "No smoke without fire", that sort of thing? But I'll bottom this.'

'You have a lot of powerful people to fight, Matt.' She touched his arm, 'You could get hurt.'

'I'm going to do it.'

Azzra held his arm tighter, 'Good. I want to help.'

'I need to get close to Romney - get him on his own.'

She looked away and seemed disturbed. Proctor said, 'You all right?'

'There's something you should know.'

'What?'

'I've had a chat with Tony Romney. Over the Master's murder, I wanted to follow up your enquiries, drug connections.'

'Yes, makes sense,' Proctor said.

'Masters was a heroin addict, He was in a bad way. Became a complete loner last six months. Seemed all he did was play computer games. I asked him why they didn't charge him.'

'What'd he say?'

She shook her head and said, 'Sweet Tony Romney said the little shit would be dead in six months, why waste taxpayers' money.'

'Yep, that's Romney all right.'

Azzra refilled their glasses and took a drink of wine. 'Matt, there's something you should know.' She sipped again and looked at him, 'Emma's made me SIO on the Master's case.'

For a few seconds Proctor was stunned. He recalled Sarah telling him how supportive Katie had been after his break up with Hannah. Now he felt he had just taken another kick in the testicles. With difficulty, he focussed his thoughts, 'That's good, Azzra. You deserve the chance. Make your reputation.'

'You're all right about that.'

He forced a smile, 'It makes sense. Whoever did that to Masters must be caught. Yes, yes, I'm glad you've got it.'

'Something else I was told...in confidence.'

'Oh, yes.'

Azzra said, 'From ACC Merritt himself.'

Proctor raised an eyebrow, 'You're getting your feet under the table fast. But listen, don't tell me anything that might compromise you, I don't want you getting into trouble.'

Azzra's lips tightened, 'Damn you, didn't you hear what I said. I want to help.'

Proctor held up both hands. 'Sorry - I seem to be saying that a lot. Go on.'

'It was a kind of aside. I was going over resourcing issues - he laughed when I mentioned seeing Romney.' She took a sip of wine, 'Moreish,' she said. Proctor topped up their glasses.

'What about Romney?'

'He was somewhat cryptic - but all is not well between Merritt and DCI Romney. He laughed and said "Belfast would suit him". I couldn't get any more from him.'

'Interesting,' Proctor said. 'Very interesting.'

Chapter 8

A brass plaque - one of six - on the outside wall of the converted factory in The Jewellery Quarter read RK Security and Investigation. The sign contrasted with others above and below it - Art Media Enterprises, Costa Studios, Image Builders, Holy Ghost Studio and Purple It. Proctor smiled as he pondered the mysteries of people in the art world. Did 'Purple It' mean colour whatever 'It' was in some shade of mauve. He pressed the intercom buzzer for RK Security. Or was the interpretation that the 'It' was already purple. Verb or adjective? A medieval monster or a world grabbing concept? Was there a primary colour purple? ROYGBIV. Red, orange, yellow, green, blue, indigo and violet. All the colours of the rainbow. Were those the same as primary colours? No, he remembered. If so maybe there was no such colour as purple. What was that novel 'The Colour Purple'? Alice Walker. Oprah Winfrey made a Broadway show. I should read more again, he thought - and listen to music. Hannah always preferred silence; he had used to listen to music a lot.

'RK Security and Investigation.' The woman's voice startled Proctor. He'd been expecting to hear Ron's bishopric enunciation.

'Matt Proctor to see Ron Kydd.'

'Just a moment, Mr Proctor.' A second passed and Proctor heard the lock click.

'Please come up, we're on floor three.'

He pushed the door and stepped into a Victorian hallway with black and white diamond patterned tiles on the floor, newly plastered cream coloured walls and decorative moulded plaster dado at shoulder height with original plaster cornices framing a high ceiling. He smelt an odour of disinfectant.

No lift. Proctor climbed a steep, stone staircase. Each tread dipped in the middle from the footsteps of generations of jewellers, metalworkers and patternmaker who had worn away solid concrete as they trudged up and down those steps for the best part of two hundred years.

On floor number three he walked down a short corridor and came to a solid panelled door, knocked and heard a chair scraped back. A woman of around sixty pulled the door open wide. She was slim and tall and wore rimless glasses, had auburn coloured hair, fine wrinkles around her eyes and mouth, high cheekbones. She smiled at Proctor like a doting aunt welcoming a favourite nephew into her home.

'Do come in, Mr Proctor.' She returned to her desk in the small anteroom and pressed an intercom. 'Mr Proctor's here, Mr Kydd.' Her accent was eastern European.

Ron came from his inner sanctum and beckoned Proctor inside.

'Thank you, Marion. Matt, meet Marion Kalkowski, my secretary, confidante and Keeper of the Records - and dear and sweet friend. Welcome to our illustrious establishment. What do you think?'

'Impressive. Half expected Sam Spade to walk through that door.'

'Sam Spade, my dear boy. This is the twenty first century. This enterprise is cerebral, innovative and twenty first century focused.'

'Hardly the place for ex-plods from the West Midlands Police then.'

'We have an excellent re-orientation programme here - we can turn street yobbos into caring doormen, ex-cons into custodians of property; Damascene conversions, Matt. No problem then with ex-officers of the law.'

'From trouncer to bouncer in one fell swoop - awesome.'

Ron raised an eyebrow towards Marion. 'I know,' she said. 'Coffee, no milk, one sugar. And you, Mr Proctor?'

'Black coffee please. Call me Matt.'

Inside his office, Ron closed the door and waved Proctor into a chair around a low coffee table. 'Marion's a star. Don't know how I'd have got this enterprise functioning so well from the outset without her.'

'How'd you find her?'

'My very first contract. Two years ago now. Steel stockholder in the Black Country, losing materials every other week. They couldn't pin it down. Had CCTV, good perimeter fencing, excellent lighting, night patrols. She worked there.'

'Doing what? Running the office?'

'Office? Marion was the entire administration. Did the lot with one junior to help. The eyes and ears of the organisation – and in my case the mouthpiece as well. I made all the usual enquiries, drew a blank. Then I invited Marion for coffee and cakes at Olga Dunn's teashop in Kinver. Eventually I prised a few theories from her…a few names…'

'The old Ron Kydd modus operandi, eh? Uncle Kindly himself.' Proctor laughed. 'The rule of the separation of seven. Find the person who knows the person etc, until you reach the person who thinks they know who dunnit'.

'Well remembered, mon ami.' Ron sipped his coffee. His mouth compressed a smile, eyes glinting. 'Now, Marion and I are the best of colleagues.'

Proctor smiled back. 'So - the old Ron Kydd charm is alive and kicking?'

Ron placed a finger across his lips. 'Now, tell me. You've thought about my proposition?'

'Yes. I'll come in with you, thanks for the offer. I'll give it my all. But I'll be honest though, Ron. I owe you that. I've got mixed feelings. But I do know one thing; I won't lie down and die because of one kick in the arse.'

'So graphic, my good friend, so image-evoking. Well expressed. Listen, I can understand your reservations but - and I'm not being trite. This business needs people like you - like us. There are good people out there who are at the mercy of cowboys and shysters. We can make this an honourable profession, Matt - an honourable industry.'

'I'm not giving up on my agenda, Ron.'

'Understood. We can help each other. I need someone else to cope and expand. Someone I can trust. But see your work here as an 'in'. It'll open doors for you.' He paused, 'I know how much you want to clear your name.'

Marion knocked and carried in a tea tray that she placed on the table. She glanced at Ron over her spectacles, a question hanging in the air.

Ron stood up. 'Marion, please welcome former Detective Inspector Matt Proctor as a crew member. We now have our very own specialist Security Consultant on board the good ship RK Security and Investigation and. Welcome aboard, shipmate.'

Proctor held Ron's proffered hand and said, 'Looking forward to the voyage, Cap'n.'

With a broad smile Marion shook Proctor's hand and said, 'Welcome aboard.' As she left she winked at him, pulled the door behind her showing a shapely leg and said, 'Hello Sailor.'

Ron opened his desk drawer and withdrew a folder, 'Ever heard of Hall's Steel Stockholders, they work out of the Smethwick area?'

Proctor said, 'Don't think so. Wait - it rings a bell, where did I hear that name?'

'Anyway, they've had a spate of thefts and even arson outbreaks. Nothing catastrophic - as yet. But the insurance company are worried; one of their loss consultants has made an investigation without any firm conclusions. But they've approached me for, how shall I phrase it?'

'A second opinion?'

'A second opinion, excellent choice of words, my dear Matthew. Precisely that.'

'So what's their take on things?'

'To put it succinctly and without mincing words - they feel they're being taken for a merry ride.'

'False claim?' Proctor said.

'A series of claims - valuable metals, special steels, copper, platinum, high value low bulk materials. Almost as if stuff were vanishing to order.'

A familiar buzz tingled through Proctor's body. Ideas and possibilities tumbled into his mind. He stifled questions that bubbled to his mouth, filed them away for future reference.

'So, the insurance company want an independent view, to second guess their own investigators?'

'Not quite, more than that. As it was put to me, we might be able to exercise more of a free hand.'

Proctor smiled, 'Snooper's Charter, that it?'

Ron raised his eyebrows, pulled his mouth down at the corners, 'Let's say, we've been asked to look beyond the obvious.'

'Owners can't be too pleased, their claims undergoing extra scrutiny?'

'True - but the insurer's angle - their line to Hall's is that we are in there to 'take an overview' of general security arrangements, you know, CCTV, access locks, perimeters, vehicle checks, etc'

'But they want us to nab someone - they think it's an internal job?'

'Precisely, my astute colleague. Graham Hall - sole owner and director - is worried. And touchy. Once he heard that RK Security and Investigation were 'on the case' - such a pleasant ring to it, that phrase, don't you think?'

'Get on with it, Ron.'

'Yes, once he heard we were advising the insurance company he starts ringing around, asking about us. I got a tip-off from an associate of mine he contacted. Yes, Mr Graham Hall is a worried man. I think you should bestow him a visit, Matt? It's that time of the year. Christmas almost with us. Wish him the season's compliments, what?'

Reaching across for the file, a memory tickled Proctor's brain. Hall's Steel Stockholders - where had he heard that name before? Katie - of course, his niece had started work there. He remembered Sarah mentioning it. Katie - thrilled to death about her first job. And Phil - he had yet to meet Sarah's new friend.

First job and three months into it - Katie Storey felt her confidence growing. She had to absorb so much that for a few weeks panic feelings overwhelmed her. Tearful at times. But that was behind her now. She was finding her feet; her expertise in word processing and spreadsheets improving all the time. She was well used to the Internet so that was simplicity itself. Smiling to herself, she flicked her tomboyish bob of blonde, highlighted hair back from her eyes and pulled her chair closer to the desk and computer screen, tucking in her short skirt. She looked around the office, there was only Teresa - the receptionist cum part-time secretary of company owner Graham Hall - who shared the small office with her. She dithered as the temptation to visit her favourite website made her fingers guide the mouse towards the internet icon. No, she thought, I mustn't. Anyway, that's secret stuff between Sarah and me. Better just get on with my work.

Hall's Steel Stockholders admin team consisted of Katie and her boss Harry Armstrong, who dealt in the main with stock purchases and sales and oversaw accounts on an ad-hoc basis. Harry was of the old school and fought shy of finance so despite her inexperience, after a short induction she was left very much to her own devices. However, her 'big' boss, Mr Hall - or Graham as he insisted on being called - often came and looked over her shoulder as she inputted data and updated income and expenditure accounts and customer invoicing. His heady scent at times was so overpowering it sickened her and she wished he would not stand so close, especially in the afternoon when even the fragrance failed to hide the reek of alcohol.

She reached in her in-basket and picked up a handwritten note. It was signed GH. She frowned and read instructions to enter a transaction of one thousand five hundred pounds in the expenditure for 'sundries' and to mark it as non-vatable. she opened the spreadsheet file using the password Hall had given her - 'Keep it confidential, Katie, okay?' She entered the transaction. She was not sure what to do with his note so she opened a desk drawer and dropped it inside.

'And how is my office angel doing today?'

Katie shot upright and her hand went to her chest. 'Oh, Mr Hall, you startled me.'

'Please Katie, it's Graham, call me Graham.' He stared at her computer screen. 'Ah, the special account. Pleased to see you're keeping on top of things.' He pulled up a chair and edged closer to her. She could feel his breath on her cheek and the reek of his deodorant made her want to puke. A strand of his curly blonde hair tickled her cheek and she made a deft movement of her head. She glanced over at Teresa who averted her eyes and dashed to the reception counter where she stood with her back to Katie and rummaged through a box file.

Katie closed down the special accounts file, opened the general accounts spreadsheet, and entered invoice details.

Hall leaned over her and pointed to a figure on the screen. 'That's a brill order; we need to keep customers like that happy.' His hand brushed against her breast. 'You're settling in well here, Katie. I'll tell you what, next time we have a decent accountholder visit us, I'll treat you to lunch so you can get to know our customers in person. Always good for business to develop the personal touch.'

He pulled his chair closer alongside hers and placed his hand across her back. 'Know what, Trees tells me you do a spot of clubbing in Brum, I know some cool nightclubs there.' He glanced down at her thighs were her skirt had ridden up.

'Anyway, got to dash, Katie, no rest for the wicked.' He stood up and strolled across the office. As he passed Teresa he patted her backside, 'I hope you're not putting on weight, Trees,' he laughed. He hitched up his trousers hard against his crotch as he left the office.

Christmas a couple of weeks away but the festive spirit was not noticeable among West Midlands police officers. Proctor had made several phone calls from home to contacts he thought still prepared to talk to him. What surprised him was how many friends turned out to be fickle - who stonewalled when he tried to elicit information, made excuses that they 'couldn't talk right now, sorry, Matt you know how it is,' one put the phone down on him without a word, a young officer he'd nurtured as a rookie. That hurt. What a culture of fear we impose on ourselves, he thought. Way of the world now. He made some progress, however, Stevie Cole helped. Azzra? She had offered, wanted to help. No, no, best not put her career at risk. He sensed Stevie's reservations but in the end he wanted to show loyalty - and concern.

Proctor leaned back in the sofa and studied the information he had compiled in his notebook of known contacts of Baz Manning; his dealing haunts and habits. But not a permanent address. Azzra had come back to him on that. No luck. Apparently Baz lived the peripatetic life. He recalled their conversation.

'Sorry I can't help more. Is there anything else I can do, Matt.'

'Don't think so, not at this stage.'

'I enjoyed our meal.'

'Yes, yes, it was good.'

She was quiet for a few seconds, 'What do you plan to do now?'

'Not sure - I think I need to press on with a few things on my own.'

'Oh - right. Well, let me know...'

'Sure, sure.'

'Okay, be in touch then?'

'Yes, Bye Azzra.'

'Bye.'

She had sounded down.

An upturned blast of Bruno Mars' singing blasting down from Sarah's room jolted him. She was getting ready to go out with Phil. Only back home a few weeks and it was as if she had never been away. Having her around lifted his spirits; he had cut back on solitary whiskey drinking in The Old Joint Stock. He smiled at her singing accompanying Brunol, the thumps as she danced in her bedroom. He found reassuring the untidy appearance the house now sported again. He leaned back and closed his eyes.

There was a time when he would have Mozart or Bach playing in the background or Katherine Jenkins alternating with the Manic Street Preachers as a matter of course. Over the years, sullen silences and disconnected small talk replaced the music of Mozart. Before Hannah finally packed up and left, there hadn't been music of any kind in the house for months. He had guessed she was seeing someone but in the end, he didn't care. His work more than compensated as the rot set in their relationship. A quick promotion from Sergeant to Inspector, further concentrated study, a bout of successful policing including a few juicy arrests took him from uniformed to plain clothes. Two promotion interviews later led to Chief Inspector rank.

But a failed marriage and now maybe losing the job he loved. Was that hard luck or carelessness - he had been naïve with Romney, didn't cover his back? Bad move.

Maybe he should have chosen the 'hard way' as ACC Merritt put it. Stayed and fought to clear his name. As Ron had thought he might. He mapped out the scenario that could have unfolded. Formal suspension - not 'gardening leave' - a lengthy disciplinary hearing, maybe criminal allegations; all the time the Chief Constable and the Police Authority press office spinning the facts to make them look good and load the dice against him. He envisaged the stories, the lurid headlines - 'Police Authority acts to weed out 'bent coppers'. 'Zero tolerance policy on city drug crime'. 'Police chairman and MP-elect vow to clean up corruption.'

Sure, he could have stayed on and fought...

He reopened his eyes and wrote a couple more names in his notebook, adding a couple of action points.

'Dad, how do I look?'

Proctor did a quick double take as Sarah twirled into the living room, her dress swirling above her shapely legs, wearing a bright blue top that showed off her slim figure to perfection. She had also done something to her hair that he was not sure of; it seemed shorter, darker and thicker all at the same time. She looked taller as well, her high-heeled shoes added at least three inches to her height. He slipped his notebook into his pocket and gave her an appreciative once-over.

'You look great, Sarah. Could pass for a model.'

Barney darted around Sarah as she struck poses, began barking. She laughed then fell into a classic model pose with her feet turned inwards and dropped her hands to her knees, her backside pushed out. 'Like this?'

Proctor smiled, 'That's it, that's how they do it.'

Sarah then threw a pretend cloak across her shoulders and did a mock catwalk stroll back and forth across the lounge. 'Or like this?'

'You've got all the moves, maybe you should try it?'

'Or how about this, dad?' She crouched back on her heels and held out her arms in a judo pose.

'Now you've got me scared.' He held up his arms, 'No competition from me.'

'I've taken it up.'

'What, boxing?'

'Martial arts in general. Really enjoying it too.'

'Good for you.' Proctor smiled at his daughter, 'You never cease to amaze me. Let's hope you don't have to use it in anger.'

She held out her hands and clasped him around the waist, 'It's good to be back home, dad.'

'And it's great to have you around. I've missed you.'

Her eyes sparkled and she said, 'Thanks.'

He held her at arms length, 'To think I once towered above you, eh?

'When I was little you once told me great things come in small packages.'

'True. What time are you going out?'

'Phil's collecting me here.' She glanced at her watch, 'About fifteen minute's time.'

'Good, going anywhere nice?'

'A meal - at Henry's'

'I know, excellent food.'

The doorbell chimed and Sarah said, 'Phil, he's early. Good thing I got ready soon.'

Barney shot to his feet, ears back, wagged his tail.

Proctor said, 'I'm sure he'd have waited for such a delectable date.'

Sarah looked conspiratorial, lowered her voice. 'Dad, you'll be okay with him, won't you? Be first time you've met him, I mean.'

'Don't worry.'

'He's a bit of a punctuality freak, hates waiting around.'

'In that case you'd better let him in, hadn't you?'

Sarah returned and sprang into the living room holding Phil's hand. He followed slowly, a hint of a smile showing on his stubbled face. His head hung forward over broad shoulders as if it were too heavy to support. Proctor called out, 'Come in, come in.'

He grasped a large firm hand that was cold to the touch. Proctor relaxed his grip as Phil withdrew his hand. Barney sniffed around the visitor for a few seconds then returned to the rug and stretched out, keeping one eye fixed on the visitor.

Sarah completed the introductions and for a few minutes they talked about the restaurant and the planned meal; Proctor got Phil to talk a little about his job with the haulage company when Sarah excused herself, 'Bathroom,' she said . In turn, he touched on his police background but skipped giving away anything about his current circumstances. He had already told Sarah he was on 'special investigation work' to explain spending his time at Ron Kydd's firm. 'Kind of consultancy work, business crime prevention.'

Sarah came back in and busied herself checking her handbag while the two talked, relaxing as the conversation progressed. Somehow, it got on to computer games and Phil became animated - he said 'It's the new religion.'

Sarah tugged his sleeve, 'Give over, dad'll think you're some kind of techie geek. Tell you what though, Phil, I'll show you what Katie and I play later, great game - Hollowcost, with avatars you know?'

A shadow passed over Phil's face, 'Great, sounds interesting.'

'Beyond me,' Proctor said. He wondered about offering drinks but decided against it. No, if his daughter was to be driven, the last thing he wanted to do was encourage the driver to drink.

Sarah intervened in any case before he found it necessary to act the host. She glanced at her watch, 'Shall we go?' Looking at Proctor she said with a tiny smile, 'We don't want to be late.'

Phil screwed up his eyes, adjusted two of several hands on his watch, and pushed a button. Proctor guessed it was a stopwatch feature. They made their farewells and set off for the restaurant.

Proctor slumped into the sofa feeling deflated. He went to the cabinet and poured a stiff scotch and ice, fetched out his notebook scanned the list of names and notes he had made earlier. He pondered over Baz Manning, Romney and Hassan's names. He had few leads on Manning - not even an address - he knew Azzra had said she wanted to help, but he was loath to go there. No, he was on his own - time to make things happen.

Chapter 9

'Hi, dad, thought I'd give you a call - see how things are.'

Proctor was startled to hear his son's voice. For two months they'd barely spoken – when he had called Chris had been curt, sullen. Proctor had decided to leave things, let time pass.

'Great to hear from you, you okay? Course going all right?'

'Yeah, I'm good. Uni doing well. Computing degree stuff interesting. Cool. Turning me into a geek.'

'Then you could help me. Sarah talks about avatars whatever they are. You know she's moved back home?'

'Yes, she texted me. Sounds like life with 'the car salesman' wasn't too hot.'

Proctor hesitated, laughed; first time he'd heard Chris sound relaxed about his break-up with Hannah; when he'd first heard he was subdued and down. His mum after all. Proctor said, 'Right, listen, can you get over this way soon, be nice to see you, maybe we could get out for a pint - a meal together?'

'That'd be good, dad. Need to ask you a favour.'

'Fire away.'

'Couple of guys here, we've decided to rent a house, move out of the Uni Halls of Residence. Wondered if you could help out?'

'Yes, be glad to.' Proctor smiled, how much does he want, he thought. Deposit?

'Sarah said you were doing some work for a private security outfit now, that so? Surprised me.'

'It's a bit complicated. But yes, for the time being.'

'Not thinking of packing in the police, are you?'

'No, no...a bit political. I'll explain it all when we get together.'

'Right, right. Anyway this move. We're going to need a van. Hire it. Unless there's any chance you could get hold of one or something?'

Talk about putting things in perspective. His career was about to be shafted while his son's priority was getting a van to move his stuff. 'Packed in the police?' that must have been how Sarah put it when she texted her brother.

'Not a problem,' Proctor said. 'Ron Kydd's outfit has a van for moving gear. I'll sort it.'

'No shit. So - no big deal.'

'Not at all.'

'Cool.'

'When?'

'Next Saturday would be good, dad. That's when we'd like to move.'

'I'll check with Ron, get straight back to you, okay.'

As they chatted Proctor felt buoyed up, he had been concerned that Chris might disconnect with him and 'take sides'. But it appeared he'd dealt with the situation, was prepared to move on. A weight lifted from Proctor's shoulders - when he finished the call he felt more content than he had done for a long time. He went to the cd player and inserted a disk. He leaned back in the sofa, closed his eyes and let the simplicity of Mozart's Serenade 'Eine Kleine Nachtmusik' flow over him. No complexity there, no complications.

Chapter 10

Proctor drove the Ford Transit along the crowded A456 at a steady thirty. How many more vehicles can the Hagley Road take before it froze into a linear car park, he asked himself. The day was bright and he drove in shirtsleeves despite the fact it was November, but a heavy fleece lay in the car boot. Very pleasant - climate change and global warming might be for real, he thought, but winter snowstorms will still leap down and bite you even if there are twenty-year gaps.

He turned up the radio and sang along with Johnny Cash as he 'fell into a burning ring of fire'. A 'white van' driver on the inside lane grinned as Proctor pulled alongside at Manor Way traffic lights and gave a thumbs up sign, mouthing the same song. The name on the side of the van read 'Romney's fresh packed meats.' Proctor's sunny mood collapsed; he recalled his 'interview' with Merritt and Carson and asked himself yet again if he had made the wrong decision; if he should have stayed and fought. Had he bottled it? Self-doubt never used to be in his character. He thumped the steering wheel with the palm of his hand and accelerated away on amber, pushed way up past the speed limit.

Car parking was a nightmare around the University so he found a street parking spot and walked to the campus. Christmas lights, decorations, and shop displays heralded the impending holiday. He would have to start thinking about buying presents, sending cards - he screwed up his eyes at the thought.

As he entered the university grounds, he wondered if he had gone to uni how his life might have panned out. Would he have joined the police? At seventeen, he left home for the Midlands and went into the building trade leaving his dad dying of grief in Wales over his mother's suicide. But after twelve months on a construction site Proctor knew he had to find something else. That was when he met the young copper Ron Kydd in a Birmingham bar with friends; they hit it off and it was not long before he had filled in an application form and took the entrance exams.

He walked up the staircase in one of the Halls of Residence buildings to Chris's room. He could understand him wanting to move out - the Spartan corridors and jaded décor exuded a feel of institutionalism. He rapped on the door. Chris was inside with two others when Proctor entered.

'This is Millie - Mill, my dad.'

'Pleased to meet you.' Proctor shook hands with the young woman, mixed race Caribbean-white girl with a huge, winning smile. She nudged Chris and said, 'You didn't tell me your dad was such a looker.'

Chris rolled his eyes. Proctor guessed with Millie around that must be a recurring gesture.

Chris indicated across the room. 'And that's Martin - we're all on the same course.'

Martin's long shirtsleeves covered his arms and hands exposing only his fingertips. He was thin, gangly and round-shouldered. He moved across the room with a strange rising and falling gait as if walking on springs. He mumbled to Proctor who said, 'Nice to meet you, Martin.' His response was to run his fingers across his pale, downy moustache and stare at his feet.

'Martin's your original computer geek, right Mart?' Chris said.

Martin smiled lowering his eyes and Chris said, 'He already knows more than most of us will learn in the next ten years.'

Millie said, 'His brain's the size of a shed.'

'Come on,' Chris said. 'I'll show you the stuff we need to move.'

Proctor studied the piles of clothing dropped around the floor, cardboard boxes crammed with tinned food, toiletries, books, computer leads, cds, dvds, players, pcs, keyboards. He did a quick double take at a box filled with teddy bears and other soft toys. A large object obscured by a wet towel rested on a kitchen unit. He moved the towel to better see it and Millie said, 'Jeremy.'

'Jeremy?'

'Stone troll.' She rushed across and laid lush kisses on the head of the statue, 'He brings good luck.'

'I'm pleased to hear it. Probably bring me a hernia.'

'Come on, Mart,' Chris said, 'Might as well start with Jeremy.'

Proctor was minded to suggest some order to the packing but as he watched the three of them pick up objects at random he concluded haphazardry was the name of the game. He picked up a box and rested it on his shoulder and followed Millie, Martin and Jeremy to the van.

As they loaded furniture and boxes, Proctor got more details from Chris about their decision to move. They had become good friends and all found the Uni accommodation claustrophobic. There also were a few problem 'neighbours' - Chris said one clown thought it a good idea to ring a hand bell walking up and down the corridor at three in the morning. Another stole someone's WC from their bathroom and placed it in the middle of the front entrance with a notice reading 'Crap's Last Tape'.

'Can't get any worse, Chris's dad, can it?' she said. 'Literature. Crap spelt with a 'C'.

Proctor smiled. 'Call me Matt. And a missing 'p', he said. She raised an eyebrow.

In a quiet moment over a coffee break, Proctor asked Chris if he was in contact with his mum; adding he hoped that was the case.

Chris said 'Yes,' then shrugged his shoulders. 'Shit happens, dad, right?'

Proctor thought that he had to agree.

Millie was chatty and friendly and Proctor found her easy to get on with. He tried to make small talk with Martin but it was like drawing teeth, although there was a flash of enthusiasm when Proctor described how useful the internet was for research.

'Have you visited any game-playing sites,' Martin asked.

Chris laughed aloud and Martin, looking abashed closed up.

Chris tried to make amends, 'Mart's into some cool games, dad, you need to have your wits about you.'

The move took a couple of journeys and by noon, they were finished and back at Uni. Proctor made his farewells and as the others moved off, Chris came to the van window.

'Right,' he waved a set of keys, 'Just need to lock up and we'll be done.'

'I can drop you all back at your new place.'

'No, thanks, we're meeting up with a few people.' He screwed up his face. 'I've been a bit arsy the last few months - sorry about that.'

Proctor said, 'It's been a difficult time - for all of us including you and Sarah. Let's hope better times ahead.

'Yeah, yeah. Listen…'

'What?'

'Sarah…' Chris frowned. 'I'm glad Sarah's home.'

'Yes, yes, me too.' He hesitated, 'Has it upset your mum?'

'Don't think so. She's got enough on her plate. Probably best thing all round.' He looked back at the uni building for several seconds, 'Listen, dad, you might think Martin's a right geek - but he's a nice guy. A bit...reserved, you know. He's in touch with Sarah and Katie and a few others on the internet, Facebook, Twitter, that sort of thing.'

'Another world to me.'

'Yeah, yeah - Second World they call it. That's what I mean, might be a good idea for Mart to spend more time in the real world.'

Proctor waited and listened.

'Would it be all right when I come to see you if he and Millie came too - would that be okay, say for a weekend?'

'Yes, sure, be great to have you all. Could do with the company.'

'Cool, and thanks - for today.'

'Pleased to help. It meant a lot.' Proctor reached out and put his hand on Chris's shoulder, 'Best be off then, see you soon.'

'Right, bye dad.'

Proctor signalled to the others and Millie waved back and gave a preposterous wink. Chris rolled his eyes.

Driving back, Proctor thought about the van he had passed coming in to Birmingham with the name 'Romney' on the side. He needed to get back to dealing with that turd. He thought about Azzra's offer of help. He had been ungracious when she'd phoned after their meal, saying he was better off pressing on by himself. He must have hurt her. Ungracious? No - as Chris put it - he'd been arsy.

Chapter 11

The bedroom was lilac-coloured, ceiling, walls, even the doors although they were a darker shade of lilac. Posters bedecked the walls, bands, footballers, moody singers, TV and film personalities. Two pcs were set up on tables that slid in and out from wall cupboards. Sarah worked on one and cousin Katie on the other, seated at right angles to one another. Sarah looked up from her monitor.

'You on Facebook now, Katie?'

'Yes, Sally's expecting a baby, did you know?'

'No! My God, she's only been with - whatsisname - a month at most.'

'Not his then.'

'Oh my God. Let me see.'

'You get on with your assignment, Miss Proctor or your dad'll chuck you out again.'

Sarah sighed and returned to viewing her monitor. 'This course is such a bore. Sometimes I think I want to pack up college. Human Resources? I thought it was about dealing with people. Come on, Katie - let's play the avatar game, it's brill. Let's s stuff 'The Nightwatchmen'.

'Not tonight, it got hairy last time.'

'Yeah, it did, didn't it? They cut up rough.' Sarah clenched her fist and punched the air with the passion of a football fan. 'Come on you Knifethrowers.'

'When we're in Second World, it's...well, another world,' Katie sighed.

'Well, that's because it is,' Sarah searched Facebook. 'You know, when our avatars are in charge I feel so confident. Weird.'

'We stuffed that Nightwatchmen clan last time, Sarah. I mean, loads of Linden dollars and land - they must be mad at us.'

'I know - and they tried some nasty tricks, Katie. Bad tortures - mean.'

Katie grimaced, 'Good job our avatars don't have balls - those electrodes look as if they sting.'

Sarah was thoughtful, 'Yeah, I didn't like that stuff. They shouldn't do that - against the rules.'

'We still shafted them though, didn't we,' Katie's voice rose. 'Tell you what; they'll want to trap us into a false move. That was a brilliant name you thought up for our clan. Where'd you get it from?'

'The Knifethrowers? From the HR course. There's a guy in our class who's dead cynical. The tutor was telling us we needed to grow our 'emotional intelligence'. This guy whispered to me, 'Bollocks, just learn to throw knives.' We'll play tomorrow night, Katie. Okay?'

'Yeah, yeah, we well beat that 'Nightwatchmen' clan last time. Hey, I though HR was all about being nice to people.' Katie pointed to the screen, 'Oh, look, we've got a new friend, Martin Ferdinand.' She read his profile and she emitted a low moan. 'Doh, a real computer geek by the look of his posting. Knows your bruv at uni.'

Sarah leaned across to look, 'Knows Chris? Let me see. Oh, my God, what a nerd.'

Katie laughed and slapped her wrist, 'Get back to your studies.'

Sarah slumped forward and rested her chin on her hands. 'No, HR's not about 'being nice to people'. It's about...well, legal stuff, employment law, health and safety, diversity and disabled and there's so much stuff to remember. And corporate culture and governance shit.'

'You won't think that when you've got a big desk in a fancy office with all these gorgeous guys running around doing your bidding.'

'That's another thing, Katie; people don't run around for other people any more. We're all...'she made quotation marks in the air with her fingers 'team workers now, sharing, communicating, business partnering. We're all co-workers now, no serfs, no bosses.'

Katie snapped up her head, her blonde bob highlights falling across her frowning face. 'You must be joking. Someone forgot to tell that to my boss.'

'Do you like it at Hall's, Katie, how long you been there now?'

'Three months.'

'That long. I missed having you round when I was living over at mom's. What's he like, your boss at Hall's.'

'It's him.'

'Who?'

'Mr Hall, the owner, Graham. He's my boss.'

There was a tap on the bedroom door and Katie looked up to see Proctor's head appear round the door. 'Sorry to interrupt, girls.' Sarah winced.

'I was thinking, Katie. I haven't seen your mum for a few weeks. Thought I'd call in and say hello. So, do you want a lift home - cold night to wait around for a bus.'

'That'd be great, Uncle Matt, ta.'

'About fifteen minutes?'

'Cool.'

Proctor pulled the door shut.

Sarah wheeled her chair round on its castors. 'Oh, I see - Graham is it. And what is this Graham like?' She leaned across to Katie, her eyes wide and rolling, 'Go on, tell.'

Katie pulled a face, looking at her monitor. 'Listen, this Martin thingy seems to spend all his life on his computer.'

'Graham. Tell!'

'He's all right, you know.'

'Katie, I think you're holding out on me.'

Katie stretched her arms behind her head and yawned. She got up from the computer and went across to a divan where she stretched full-length, holding up her arms and examining her fingernails. She picked up a copy of Hello mag and flicked through the pages.

'You are, Katie?' Sarah's voice went sing-song.

Dropping the magazine, Katie turned her head to look at Sarah. 'He's well…a bit weird.'

'How weird?'

'You still seeing Phil?'

'Sometimes - not as much as after I went to live at Mom's. He's all right - in small doses. I don't know. I started going out with him when I moved in with mum and…'she giggled, 'the car salesman. That's what dad calls him.'

Katie looked blank. 'What?'

'Ted, you know, mum's boyfriend.' Sarah pulled a face. 'Doh, he sells cars!'

'Do you find Phil weird?' Katie stared at the screen. 'I mean, anything…strange about him?'

'You're changing the subject. Katie, what is this? You sound just like my dad when he's in cop mood. Questions, questions, questions.'

Katie shifted on the divan, crossed her legs and fiddled with the coverlet. 'It's just…well, I think I'm crap at boyfriends. The guys I fancy don't fancy me and I seem to attract right arseholes.'

'Katie, you finished with Phil ages before I went out with him.'

'No, no, Sarah, I'm not saying that or anything. It was over between us when you started dating him. It's just…'

'Just what?'

'Are you and he…do you think you'll stick together?'

'I don't know. He can be, well, a bit…strange.'

'Has he…done anything?'

'Katie!'

'No, I don't mean…' Katie ran her hands through her hair cascading it over her face. 'Like…has he hurt you?'

'No, no! Why? Did that happen to you? Did Phil…?'

'Doesn't matter.'

Sarah became silent for a time, tapping at her keyboard and reading the screen. 'I've been thinking about things', she said, not looking up. 'Last few times we've been out, well, I got bored.' She heaved a sigh. 'Hated it, yuk!' Looking straight at Katie, her chin held high, she closed her eyes and paused. 'I think I'll dump him.'

Katie stared at her fingernails, 'That'd be good, Sarah'

'What?'

'Listen, things between me and Phil got a bit - well, shitty. I don't want to go into that but you're my cousin, best mate. It might be good.'

'To dump him?'

'Yeah, yeah.'

'I didn't know…what's this about crap boyfriends, this Graham, is he crap too?'

'He's old enough to be my dad, and he's tried it on. I think he's a real perv.'

'Leave then.'

'Why should I?' Katie's face became spirited, her eyes fiery. 'I like the job, there are some nice people to work with. Why should I pack it in just 'cos he can't keep his pervy hands to himself?'

Sarah went across to the divan and put her arms around Katie. 'I didn't know...any of this. You should've said.'

'Well, you'd moved other side of town and what with the trouble between your mum and dad I didn't want to bother you.'

'You're not bothering me. I care about you, K.'

Katie's eyes softened but her mouth tautened, 'I'm such a load of shit, aren't I?'

'Katie, you're not. Never, ever think that. Now listen, I want to hear all about this Graham. And you know what; I have made up my mind. Never thought it through all the way but Phil's become a bore. I'm going to finish with him.'

Katie wiped her running nose with the back of her hands. She took Sarah's hands in hers. 'You're not angry with me, for saying Phil's not good for you?'

'Course I'm not.' Sarah placed her arms around Katie. 'You've helped me make up my mind.'

'Still best friends, cuz?' Katie nuzzled her face into Sarah's shoulder.

'Yeah, still best friends, cuz.'

'Tell you what, let's plan a big night out clubbing before Christmas with our mates - get well slaughtered.'

Chapter 12

He had a habit of cracking his knuckles, something he did more and more often. Sarah wondered if she was deliberately searching for things about him that she disliked. She knew it wasn't going to be easy. Maybe she should just have texted him, 'I want us to finish, Phil - sorry.' That's what girls did these days, why am I putting myself through all this hassle?

He had big hands, she had noticed before but folded they looked like a pair of hams. She tried to think how she would broach it. He stared into space - that was something else; often she'd chat away and she'd think he was listening; now...she began to wonder if he did listen. At times he drifted off into a world of his own, a private and personal place he wouldn't share.

'Penny for them?'

'What?'

'What are you thinking about, Phil, just now?'

'Nothing'.

'But you must be thinking about something. Nobody can think of nothing – unless they're asleep or dead.'

'Don't use that word.'

'What word?' His tone upset Sarah, it was as if she'd intruded into a part of his mind that was off-limits.'

'Dead - a word you shouldn't use.'

'What do you mean? It's a word, isn't it? I'm allowed to use words I choose, aren't I.' She could hear her own voice as if watching a film – was she trying to start a row, was that how her sub-conscious was working? Make him angry, have a fight, storm out. For some reason, there was anger rising inside her.

'Why shouldn't I use that word?' She tried to look him in the eye but he stared straight ahead.

He shifted his position, looked at his hands, clasped and unclasped them. 'You should know why.'

'No, I don't. What is this?' She curled her lips at the side and opened out her palms. 'Huh?'

'Brings back memories.'

'What memories?'

'I've told you – when I was in the army. I saw people die - mates.' His eyes shadowed and he leaned across staring into her face. 'They died - became dead. That's why I don't like the word.'

She was taken aback, a glimmer of understanding flickered across her eyes, but a devil inside prodded at her. 'How can I know, Phil, you've never talked about these things.' Her voice was shrill.

'People like me don't'

'But sometimes talking can help you - come to terms...'

His shouted words were like a physical attack. A couple of heads turned nearby. 'You don't know what the fuck you're talking about. Psycho mumbo jumbo.' He pointed his forefinger at her forehead. 'Just shut the fuck up, right?' He bent his finger back as if pulling the trigger of a gun.

Sarah felt the strength drain from her. 'I've never seen you like this before...'

'No, you haven't. Count yourself lucky.'

'I think...'

'You think what?'

'Maybe...you ought to see someone...'

'See someone about what?'

Sarah drew a deep breath. 'Phil, I can see you're upset. I don't know what happened in Iraq. Maybe I can imagine some things. I see you're angry...'

'Too right I'm angry. Now let's leave it'

'I don't think I can.'

'Leave it!'

Sarah became quiet, folded one hand over the other, 'I've been thinking.'

'What?'

'I...I want us to finish. I don't think there's any future in us...'

He leapt to his feet, his chair falling backwards, forehead creased, teeth bared. He reached out and snatched her arm, pinching flesh. 'What did you say?'

Sarah felt her stomach hollow, her legs weaken. This wasn't what she'd planned; she'd lost control of this exchange. She wanted out, to get up and run off, to flee. But his powerful grasp was like a vice, numbing her arm. He brought his head close up against her. 'You saying you're dumping me. That it?'

She couldn't reply, no words would come.

'Is that it?' he yelled. Through a mist she could see people moving away nearby. Urgent, whispered conversations penetrated her mind. He yanked her forward twisting her blouse, 'Listen you bitch, nobody dumps Big Phil, you got it?'

Sarah's eyes streamed. She summoned all her strength and yanked her arm away, pulled herself up and staggered to the women's toilets. Phil tried to follow her but a restraining arm of a pub customer caught hold of him. He yelled 'Bitch' after her. She glanced back and saw a pale-faced guy holding Phil. Without any warning, Phil caught hold of the man by the shoulders and head butted him. The man crumpled and Sarah watched in horror as blood spurted from his mouth and nose. She stifled a scream and rushed into the toilets, fell into a cubicle and heaved up her guts.

A short time later a girl and an older woman came in and helped Sarah to her feet.

'Are you all right, love?'

She struggled to speak, mouthed a silent 'Thanks'.

'I think you'd better stay here until he's calmed down.'

'I think the landlord's called the police,' the girl said.

The woman wiped Sarah's face with a tissue. 'Maybe you should get a taxi home, love. Shall I call one for you?'

Sarah took the tissue and blew her nose, 'Thanks, I'll be all right.' She thought of her avatar in the game called Rhea - from the legend of the Goddess who fed stones to Kronos and saved the baby Zeus. She thought of another Goddess who threw knives by using her mind; her brains. She thought of her clan 'The Knifethrowers' and steeliness dried her eyes and stilled her trembling hands.

Chapter 13

Proctor poured himself a nightcap. He listened for sounds from upstairs but guessed Sarah was home and asleep - the trail of shoes, bag, coat on the hall and stairs didn't overstretch his detection skills. He had hoped to catch up with her, have a chat. Over the last few days, he'd sensed a change of mood in her; she didn't show her usual vibrancy. He sipped the iced spirits and studied his notebook. Azzra's information gave a new urgency to his enquiries. And if Romney was destined for Ulster his task would be a lot more difficult. No, he needed to pin down Romney and press him for answers. If he failed there, he could turn his attention to Carpenter but of the two, Romney was more likely to know Baz Manning's whereabouts.

Proctor climbed the stairs slowly. He thought, one whisky too many on top of the bottle of wine. Going upstairs, he held on to the banister rail and went into the bathroom where he sloshed cold water over his head and face. He made his way to his bedroom and frowned as he passed Sarah's room. He thought he heard a stifled sob. Hesitating, he waited several seconds. Again he heard her short abrupt intake of breath and another sob. He knocked softly on the door.

'Sarah, Sarah, you all right?'

He waited for a reply and not hearing anything decided his best course was to go to bed, he could ask her in the morning when she was fresh if everything was okay. Her bedroom door opened and she stood holding onto the door. In the landing light he saw her reddened eyes. She twisted her face and took a shaky intake of breath.

'Sarah, what is it, darling? Is everything all right?'

She bit her lip and he felt her vulnerability, a frailty that took him back years to when she was changing schools, and while desperately seeking reassurance, was not going to show her fear.

He reached out and embraced her, 'There, now, Sarah, it's all right.'

She leaned all her weight against him and he steered her towards her bed. She slumped on the coverlet.

'Do you want to talk? Is there anything I can do?'

She lay on her stomach across the bed; her head buried in the duvet, a slight shudder ran across her shoulders. Turning over she said, 'Dad, I've split with Phil.'

'I'm sorry,' he touched her shoulder.

'I'm glad, though.' She ran the back of her hand across her nose. Proctor went to the bedside table and passed her a tissue. She cleaned her face and wiped her eyes. She sat up on the edge of the bed, 'I'm glad I did it - we were going nowhere.'

'Try and get a good night's sleep, eh? We can talk more in the morning if you want.'

Barney appeared from downstairs and looked at Sarah, his head to one side. She sniffed and a small smile crossed her lips, she patted the dog's head.

'Thanks, dad. Goodnight.'

She dragged the duvet over her shoulders and Proctor kissed her forehead. Her muffled voice sounded resolute, 'I'm glad it's over. He frightened me tonight.' She turned on her side and Proctor sat for a while on the edge of her bed, his body tensed and jaw tight; listening to her breathing slow down and her body relax. Barney stretched out on the bedroom floor watching Proctor.

Chapter 14

Proctor looked at his watch for the umpteenth time that morning. He had been waiting for the best part of thirty minutes and had exhausted reading the newspapers laid out across the reception area table. He went to the window and the nervous young receptionist smiled at him.

'I'm sorry but I have a few other appointments today,' Proctor said. 'Can you check again when Mr Hall can see me, please?' He smiled, tried not to make her nervous.

'I'll call him again.' She tapped a number into the phone and looked apprehensive as she spoke in quiet tones. Her face tensed as she listened, then in a very controlled gesture she replaced the phone in its cradle. With an effort she donned her sunshine smile and came to the window, 'Mr Proctor, Mr Hall can see you now, I'll show you to his office.'

'Thank you.' Proctor followed her along the corridor and up a flight of stairs, trying not to stare too much at her tight little backside. It occurred to him that he hadn't had sex for over six months since he and Hannah split - and that hadn't been much fun for either of them.

Graham Hall had yellow blonde hair that curled over his head to his shoulders; he wore a gold chain around his neck and the largest Rolex watch Proctor had ever seen. His pink shirt collar was open down to the third button and blonde hair sprouted over the edges.

He took several seconds from when Proctor entered the office before looking up. When he did, his face was blank. Proctor squinted against the sunlight streaming through the window behind Hall's desk. Hall rose from a black leather, high-backed executive chair and smiled, watching Proctor but not saying anything.

With an effort, Proctor returned the smile and said, 'Good morning, Mr Hall.'

Hall laughed and shot out his hand across the desk for Proctor to shake. His gold ring felt clunky and cold against Proctor's hand. He walked round his oval shaped desk mounted on a six-inch high plinth that elevated both his desk and the tall chair behind it. He waved to a side table and said, 'We'll sit over here.' At five feet eight, he was three inches shorter than Proctor. Raising his voice, he shouted, 'Teresa.'

Proctor sat down and removed from his bag the folder Ron Kydd had prepared for him. Hall's smile thinned and he indicated the folder, 'Always a good sign to see a man prepared. Now, then, Matt isn't it?'

Proctor nodded.

'Now tell me, Matt. What's your experience of the security industry?'

A timid knock on the door was left unanswered by Hall while he waited for Proctor's reply.

'I'm knew to the security industry. But I learn fast.' He flicked open the folder, 'You've got your hands full of trouble here, haven't you?'

Hall pursed his lips and shouted towards the door, 'Come.' Teresa edged her head around the door and waited.

'Tea, coffee?' asked Hall.

'Coffee, black.' Proctor looked across at Teresa, 'Thank you.'

'Usual for me,' Hall said. 'And let's see if you can get it right for once.' She withdrew her head and her quick footsteps retreated along the corridor. 'Now, then, Matt. Let's see the quick learner at work. Where do you want to start, man?'

'I suggest a brief tour of your premises might be useful. Give me a feel for the place. Then maybe we can have a chat. Is that all right?'

'Ah good. Man of action, eh? I understand from Ron Kydd that you're ex-police. Thought you'd take an early pension?'

'No. I thought...why not get my snout in the trough with the real entrepreneurs.'

'Ah, right...' Hall laughed out loud, 'I get you. Like it, Matt, like it.' He tapped the side of his nose. 'Only one reason for being in business, eh?' He rubbed his forefinger and thumb together, his ring glinting in the December morning sun streaming through the window. 'Come on, I'll show you around.'

'Thank you, Mr Hall.'

'Hey, man, call me Graham, we don't stand on dignity round here.'

Proctor smiled and reached into his bag and fetched out a Sony camcorder. 'No problem if I take a few shots for the family album...Graham?'

Hall's eyes flickered briefly and his eyes narrowed. He smiled again. 'No, no, of course not. Professional touch, that. Very good.'

He reached across the desk and held up a framed photograph. 'Hey, talking of families, what about these three beauties, eh, man?' The photograph showed a leggy blonde haired woman in her early forties in a smart white two piece suit seated with two equally blonde girls aged about eight to ten on either side, with perfect features and wearing white party frocks and ankle socks.

'My wife Sandy and daughters Mandy and Candi. Aren't they beautiful?'

'You have a lovely family.'

'You a family man, Matt?'

'Yes. Two, grown up now.'

'Good, good. As I said, a man of action, eh?'

Hall pecked a kiss on the photograph and replaced it on the desk. 'Finish your coffee, then we'll make a start.'

They walked back along the corridor past Teresa in the reception office who flashed a quick smile at Proctor. Behind her in a small office, he glimpsed another young woman at work. He did a quick double take and frowned. Katie Storey caught his eye and waved. Without thinking, Proctor put his hand to his lips. Katie got the message and with a bow of her head, turned her attention back to her computer.

Proctor followed Hall through a heavy door fitted with stout bolts and locks into a warehouse. Palleted boxes were piled high, separated by aisles each about ten feet wide. A forklift truck driver manoeuvred his vehicle along an aisle, slid the forks under a pallet and raised a wooden crate. The driver gave a thumbs up acknowledgment to Hall who flicked his hand in his direction. The truck moved down the aisle towards a loading bay where a lorry waited with its rear doors open like a gaping mouth.

'Are all the trucks yours, Graham?'

'Most. If we're pushed I'll bring in hire vehicles to get over the peaks.'

'Your own drivers?'

Hall said, 'No, contract drivers.' He then became vehement, 'I have them all checked out, mind you.' His smiles came less often.

'Good, good.'

For about an hour Proctor surveyed the operation, taking plenty of still photographs and camcorder shots of loading activities, storage facilities, close ups of door and window locks and potential CCTV locations. In the office with Hall, he asked for inventories of the fleet, registration numbers and an employee schedule including dates of birth and addresses, key holders and key storage arrangements.

'A lot of this stuff is confidential', Hall complained.

'We're good at confidentiality, don't worry.'

Proctor asked for a list of contracted staff used over the last twelve months. Hall became perturbed and challenged him. 'Hang on; this isn't some kind of management consultancy job, I just want recommendations on security.'

Proctor said, 'I'll also need to look at computer data about stock movements. It's all part of the insurance remit, Graham.'

'This is going way over the top.'

Proctor said, 'Risk analysis. I can't do it without that information. The better armed with facts we are, the better the recommendations and the more secure your operation will be.'

Huffily, Hall said he'd need time to pull together the information requested. 'This stuff is commercially sensitive, you know.'

'I understand.'

'You'll need to be specific.'

'Of course.'

Proctor hunched up his shoulders and pulled his jacket collar against his neck. He looked across the car park, shimmering in the wet, swore under his breath and taking a deep breath dashed towards his parked Audi Sportback 3, his one extravagance he would not deny himself. He swore again as he splashed into a deep pocket of water that soaked his shoes. He pointed the remote at the car and the amber lights still flashed as he tried to wrench open the door. It remained locked. He closed his eyes and tried the remote again, waited, pulled open the door and threw himself into the seat.

His mother's words spoken in their lilting South Wales accent flooded into his mind. 'There, there, young Matt. More haste, less speed'. Weird, some forty years on and those gentle, chiding chastisements still returned. 'Mother. What a bloody way to die!' With a savage twist of the key he fired the engine and looked in his rear view mirror at the illuminated works sign perched high on the warehouse roof, 'Hall's Stockholders'.

Proctor pushed his hand through his soaked hair. He revved the engine and sped through the car park sending sheets of spray arcing through the fading afternoon light.

'What a wanker.'

Chapter 15

They sat around a plain table each facing a computer terminal. All five wore military camouflage jackets; one or two had blackened their faces. A few empty Budweisers lay on the floor. A dim overhead light cast shadows down their faces.

The Man leaned forward and looked at each in turn, 'We have an enemy. It's serious. We must take out this enemy.' He looked at a face to his right. 'Swordman, how do we beat them?'

'Going to be tough, Man.'

'So?'

'They have worked out a strong strategy - skilful.'

Another cracked a bottle down on the table. 'Just kids - birds! We can't have them taking the piss.'

The Man held up a hand. 'So then, they have a strong strategy, right?' He turned again to the man on his right, 'Any ideas?'

Swordman said, 'Well, they have won much land, a lot of Linden dollars, captured a lot of our tribe. In the game, we're struggling.

The second man shouted, 'Let's take 'em out. Not piss around!'

'Maybe you're right – but not straight away. First, we frighten them. That's part of the game. We use torture, right. They must get shit scared. Agreed?'

They all indicated assent. 'Now then, we lean hard on them outside; find their email addresses, networking sites, mobile numbers. Got it?'

Swordman waved his forefingers together, the second man stabbed his bottle towards The Man, 'And if that doesn't work?'

The Man looked at him for a few seconds. 'If that doesn't work, we cross over, that's what we do.'

A broad grin passed over the questioner's face. 'That's what I wanted to hear.'

The Man sat back and tapped on his keyboard. 'Winner takes all.'

Swordman reached his hand out and placed it on The Man's arm, 'My kill, my kill this time?'

The Man placed his hand over Swordman's and said, 'Two kills this time, yours first, then mine.'

The beer man jumped up, demonlike and whooped, pointing at Swordman, 'Your first,' then pointing at The Man, 'He's lost count!'

Chapter 16

A swirling December fog descended over Hall's car park smothering the tall lighting columns. Damp leaves shivered as they clung to the black asphalt surface against a biting wind. Teresa looked out chewing her fingernails as Katie started clearing her desk.

'I shouldn't walk all that way to the bus stop tonight, Katie I'll give you a lift. Looks like a nasty night out there.'

Katie looked up from her screen. 'Sod it! It is a bit thick outside. I didn't know it had come down so much.'

Teresa gave a short laugh, 'Never known anyone like you. Once you get your teeth into something you don't notice what's going on around you.'

'I've got a bit behind today what with Graham tied up with Matt - Mr Proctor's visit.'

'He's nice, that Mister Proctor, isn't he? For an insurance man I mean.'

'Yes, yes...he is.' Katie wanted to tell Teresa that Matt was her uncle but he'd indicated to keep it quiet; she wasn't sure why but she sensed it was best to follow his lead.

'I just need to finish this off,' she said.

Teresa smiled across at Katie, 'You do like working here, don't you.'

'Yeah, job's great...'

Teresa's smile vanished as she glanced over her shoulder, 'I know, great job but...' She mouthed the words 'Mister Hall'.

'He's not that bad,' Katie said. 'Suppose we have to put up with his wandering hands.'

'Would you, I mean…'

'What, go off with him?'

'No, no, I didn't mean that, like tell anyone, report him.'

'Who to? Harry Armstrong?' Katie laughed aloud, 'He'd run a mile if he thought he had to follow up a complaint.'

'But it is, isn't it, I mean…' Teresa shot a worried look through the glass partition and lowered her voice to a whisper, 'I mean, it's harassment, isn't it?'

Katie shrugged, 'I don't know, so long as he doesn't push it too far.' She looked at Teresa and said, 'He ever tried anything on with you, Trees?'

'No, no, why would he? I mean - you're attractive - me, well…'

'Don't put yourself down, I'll tell you what, you've got great bone structure.' She reached over to Teresa and pulled her hair back from around her cheeks, removed her glasses. 'You get round to me and my cousin Sarah's. We'll give you a makeover; Sarah's brill at it. What do you think?'

'Well, maybe - do you think you could make a difference?' She pulled at the corners of her mouth and dragged her fingers through her hair. 'Oh, I couldn't - I'd feel so self-conscious.' She gathered her bag and took a last look around the office. 'Please, let me drop you off home.'

'It's out of your way, Trees.'

Teresa looked out of the window. 'Oh, that fog's getting worse. I hope I can see well enough to drive. Come on Katie, I'd like to.'

'Go on then.' Katie smiled, 'But stop being such a worry guts. I'll just switch things off and lock up.'

'I'll start up the car, get the heater going. You know where I'm parked?'

'By the loading bays.'

'Right.'

Through the glass partition Katie watched Teresa hurry along the corridor, her head down and shoulders rounded. She wanted to rush after her, grab her and straighten her shoulders, tilt her head upright and demand, 'Think and act beautiful and you become beautiful.' It was something she'd read in an advice column and always stuck with her - it made sense. Katie knew she had fine features and good skin and a practised upright posture. So then - if you got it, flaunt it.

She closed down her computer, checked everything was put away and switched off the office light as she left, locked the door behind her. She left the outer reception light on, as Harry always was last out and locked the main outer door. As she stepped outside, she pulled her coat collar closer around her neck. It looked like it was going to be a real pea-souper. She was pleased Trees had offered her a lift home. She'd talk with Sarah, organise that makeover.

Katie thought she heard footsteps behind her, she looked back faltering in her stride across the car park but couldn't pick out anyone in the gloom. She increased her pace and glanced up at the ever more obscured car park lights. She felt her hair become damp from the heavy moisture in the air. Her breath steamed and she wished she'd worn a thicker coat this morning. There they were again, footsteps that seemed to go in time with hers. The loading bays were but a hundred yards or so away. She ran in short bursts trying to make it look as if she wanted to get out of the cold, nor fearful. As she hurried, she felt more sure than ever there was someone behind her. She started running flat out yet felt deadly cold as if the night air seeped right into her bones. She glanced behind; there was someone following, she could make out a shadowy figure keeping the same distance. Let me get there, to Teresa's car, quick, quick, I hope she's left the door open, engine will be running to operate the heater. Trees there in the car, warm, safe, hurry, hurry.

An arm grasped hers before she was aware there was someone so close. She wanted to scream but nothing came out.

A breathy voice; 'Katie, wait, wait.' The man laughed and said, 'I couldn't catch up with you, didn't want to shout out and frighten you.'

Katie froze and looked at the tall, burly figure alongside her, his short gasps of breath spurting out and clouding the night air.

'Phil, what – what are you doing here?'

'I decided to check out the office, see if everyone was all right. For people to get home I mean. I'm used to it, driving in all sorts of weather. Know the roads like the back of my hand, could do it blindfold. Very dodgy night to drive in if you're not used to bad conditions.'

He swung round and she saw a rucksack on his back. 'But what are you doing here…where are you going? '

'Contract delivery, had to drop off an urgent load here today.'

Katie continued to stare at his rucksack.

'What, this?' he said, 'My gym night, three sessions a week. I never miss out.'

'You frightened the life out me.' She controlled her breathing as she kept walking, fought to ignore his restraining hand on her arm. 'I need to hurry, Phil, I don't want to miss my lift. Trees is waiting for me in the car park.'

He laughed, 'You'll be lucky if she gets you back in one piece tonight.'

'That's a comfort then,' she spat. His failure to apologise for frightening her angered her; she just wanted to get home, have a hot shower and curl up in front of the television.

'Katie, there's something I wanted to ask you.'

'What?'

'Did you know - has Sarah mentioned we've split up?'

Katie was about to blurt out that she knew everything, that Sarah had told her about his freak-out when she'd said it was over between them. But an internal alarm bell rang; she thought quickly.

'I don't see that much of her these days since she moved to the other side of town.'

'Right,' he moved closer to her and she smelt beer on his breath. 'We were good together, Katie. Should have stayed together. I know me going out with Sarah was a mistake, you were the right one for me, Katie.' He emphasised his words as he spoke, willed her to believe him.

'Phil, please, I don't think this is the right time...' She bit her lip, saw the lights of Trees' parked car blur through the murky fog, sniffed a whiff of blue grey exhaust smoke. She just wanted to be there, get into the warm car, curl down into the seat, get home.

'Katie, how about - can we get back again. I know I was a bit off last time but I realise now you're the right girl for me, how about we go out together, see if it works, eh?'

Katie wanted to tell him to bog off; that once he'd gone from her life she was never so relieved. After what happened between him and Sarah - there was no way it would happen. Again caution stilled her tongue, made her think through her words.

'I'm a bit tired right now, Phil, and freezing. Let me think about it. I'll give you a call.'

The parked car loomed into view; Katie wanted to run to it. She stared ahead, please, please, let Trees see me, shout out to me.

The car lights switched on and off, she could hear the soft purr of the running engine, she wanted to break into a dash, her pulse quickened. Good, good. She reached for the door handle; Phil held back, then snatched out and grabbed her arm, tightened his grip. She wanted to pull her arm away, to fight to shake off his grip. She restrained herself, forced a smile and raising her voice so as to be heard said, 'This is my lift, Trees' been waiting ages, I got to go now. Listen, Phil, have a good workout, I'll call you, okay.'

Trees leaned across from the driver's seat and looked through the passenger side window. Phil froze as he heard the window mechanism whirr. He stood still then whipped his arm away.

Katie squeezed into the door held open by Trees and sank into the seat. The warm air inside the car enveloped her like a comforting duvet. She gripped Trees' hand and looked out the window to say goodbye but he had melted away into the night fog.

Chapter 17

Katie peeped through the side of her bedroom window curtains, early evening and getting dull but she didn't want to switch on the light. She felt sure it was the same car. Red, darkened windows, a VW Golf GTI. She knew the model because it was the kind of car she wanted to buy now she was earning good money at Hall's. Especially as she had gotten two raises from Graham already and her only there a few months. Still - that was all right but she didn't like the way he kept touching her. It was weird though, he kept asking her to go out with him to Brum, to a club where he was a member.

She'd seen the photo on his desk of his wife and kids, he was old enough to be her dad she knew but a part of her thrilled at the idea. She pictured herself in a plush, swanky club, heads turning to watch her as she walked through the place, sipping a sophisticated drink - and Graham wasn't bad looking. Kept his figure, she knew he worked out ; she'd entered the gym subscription in the books. It was tempting but another part of her advised care, don't get your fingers burned, playing around with married men was dangerous. But then again you only live once, don't you?

She'd noticed the car on several nights, parked about ten houses down from her parents. No point asking mum or dad about it - lived in a world of their own, they did. The fact that she'd spotted it made her think that others along the street would have as well. But would they? And even if they did would they think twice about it? This was typical suburbia - she knew the people living on the adjacent semi, they'd been there years since when she was at school. An elderly woman called Gwen - she'd never known her full name - lived the other side. She hardly ever saw her. Hadn't seen her for months and months - a year maybe? God, perhaps she was dead. Over the years, most of the houses had changed hands as the area improved and long staying residents cashed in on their investment. Not any more though. No, there was no point in asking around about the car - she'd be taken for some kind of nutter. Maybe it was perfectly innocent, a visitor or relative calling on someone, someone with a new partner, new marriage, could be anything. But she was touchy, apprehensive. She'd never seen anyone get in or out of the car. She stood a little distance from the window so as not to be seen. She put her fingers in her mouth and chewed at a small piece of fingernail. The sooner she bought a car the better, ages now since she'd passed her test, six months.

Over the last few weeks Katie had become more and more twitchy. She moved away from the window and flung herself on the bed and lay face down. Then she sat up with her arms pulled across her knees. Her mobile was on a small table in the corner of the room. She went over and dallied before opening it. She muttered 'shit' when she looked at her text messages. Her heart gave a jump. He was in contact with her again, 'Swordman'. She went to hit the delete key but an invisible hand stayed her, told her not to be such a wimp. She read the message.

'R u rdy yet to meet. U want 2, gv u gr8 time, yes, babe.' Katie flipped back to his previous text. She'd accepted him as a friend on Facebook, he seemed to have a nice profile, now she wasn't so sure. Who exactly was out there? She went to the window again and her eyes drilled down to the parked car; still not able to see the driver. She thought about going outside and passing the car, see if she could see through the windows. It was getting dusky outside, she called Sarah's number.

She chewed her fingernails and stared at her mobile screen while she waited for Sarah to come round. She read and re-read the text messages until she could recite them from memory, a deepening chill crept through her. Who was 'Swordman'? Why was he doing this? What did he want? She rushed to the door to let in Sarah.

'I haven't told you this yet but he - well - kind of followed me.'

'Who?'

'Phil, leaving work last night - it was foggy and he followed me through the car park. Didn't know who it was. Trees waited to give me a lift. He scared me, Sarah.'

Sarah held Katie's hands, 'Did he do anything?'

'No, no, but he asked me - he wants to get back with me.'

'You didn't agree?'

'No, no, kind of, well stalled him. I was frightened, he followed me before he caught up and just like that asks if we can get back together. I was dead scared knowing what he was like after you dumped him.' Katie tightened her grip on Sarah's hands. She was pale faced and said, 'When I got into the car he'd vanished in the fog. But as we drove off I looked out the window.' She pressed her hands over her mouth. 'Sarah, I saw his face again through the back window. That look...it was terrible. He looked as if he hated me, as if he could kill me.'

She handed over her mobile to Sarah. 'I keep getting these weird texts and emails.'

Chapter 18

Proctor looked at the nameplate, sighed as he waited for Marion's voice. Hit the code, climbed the stairs. Her voice was as good as ever, familiar and caring.

Once inside he sat at his office desk, his chin resting on his hand. He tapped his pen on the desk, threw down the pen and went to the window. An Asian man and woman looked at the jewellery display in a shop window opposite that advertised 'gold bought and sold'. A Mercedes and BMW slid past each other in the narrow street. Ron Kydd walked in.

'No joy?'

Proctor said, 'That's about the fifth message I've left. No reply.'

'You're keen to speak to him.'

'I am.'

'Umm, you understand why he won't talk to you, Matt. Romney has ducked and dived all his life. He avoids confrontation unless it's on his terms. He's not going to face up to a verbal onslaught from an angry Matt Proctor, is he?'

Proctor grunted, 'Who said anything about verbal?'

Ron smiled.

Proctor said, 'You're right though. Nearly got through on his direct line but as soon as he heard my voice he put the phone down. I'm going to have to see him in person.'

'But you won't be able to get into Police HQ, Matt.'

'I know. No pass, reception staff - uniformed and civilian - will have had their cards marked. No, I'm going to have to see him on neutral ground.'

'At his house?'

'No, I'd be in even deeper shit if I tried that.'

'True.' Ron stood up and stretched. 'Aren't you being - as our American cousins say - a tad overanxious, patience is the proverbial virtue, my friend.'

'I haven't time to be patient.'

'Is that so?' Ron's furrowed forehead invited a reply from Proctor who didn't respond.

'Did you know he's a bit of a gambler?' Ron said.

'Romney?'

'Yes, I'm surprised you didn't know. On the other hand, he always was a secretive character, something of the skulker about him. When I was a young staff officer to the Chief there were some concerns expressed about Romney's extra-curricular activities. We did a spot of surveillance, as well as gambling he had something of an appetite for the ladies of the night - frequented haunts off the Edgbaston Road. We told him to watch it. I think he laid off the casinos for a time but as with all addicts I suspect he soon succumbed.'

'Right, that's good Ron. Where was his gambling den?'

'Hagley Road. Caribbean club.'

'Maybe I should try my hand at a game of blackjack.'

Ron smiled and removed his wallet from his jacket, got out a small card. He flipped it across to Proctor who caught it, 'You might find that helpful.'

Proctor examined the card, Caribbean Nights Casino Membership.

'Stakes are high on Friday nights. Romney enjoyed playing for high stakes.'

'You're a dark horse, Ron.'

'Comes from too much time to spare in Her Majesty's Royal Naval service. I had quite a penchant for seven card stud poker in my prime.'

Chapter 19

Proctor reviewed his notes from his last meeting with Graham Hall. He'd focused on the insurance reports' theft details and made links with stock movements in and out of the plant. He saw a pattern emerging - thefts soon followed deliveries of high value materials. Definitely looked dodgy. He thought ahead to his visit to Hall's the following morning. He opened his mobile and phoned Katie's number.

'Uncle Matt here, listen, are you free to talk?'

'Yes, go ahead.'

'I'm coming in tomorrow morning to meet Graham Hall.'

'I know.'

'You know!'

'Yes, naughty but I looked at Teresa's appointments diary. Nosey, I know – curiosity killed the cat and all that.'

'You know about this review I'm doing then?'

'Yes, mind you - after you left last time Graham was like a bear with a sore head.'

'Yes, yes, well...look, Katie I think it would be a good idea if you kept it to yourself that you're my niece. Is that all right?'

'Oh, goody. It's sort of...a secret?'

'Yes, you could say that. Thing is, Graham Hall isn't too happy with this review. Forced on him by the insurance company.'

'I see - so he doesn't want you poking around then?'

'Spot on - so no 'Uncle Matt' then, right?'

'Yes, yes, I'll wait to be formally introduced to Mr Proctor.'

'Good girl, take care. See you later.'

'Do you want to speak to mum?'

'Not now, I've got some more work to do tonight, tell her I'll call round soon.'

'Okay - bye then.'

This time on visiting Graham Hall, Proctor took his laptop. He judged Hall was someone who needed to put others down, to exert superiority; so Proctor decided he'd make use of the time he'd be kept waiting. He was not disappointed; Teresa grimaced as she said, 'Mr Hall has an important customer on the phone but he'll be with you as soon as he can.'

He worked for about ten minutes drafting ideas for CCTV locations when he noticed Teresa chewing her nails as she stared at a sheet of paper. She took it into the inner office and placed it in an in-tray. After a short interval, Katie came through the reception area. She pointedly ignored Proctor giving only a slight nod of her head. She referred to the paper and called through the open door to Teresa.

'Another one?'

Teresa shrugged, 'He popped it in first thing...' her voice dropped...'this morning.'

Hall bounced into the reception area beaming at Proctor. He had changed his pink shirt for a lime green coloured crew neck. He did not have his medallion on but a gold bangle hung over one wrist and his hair seemed more yellow than ever.

'It's great to see you again, Matt, come on through. I've been thinking about what you said last time. Now I want to get things right, think through our operation from a security point of view. Going thorough some figures since you were last here has made me realise what a drain these thieves are having on our bottom line. Not on, mate, not on'

Teresa looked up and asked, 'Would you like me to bring through some coffee, Mr Hall?'. Hall ignored her and his manner switched from bonhomie to theatrical seriousness. Raising his finger, he wagged it in Proctor's face and said, 'Make no mistake; I want it stopped – like now.' He glowered at Proctor as if he were personally responsible for the 'drain' on the 'bottom line.'

'Pleased to hear that, Graham. I'm sure we can change things for the better.'

'Damn right you can.' He pointed sharply at Teresa, 'Two coffees, right now, got it?'

As the meeting progressed, Proctor fought to control his temper. Hall's arrogance and bullying front stretched his impatience to breaking point. It was as if he wanted Proctor to take him on, challenge him. He listened as Hall railed against the 'thieving bastards' who thought they could take what they wanted, how law abiding businessmen like him were being driven to the wall, how the whole country was in terminal decline not least because of all the immigrants who came through without any attempt to control their numbers.

Proctor relaxed as the tirade wore on; the more extreme Hall became the more comfortable Proctor felt about dealing with him - the man was an exhibitionist, a performer; a motor mouth who just had to confront. However, when he said he wanted razor wire on top of all perimeter fencing, Proctor decided he needed to rein him in. He took the legal line in the first instance, 'Graham, you can't do that, it's illegal.'

'I want it - and you'll supply it, install it.'

'It would mean the firm would be in serious breach of the law.'

'I don't give a shit. I want the bastards to suffer, If I could have my way I'd not just slice their hands with razor wire, I'd cut them off.'

'I can't recommend that'

'Listen, I call the shots. This is my business, my contract. You do as I say.'

'You talked bottom lines earlier, right?'

'Yes, and that's what this is all about.'

'Here's the real bottom line, Graham. Do you want me to keep you out of jail?'

For the first time Hall was lost for words. Proctor let him stew for a few seconds. 'I don't think you being locked up would do anything for your bottom line, Graham, would it?'

Hall leaned back in his chair, chewing on a pen and studied Proctor. 'You're very persuasive, Matt, aren't you?'

'You'll get a good job from us, rest assured about that.'

'Okay, now then, CCTV. I want that installed in all the toilets, see what the sods are up to.'

Proctor shook his head. 'I don't think that would be a good idea. Do you want to know why?'

'You want to keep me out of jail?'

'Yes. And I don't want you lynched by your own employees!'

Hall screwed up his face. He slapped his thigh and burst out laughing, pointed his finger at Proctor and rolling his hand back and forth he said, 'Nice one, Matt. See what you mean. Right, I'll wait for your report.'

Proctor rose to leave, 'By the way, Graham, that list of employees, I can get that from your personnel or payroll file. That all right?'

After a moment's hesitation Hall said, 'Yeah. Yeah, see Harry Armstrong, looks after admin, he'll sort it.'

Proctor left Hall's office feeling buoyant, he thought he'd got the measure of Hall, a bully and an exhibitionist - and weak. He recalled the framed photograph on his desk of his wife Sandy, the two little girls Mandy and Candi - he wondered how much a narcissist like Hall could feel affection, love for others - or were they simply his 'trophy' family?

He returned to the reception area and asked Teresa if she could get hold of Harry Armstrong. Looking past her into the inner office Katie glanced up and gave him the briefest of acknowledgements.

Harry Armstrong looked as if all the cares in the world rested on his shoulders. His hangdog jowls hung from the sides of his face like a pair of onion bags on a bicycle crossbar, rheumy eyes darted around in a state of perplexed anxiety. He almost fell through the door wiping his hands with an oily rag and muttered, 'Sorry, sorry, couldn't get to you any quicker. What can I do for you? You're doing the security checks, is that right?'

'Yes. Matt Proctor.'

Armstrong ran his hands down the sides of his overalls before extending his arm to shake Proctor's hand, then pulled it away. 'Better not, filthy hands.'

'I understand you look after admin?'

'Well, in a kind of way. I'm not one of these office wallahs you know.' He indicated the inner office and said, 'Young Katie is the one you want to talk to - picked things up quick. She knows the ropes a lot better than me. I think I'm too late for computers.' He stuffed the cleaning rag into his overalls and ushered Proctor towards the door. 'Come on then, I'll get Katie to speak to you.'

Katie smiled as they approached her desk. She was dressed in a crisp white blouse and grey plaited skirt, her blonde bob newly streaked. Proctor felt proud how professional his niece looked.

'Katie, Mr Hall's said can you let - this gentleman know - sorry, sorry, Graham said your name but I'm terrible with…

'Matt Proctor.'

'Ah, Mr Proctor, that's right. So, I'll leave you with Katie, then...right?' He retreated, scuttled to the door as if departing from an alien world.

Katie laughed and held out her hand, a conspiratorial grin on her face. 'Good afternoon, Mr Proctor, I'm Katie Storey. What can I do to help? Would you care to sit down?'

Armstrong softly pulled the door shut.

Proctor sat down and pulled a chair up to Katie's desk. 'Thank you...Katie.'

Teresa waved to catch Katie's attention and called out, 'I need to take these schedules over to despatch. Can you mind the phone, please Katie?'

'Yes, okay.'

Proctor said, 'You seem well settled. Enjoying it?'

'Yes, Teresa's very nice. Harry - well, you can see...he just lets me get on with things, hardly a boss, more a friendly old uncle...'

'Less of the 'old' if you don't mind.'

'Oh, I'm sorry, Uncle Matt.'

'I think you're old enough to drop the uncle, Katie. Matt'll do fine.'

'Right...Matt.'

'Can you run the payroll file, please? I need to get a list of employees.'

Katie accessed the menu and typed in her password. Proctor concentrated as her fingers scanned the keyboard. Five alpha digits, he didn't get the sixth, a numeral. She opened the file and scrolled the list as Proctor glanced down the names.

'Shall I print it out?'

'Yes, please. Is access to all files password controlled?'

'Yes. I've made the list bang up to date for you. I guessed you'd want it.'

'Clever little you.'

'Less of the little - Matt.'

'Touché.'

She started to print out and Proctor glanced at her in-tray. A handwritten note lay on top with the words 'Expenses £1600' - the note that Teresa had passed earlier to Katie. Proctor picked it up and said, 'You keep accounts on here as well?'

'Yes,' she said. 'Now that definitely is passport controlled.'

'How do you mean?'

'Graham - Mr Hall changes it every week.' She glanced around and said, 'He's makes sure he does that himself.'

'So - who knows the password, you and Hall - Armstrong?'

She laughed, 'Not Harry – even if he knew it he'd forget it in five minutes.'

'Umm, quite a responsibility Katie.'

'I don't mind, I like the freedom.'

'Yes, I can understand that.' He picked up the note, 'You'll make an accounts entry from this?'

'Yes,' she giggled a little. 'Graham updates things on his own computer at the end of the month. Transfers files across. I'm glad of that. I hate figures. Oh, Sarah's coming round to see me tonight.' She licked her lips slightly and looking down at the keyboard said, 'She phoned to say she'd finished with Phil.'

'Yes, she was very upset.'

'I'm glad, Uncle Matt.'

'Matt!' he said in exasperation. 'God, I'm beginning to sound just like your boss.'

'No way. Anyway I'm glad for Sarah.'

'You're glad?'

Katie gathered the printout pages and stapled the sheets together. She passed them to Proctor. 'I don't think Phil and her were suited.'

'I didn't really get to know him, only met him once,' Proctor said.

'No, it was the best thing. He has a temper. Sometimes he was, well, scary.'

'So you knew him then.'

'Yes, I used to go out with him before Sarah.'

Proctor looked bemused. 'I never knew that.'

'It's all right, we'd finished months ago. Katie knew all about Phil and me. But I must say I'm glad she finished with him.'

'Right, right.' Proctor put the payroll list in his bag. 'Must make it a bit awkward, him working here?'

'Not that much, he's on contract delivery, sometimes he's around in despatch and warehousing but I seldom ever see him.'

'Good, good. Not on the payroll, then?'

'No.'

'So, that's that then. You and Sarah going out tonight.'

'Later, maybe, but we'll have a session with our 'Hollowcost' game first.'

'Holocaust - as in the Jewish holocaust?'

'No, nothing like that. It's a computer game, we use avatars and it's great to play'

'Well you're certainly breaking the stereotype of girls and computers. Sounds to me you're both big - what is it ? Gaming fans.'

'We grew up with it. Don't you remember when we were kids? Chris was the expert but we kept well up with him. It's another world, literally - it is.'

Proctor watched the brightness grow in her eyes. He said, 'I think I'm more in the Harry Armstrong school.' He stood up, 'Thanks for this, Katie. By the way, are you studying accounts on your course?'

'No way,' Katie smiled. 'Far too boring.'

Proctor said, 'Yes, thought that might be the case. If anyone here wants me, I'm just making a warehouse inspection for my report. I'll shoot straight off afterwards.'

'Right, be seeing you, Uncle Matt.'

Proctor touched his lips with his finger. Katie giggled, 'Sorry.'

He walked along the main aisle of the warehouse noting the racks of steel stock in bars, EN8, EN 47, specialist steels. Coils of steel were stored in one central area, copper and aluminium in separate pens surrounded by strong metal mesh walls. Proctor carried on towards the despatch area hoping Dutson wouldn't be around. He didn't want to renew his acquaintance after what had happened with Sarah. Dutson would also know he was Katie's uncle and while it probably didn't matter too much, Proctor guessed that Hall would welcome any excuse to foul up his review. That it might put Katie in trouble with Hall was more important and he didn't want to harm her job prospects.

Armstrong appeared as if from nowhere and said, 'Everything going all right, Mr Proctor?'

'Yes, thanks, Harry. I just wanted to check out a few thing in situ. Thinking ahead to lighting and possible siting for CCTV.'

'Good idea, we thought about it but felt as we had cameras on the outside gates that should be enough.'

'I know - it's about weighing up options at the moment. Cameras are expensive. But well positioned can be cost effective.' He looked up to the ceiling where a line of overhead fluorescent tubes shone down over the main gangways and into the loading bays. He pointed up and said, 'Even if we rule them out on cost grounds I need to get up there and have a look at possible securing positions. Have you got a ladder I can use?'

Proctor was surprised when Armstrong smiled - that was a first for him - and said. 'You don't want to go there using steps Mr

Proctor, that would get us into trouble right enough with the insurers. Health and Safety, you know?'

Proctor indicated his agreement, 'Of course, the dreaded H and S.'

'You can say that again. I'll get one of the lads to bring over a tower hoist and get you up in that. I'll get him to bring a hard hat as well.'

'Thanks, Harry.'

A burly man with a crop of ginger hair wearing blue overalls appeared a few minutes later with the tower. He indicated the platform and said, 'I'd better go up with you.'

'I'll be awhile, need to take measurements, notes, a photo or two. I've got a head for heights, used to work on the building.'

Ginger Top appeared dubious scratching his chin, 'Well, I'm not sure…'

'I'll be all right. Anyway I'm sure you're busy enough without having to nursemaid me.'

'Well, that's true enough. If you're sure…'

'No problem, just get me up to that girder and give me about thirty minutes.'

'Okay.'

Proctor put on the safety hat, strapped it under his chin, and climbed into the platform. Ginger Top operated the hoist and Proctor held the rail as it ascended up into the roof space. When he was some fifty feet up he raised his thumbs and shouted. 'Thanks. Don't forget to come back and get me down.'

Ginger Top looked up and waved, 'Half an hour's time.'

Proctor looked around for a few minutes and then got out his camera and took several shots from different angles. Some of the workforce clocked him. He photographed for several minutes then pulled out a tape measure. As he noted dimensions, he watched the workers below until they got bored and weren't paying any attention to him. He manoeuvred himself into a position where he was shielded from their view and got out from his bag a miniature battery operated cctv camera. He set the on/off time and time lapse between shots, disabled the flash setting and switched it on. He cut lengths from a strip of black adhesive tape and strapped the miniature camera to a roof truss, directing the lens towards the loading bay. A truck drove into the bay and an operative loaded steel coil using a remote controlled crane. Proctor grunted in satisfaction. After a few final adjustments he was finished setting up the camera.

Ginger Top appeared below and gave a thumbs up sign. Proctor indicated he was ready to come down. As he descended in the tower he motioned upwards and said, 'Higher up there than I thought, wouldn't fancy a maintenance job on lighting changes. Do they blow often?'

'Hardly ever blow these days, modern lights. Can't remember last time anyone got up there.'

'Well, pleased to hear it.'

'Harry says you might put CCTV up there?'

'Not sure, not very good sight lines. CCTV might be better used outside on the perimeter fences, but you never know.'

'Right, that it then?'

'I'll send a contractor round in a week or two, get a camera fitted up there as a trial, see how it goes. Thanks a lot.'

Proctor walked towards the exit. He glanced back and saw Ginger Top in deep conversation with Graham Hall, both pointing up to the warehouse roof.

Back at Ron's offices Proctor made a couple of phone calls. One was to a security equipment installation company that Ron used and trusted.

'I'd like a camera installed next week on a trial basis. Hall's stockholders in Smethwick. Contact's called Harry Armstrong, can you do that?'

Proctor specified what he wanted and said, 'Now listen. There's a miniature camera fitted above Aisle 3, section B. Remove that and put the CCTV camera there in its place. I'll give you other locations later. I'll collect the miniature from you in person, okay. And make sure you keep quiet about the miniature. You know what this is about, don't you?'

'Got you, no problem.'

His second call was to DS Stevie Cole at Brasshouse Lane police station.

Chapter 20

Proctor drove into the multi story car park opposite Police HQ at around seven pm on a Friday evening and drove the floors and aisles until he located Romney's silver Toyota Celica. He not only recalled the car but Romney boasting about how he'd knocked the car dealer down by a thousand through flashing his warrant card and saying,' I'm sure everything's above board here but it's a pain to have a police car parked outside your premises all day, John, right?'

He parked his Audi Sportback one level above but with Romney's car in sight. He settled down to wait.

An hour later, his patience was rewarded. The burly figure of Tony Romney ambled through the well lit car park.

Proctor waited until Romney's car had moved off and down the ramp before he eased the Audi forward, leaving switching on his lights until he exited. He picked up Romney's trail and followed him into Colmore Circus, along Snowhill Queensway and up Great Charles Street. The traffic crawled around Paradise Circus, along Broad Street and under the Five Ways Island. On the Hagley Road he didn't get too close to Romney as he was now certain he was heading for the Caribbean Nights casino. He slowed down as he drove past the casino watching Romney park up, lock his car and walk to the entrance. Proctor drove a little further along the Hagley Road, took a left and did a three point turn returning along the Hagley Road in the city centre direction and then into the crowded casino car park.

He flashed Kydd's membership card at the door attendant who waved him through.

Hugging the dimmer areas, he located a bar where Romney was ordering a drink. An Asian man approached Romney and they exchanged a few words until the Asian left and went outside. Romney soon followed him. Proctor waited a minute and then stepped outside as well.

He watched the two men talk in the car park between a couple of parked cars. Proctor kept low, sidled along an external wall, and crouched behind a vehicle peering through the side windows. The Asian looked around, opened his car door and removed a package that he handed Romney who shoved in into his pocket. Proctor edged closer.

'Good man, Ranjit,' Romney said. He opened his car and slid the package into the glove compartment. Hassan walked back towards the club. Proctor noted the registration number of Hassan's car, repeating it until it stuck. Romney lit a cigarette and took a few pulls before dropping it on the ground and stamping it out. He went back inside. Proctor gave him a few minutes then re-entered the casino. Romney returned to the bar and ordered another drink, looked at his watch and walked towards the toilets. Proctor moved after him.

Inside, Romney went to the urinal. Proctor waited until he'd started pissing then stepped up alongside him.

'Good evening, Tony, long time no see.'

Romney looked around and his ruddy face turned a shade pasty. 'What the …'

'I've been looking forward to having a chat, Tony. You're an elusive man.'

'I've nothing to say to you.'

'That's not the way I see it.'

'Piss off.'

Proctor snatched Romney's arm up his back, causing his still trickling piss to run down his trouser leg.'

'Ah shit.' Romney fought to free his arm but Proctor pressed him against the urinal.

'I want to know his whereabouts, Tony.'

'Who - what the hell you talking about?'

'The little toe rag you and Romney connived with, Baz - Barry sodding Manning. Where is he?'

'I don't know, anyway it's all done and dusted. You're stuffed and that's an end to it.'

'Not the way I see it, Tony. I want to find him and I'll haunt you until I know. Where?' Proctor balled his fist, turned Romney around and drove his fist into the big man's flabby midriff. He stumbled over and went down clutching his stomach.

'Where?'

'Don't know.' He fought for breath.

Proctor pulled him to his feet and rammed him in the solar plexus again. Romney crumpled and gagged vomiting into the urinal. Proctor kneeled over him, 'You'd better start remembering or this might become something of a ritual.' He pulled back his fist and Romney raised an arm, 'No.' he wheezed.

'Where, Tony? Where's little Baz?'

'He hangs out in The Old Turk, Aston.'

'Now that wasn't so hard, Tony.'

'Won't do you any good, wasting your time, Proctor. You're well beyond the Pale.'

Proctor put his face up against Romney's and said, 'Has anyone told you Tony, you smell like shit.' He walked away and stopped at the door before looking back. 'By the way, I thought Hassan looked very smart tonight. Dental work must be paying well these days.'

127

Romney's eyes slitted as he followed Proctor's departing back. He held his hand against his stomach and winced as he dragged himself to his feet. He wiped the back of his hand across his mouth and shuffled to a cubicle where he flopped on a seat. He pulled out his mobile phone and tapped in a number.

Proctor stayed in the club to have a drink. He was quite happy for Romney to see him sticking around. Romney would be licking his wounds for a few minutes but he'd given a starting point to find Baz.

He looked around the gambling club, it mirrored cosmopolitan, multicultural Birmingham all right, Afro Caribs, Asian, Chinese, White, and all shades in between. Voices were mostly quiet, a few raucous laughs broke out, muttered conversations here and there into mobiles. Most punters were casually dressed with plenty of bling visible, some suited with ties hanging loose - straight from the office. Most open necked. A fair number of women around the roulette table; the world of equal opportunity spreading. He spotted Hassan; the good dentist pushed a large pile of chips across the roulette table. Yes indeed, orthodontry was paying well.

Proctor got tired of waiting for Romney to reappear. He downed his scotch and decided he'd have a drive round to The Grand Old Turk's Head about half an hour away in the Aston area. He stepped into the car park and unlocked the door with the remote.

The crack on the back of his head was abrupt and loud, like a light bulb blowing. As he fell to the ground he glimpsed a shadow, a dark-coated figure wielding a baseball bat – he tried to break his fall but his arms were leaden lumps that folded beneath him. His forehead hit the wing mirror and he slumped on the car park tarmac. A boot whacked into his stomach and again against his ribs. Some residual strength grew within him and he grabbed a leg and pulled hard. His assailant lost balance and tried to shake free but Proctor held firm and staggered to his feet. The black-coated figure wore a beanie pulled low down to his eyes. Proctor couldn't make out features in detail but glimpsed he was dark-skinned. He tugged at the man's leg; the baseball bat smashed against his arm. He glimpsed a gold double-banded ring on his finger. The assailant kicked himself free and ran off in the direction of the Hagley Road. Proctor tried to follow but the blows had taken their toll. His strength ebbed as the pain in his ribs and face struck home. He slumped to the ground and sat still until his head stopped swimming and the nausea passed. Vigilance, that was the word that came to him. Losing your touch, Proctor, too many years sat at a desk staring into a computer screen, the bane of modern policing. He shuffled into his car seat and took several deep breaths before switching on the engine and drove home nursing his ribs. The Grand Old Turk's Head would have to wait - lucky Baz Manning.

Chapter 21

In bed, one hand pressed against his ribs, Proctor went over his visit to the casino. Who had whacked him? Was it a random attack? A mugger after a punter with big winnings? Someone who took fright when he fought back. Not Cartwright, he'd probably be with Romney - anyway, didn't have the bottle. Had Hassan clocked him? Unlikely - thumping people on the back of the head with a baseball bat hardly conformed to the Hippocratic Oath. Who then - Baz? There's a thought. Yes, a visit to The Old Turk Head was certainly called for. He groaned and retuned his mind to his last visit to Hall's.

During his tour of the site he had noted a number of obvious improvements to security that would be neither difficult nor expensive. He was struck by Hall's reluctance to open up his computerised data. His police officer's antennae leapt to the obvious. What was Hall hiding, what was his secret? Katie kept 'the books', she had the computer password. She'd mentioned her mum. Penny. What with his personal life in turmoil he'd neglected his sister of late. Keeping some semblance of solidity in Chris and Sarah's lives had been his priority. He decided to call in on Penny – not tomorrow though, healing day tomorrow.

'I know you won't believe this Matt, but I knew you were going to walk through that door.'

'The old telepathy between twins.'

'Must be. Not the first time we've had that kind of experience.'

'True.' He hesitated, 'We felt that when Mother died.'

Penny came across to Proctor and held out her arms. 'Come here, little brother.'

They embraced and Matt smiled, 'Little brother by all of five minutes, sis.'

'I know, come and sit down, I'll put the kettle on - unless you fancy something stronger?'

'No, cup of tea will be good. Cyril working late?'

'Afraid so, you'd think teaching meant early finishes but he's taken on quite a few extra responsibilities - desperate for that deputy headship.'

'He deserves it.' He paused, 'You've heard I've taken on some security work.'

'I have. Our daughters talk. But Matt, I still think you're keeping something to yourself. I can't see why you resigned.'

'I haven't resigned. It's complicated. It'll become clearer when I'm ready. Trust me. What I wanted to ask you is about Katie. I was surprised she'd started work?'

'Yes, Hall's Stockholders. Enjoying it too.'

'You didn't say last time I popped round - when I dropped Katie off.'

'Few months ago that,' she glanced under lowered eyebrows. 'I must have forgotten to mention it...'

'Penny...?' His intonation carried a faint Welsh uplift.

''Well, you know how it is. I had enough earache from Cyril - didn't want the same from you. You know what he wants for Katie. University! The be-all and end-all. I didn't think I could take more criticism from you as well. Your Sarah, taking 'A' levels next year?'

'No, no. She's also decided Uni's not for her either, doing an FE College course.' He turned the subject back to Katie, 'Has Katie given up college?'

'No, she gets time off to go - and she's earning money at the same time. Best thing for her, She isn't as academic as your Chris and Sarah. She just didn't want to know about university. Cyril's disappointed but it's the best thing.'

Proctor stared at her.

'It's what she wants, Matt!'

'Fair enough. Reasonable job she has there, and it's good she's continuing with College.'

'You seem to know a lot.'

'I'm doing a security review there. A contract I've had through Ron Kydd.'

'I haven't seen Ron for ages.' She smiled; 'He makes me laugh with those strange phrases he uses. Still wear the dickey bow?'

'Oh, yes - more outrageous than ever. Listen, Penny, I'm going to be paying Hall's a number of visits. I think it might be wise for it not to be known Katie's my niece. I don't think I'll get on with Hall - but he's her boss, I wouldn't want any ill-feeling to affect her. I've mentioned this to her but I'm not sure how serious she takes it. Can you tell her it's important.?'

'Yes, sure.' Proctor became quiet for a few seconds.

'You all right, Matt?'

'I still have that dream.'

'About mother?'

'Yes, crazy, but I can't seem to shake it off.'

Penny took Proctor's hand, 'You've had a stressful time lately. It'll pass.'

'Bloody stress, R and R...'

'Hey, take it easy.'

I know, I know,' he said. 'It shouldn't have happened. She shouldn't have died in that way.'

'I know, I know.'

'Sometimes I worry about Sarah.'

Penny continued to hold his hand, 'We all worry about daughters.'

Chapter 22

A snap frost fell around three o'clock in the afternoon. As the sky darkened and gloom set in Sarah stared out of her college classroom window. She cursed her car. Smart car - bloody stupid car! Of all days to fail to start - up until today the weather had been autumnal mildness - now comes winter fog and frost.

She checked her watch again and wondered whether to leave early; she had to catch two buses to get home and their reliability was hit and miss. Perhaps she should phone dad to collect her, she thought. She discounted that telling herself she was a big girl now, quite capable of getting home despite a bit of fog and frost and besides he had enough on his plate at present. During chats at home she read between the lines as he dripped information. She recalled the way he'd held her eye when he used the words 'gardening leave', looking for a reaction, gauging her feelings. Dad was both stubborn and proud. He wouldn't admit even to an accusation being made against him; would have felt it was an implied criticism. She'd shown sympathy and expressed her faith in him. Nonetheless there was a look of inward disappointment in his face, as if he'd let her down somehow. Stubborn pride, not letting down those close to you; yes, familiar characteristics - like not being willing to phone for a lift for fear of appearing a wimp.

Like father, like daughter - she smiled to herself.

'Sarah, did you hear me?'

Mister Quigley's high pitched voice brought Sarah out of her reverie. 'Sarah? Any views on the difference between objectives and goals in the performance review process?'

Sarah threw him a blank look. She couldn't connect with what he'd said and was aware of the rest of the class watching her.

She said, 'Yes, I've been looking out the window and decided that while my objective is to get my car fixed - that'll take a few days - so, my immediate goal is to catch the 226 bus home and preferably an earlier one.'

A gurgle of laughter ran round the class and Quigley sat up looking anxious. 'Oh, dear,' he said staring outside, 'It is getting rather nasty indeed. Does anyone else foresee problems getting home?'

A ripple of assent travelled through the room. The 'Cynic' as Sarah had christened him - the guy who gave her the idea for the clan name 'The Knifethrowers' - stuck up both thumbs and mouthed 'Nice one'.

Quigley licked his lips and said, 'Right, right. By the way that was a very good analogy. Yes, yes, goals are short term, objectives long term.' He walked to the window and rubbed his chin, 'Yes, getting murkier I think. We'll carry on for another fifteen minutes and if it hasn't started to clear then we'll have an early finish. Is that all right for you, Sarah?'

'Yes, thank you, Mr Quigley,' Sarah said in her most effeminate voice again triggering a surge of sniggers and a few loud, squeaky 'Oohs' from the lads. Colour flushed Quigley's cheeks and he darted back to his flip chart and said, 'For the next few minutes then can you call out the five characteristics of a well defined objective.' In the silence that followed he wrote in a vertical line on his flip chart the letters S.M.A.R.T.

As Quigley wrote the responses 'Cynic' passed a scribbled note to Sarah that read 'Sarah Makes A Real Tit (of Quigley)'. She puffed her cheeks and mouthed 'sad'. She began packing away her books and laptop and grimaced as she thought of lugging the laptop on the bus; what was it Katie once said; 'I can't wait to get a flash car - only poor people and oldies go on buses.'

Her toes were the first part of her body to feel the cold. She wiggled them inside her shoes as she waited at the crowded bus shelter. There was a mix of college students, women shoppers and elderly people. Two figures hovered some distance from the end of the queue well away from the bus shelter. They wore zipped up leather jackets, gloves and beanies that looked more like balaclavas. Both stared down at their feet and stamped the ground. They looked more suited to ride off on motor bikes than public transport.

She was glad Quigley had let them go early. She fumbled in her purse to sort out the right change. The driver had been irritated in the morning; gave her a dirty look when she handed over a two-pound coin. Most passengers had presented free bus passes or travel cards.

She clutched her fare change in her hand and blew several short breaths to warm her fingers. The sodium lamps along the road gave off a murky amber dazzle and grew into dim orbs further along the road. She sniffed and wiped her nose with the back of her hand, unwilling to ferret out a handkerchief and see her change go spilling along the pavement.

The bus pulled up and Sarah took the first available empty seat about three rows in. She stared out as passengers embarked and shuffled into seats, tucking overcoats around their legs and poking shopping bags and carriers under seats. The air smelt damp and the fogged up windows grew denser. When the bus pulled away, Sarah sat back and hugged the laptop close to her. She hoped her wait at the terminus for her next bus wouldn't be too long.

At the terminus the fog grew thicker and Sarah felt a pang of anxiety as she waited for her connection. Only a few other passengers from the previous bus had alighted along with her. She was a little relieved that the two 'balaclavas' appeared to have left the terminus; it was stupid she knew but they had intimidated her.

She checked her watch and willed the bus to appear. A woman behind her started a sneezing fit and someone muttered 'Bless you'. Sarah peered into the gloom and felt a wave of relief when she saw the lights of an approaching bus. Several shoppers picked up bags and shuffled closer to the shelter exit. Sarah slung her bag containing her laptop across her shoulder and bent to gather her small notecase. The people ahead of her boarded the bus.

The blow against her side confused her. At first, she thought someone had stumbled into her. She staggered forward and then felt an arm close around her midriff and take her weight pulling her back outside the bus shelter. She opened her mouth to shout when another arm closed around her neck and a piece of material was pressed into her mouth. The cloth had a sickly sweet smell and Sarah gagged feeling weak in her stomach. She had an impression of the bus shelter moving away from her, the passengers climbing aboard as in slow motion. By now, she was nearly horizontal with her legs dragging on the ground. She tried to scream, to call out but only a short croak came from her. Sarah looked up at the figure holding the gag over her mouth; a balaclava-covered head was all she could make out. She was now several metres away from the bus stop and the fog seemed denser than ever.

'Take her.' She heard a muffled male voice cry out. The one holding the gag released his grip and Sarah felt something cold and metallic pass around her throat. There was fumbling behind her as her assailant arranged a tighter grip on his stranglehold. A curious strength ran through Sarah. She let her body go limp and her sudden dead weight unbalanced the attacker; he stumbled and at the same time, the cold wire around her neck lost its grip. She summoned every ounce of strength she possessed and swung her arm upwards and across the head of the strangler. She felt a sharp pain as her elbow connected with the side of his head and he yelped. She scrambled away on hands and knees and saw the second attacker rush to pin her down. She remembered her martial arts instructor's words - balance, impetus. She swung the loose laptop case against his legs and he fell forward. Throwing herself towards the bus, she banged against the steps just as the pneumatic door closed pinning her halfway in the door.

A wide-eyed driver stared down at her. A woman passenger in the front seat held her hands across her mouth; Hands pulled at Sarah's legs.

She kicked out, felt her shoe connect and heard him wince and snap a sharp cry of 'Fuck'. A woman in the bus doorway lunged downward and grabbed Sarah's arms while shouting to the driver, 'Move off, move off.' The bus lurched forward and Sarah's legs came free as he released the door. The woman pulled her inside and Sarah lay prostrate, relief flooding thorough her as the bus doors hissed shut. The pale faced driver accelerated away, looking between Sarah and the road ahead.

Several passengers helped Sarah into a seat while the bus built up speed, leaving behind a wall of swirling fog and fading streetlights.

'Are you all right, love?' The woman's attentive face was close to Sarah's as she crouched over her. Someone held her hand and she fought to control her breathing, stop her spurts of breath turning into sobs.

'Were they anyone you know?'

Sarah shook her head, 'No, no, I don't think...'

'It's getting terrible around here,' a second woman's voice spoke. She raised her voice to the driver, 'Will you get the police then?'

The driver stared straight ahead into the thickening fog. 'I'll report it.' He indicated ahead and said, 'Waste of time trying to get a response on a night like this. They'd never come out.'

'Well,' the woman pulled herself up straight and with a note of huffiness said, 'I certainly think you must make a report. Don't know what the world's coming to.'

The second women spoke with sympathy, 'Is there anything I can do, love. Are you hurt, maybe you need A and E?'

Sarah grimaced as she moved her arm aware how much pain she felt in her elbow. 'My mobile, it's in my pocket, if you can get it out…'

'Of course, love, here.' She fumbled in Sarah's pocket and handed her the phone. Sarah drew a deep breath and hit Matt Proctor's number.

'Husband, boyfriend?'

Sarah smiled and said, 'My dad.'

The woman held Katie's eyes, 'Dad's are best.' She turned away and stared out the window watching the silent fogbound night speed past.

Chapter 23

Proctor listened outside the bedroom door for a time before he went downstairs. Sarah's bruising would only come out over the next few days, but she was young and strong. She refused to go to the hospital - no surprise there. Downstairs he sat on the sofa, clenching and unclenching his hands. He still felt an occasional throb from the back of his head and knew he should have it checked out. But he wouldn't. He leaned back and closed his eyes forcing himself to calm down.

He poured himself a large scotch and soda. He had barely moved for over an hour after saying goodnight to Sarah, listening as she ran a bath, heard her sobs as she went upstairs, returned her final soft 'Goodnight', listened to her door open, close, the soft murmur of music followed by silence.

He clenched the glass so hard it was miracle it didn't shatter in his hand. His anger was uncontainable. As Sarah recounted the events of her journey from college, his mind raced through all the possible scenarios that could have happened. Several times, he put his hand across his forehead squeezing out from his imagination what might have been. Too horrible to even think about. He remembered some cases he had been involved with, recalled distraught mothers, and devastated fathers as the reality struck home that their lovely daughter was no more. That the worst thing any parent can fear had happened.

And now this evil had visited his doorstep. He forced himself to think coolly, assess the possibilities, motives, try to pin down names. He knew it was most likely people she knew who did this, perhaps the last you'd expect. He hadn't been there to protect her; he'd never let her be exposed to such danger again. Proctor lowered the whisky glass on the table, turned off the lights. He double-checked the door locks front and back before going to bed; doubtless a restless night ahead. He tried to shake off the memory that filtered through of his mam and a stalker.

He stood upright. Right then, tomorrow he'd visit the Grand Old Turk's Head. He decided he'd ask Penny to look in on Sarah. Better let Hannah know as well.

He thought about Azzra Mukherjee.

Proctor twisted and turned in bed. He was tired and wanted sleep yet the thought of falling asleep filled him with dread. The cyclical dream kept recurring; now here it was again as vivid and terrifying as ever. He looked at the bedside clock and rubbed his eyes, five a.m. His head throbbed and a wad of cotton wool felt bunged in his mouth. He shouldn't have had that last whisky. What was that with Sarah? He hoped she'd be all right, was her attack to do with falling out with Dutson? Had he been violent before? He was an oddball. Proctor recalled his one and only conversation with Phil. Didn't give much away. Seemed a bit of a control freak. Into gadgetry in a big way. He'd said something about computing - what was it? Social networking, that was it, the new religion he called it. Must pack up drink, must find Baz Manning, where is he, see Romney, Northern Ireland Police Service, going there, old RUC, Sarah check she's okay, Baz Manning, Manning...in morning...sleep...

'Stalker...Penny, what's a stalker?'
    'Shush, listen'
    'I can't hear anything, what are they saying?'

'Mam telling dad, she's feels she's being – stalked'

'What's stalked?'

'Followed, someone keeps following mam'

'Why, why'd someone do that?' Who?'

'A man…Mam says she's scared.'

'Here, move over, let me listen…she says she's going mad over it. Dad's angry, Penny, yelling out, can you hear him?'

'Of course I can…they'll hear him in the chapel the way he's shouting.'

'Quick, Penny, I think they're coming out, get into my room, we'll hide, quick, quick.'

'Mam, mam, I sang in the school choir today, it was great, we sang Adeste Fidelis, do you want to hear me sing, mam…?

'Round and round the garden, like a teddy bear, one step, two step, tickle under there…

'Mam, don't, I can't stop laughing, do the teddy bear tickling, no, stop, stop, mam

'So green, soft rain, I won't go in yet, I won't, I won't, another swing, push me, Penny, higher, higher, up, up into the sky, look, a patch of blue, see, Penny, I told you it was getting nicer.

'Penny, did you see that big dog again? You did. Was it like yesterday, like when you closed your eyes? You frightened me. Penny, you can see what I see, is it because, like we're twins? I'll close my eyes, think, think. No, don't tell me, just you look, don't tell me what you see. Is it…is it…you see a tree, a tree and…and…there's a squirrel climbing up the tree, it's reached the end of a branch, lying flat on the branch, grey with a little brown face darting this way and that. Is that what you see, Penny, is it, is it? You do, it's like kind of magic, isn't it. You can see what I see without you looking. I can see too, my eyes closed - I can read your thoughts, right. And you can read mine…Penny, at times, at times it's as if as if we're one person. Sis, it's scary, isn't it?

'Mam, mam, are you all right, wake up mam. Oh, mam, wake up, blood, your head's all bloody, so still, mam, you're all cold, cold all over, I'll get dad from the steelworks, Penny, come home, come home, now. Listen, listen, Penny, it's mam, she's hurt, in the house, listen to my thoughts, I think, I think she's fallen down the stairs, there's pills, little pink pills, all over the place, Penny, come quick, come home quick.

'Matt, Matt, I was at next doors, I heard you, in my head, you were calling me, Oh, God, mam, mam, mam wake up.'

'Is she...dead, Penny?'

'I don't know - these little pills, quick, gather them up, Matt, we must hide them.'

'Why?'

'I don't know, but we must. Something bad will happen if we don't.'

'Pills, little pink pills rolling around like tiny marbles, a lot of them, mam, we didn't want you to die, who'll push the swing, do the teddy bear thing, I want to hear you sing mam, I want to sing Adeste Fidelis to you again. Please mam, please come back.'

'Matt, mam's dead, she's not coming back.'

'I didn't see...the stairs are so steep, down, over and over, the blood, Penny, so much blood on the stairs, her face was grey, grey as the clouds over the steel factory, Penny, grey, and the red blood, I kissed her head, Penny, salty taste, the stairs, so steep.'

'I know, here, here, dad will be home soon.'

'Penny, can you do the teddy bear rhyme?'

'Yes, yes, give me your hand, round and round the garden, like a teddy bear one step, two steps, tickle under there.'

'It doesn't seem to work, Penny. Doesn't tickle, don't feel able to laugh any more.'

Proctor woke up shouting; he could hear his own screams before he became fully awake. His body was drenched in sweat; he could taste salt on his lips. He sat up and wiped the sweat from his face with the sheet. Six o'clock. His heart raced and he felt drained, he tried moving his legs but they felt as if they lay under sandbags. With an effort of will, he heaved the cover from across his legs and felt the cool morning air dampen his soaked legs. He pulled himself out of bed and shivered. What brought that on? He thought he'd put that dream behind him. No, no, the demon wasn't exorcised yet. The Cardiff stalker: mam hadn't been the first woman to be terrified in that way, they never caught the stalker and there were many women who'd been near enough frightened to death, looking over their shoulders, with husbands and boyfriends out in vigilante groups chasing a shadow. Mam was terrified, driven to suicide, there were others whose nerves got the better of them, lived shattered lives. As suddenly as he'd appeared, the stalker vanished. There were rumours; an unidentified body fetched out of the Taff but nobody knew the truth. What was known was that at five years of age Proctor and his twin sister Penny were without a mam.

Chapter 24

Since the ban on smoking Proctor found the inside of pubs a strange experience. As a converted non-smoker, though, he appreciated the freshness of the atmosphere. But he still had a problem over what to do with his hands, especially when alone in a bar. Handling a glass wasn't enough - too transitory. When a smoker he wouldn't have bothered with a newspaper but now he felt the need for some kind of diversion, some activity to engage his restless hands - he detested waiting

He bought a scotch and found a corner table where he sat looking out across the bar. He opened the paper, turned to the back page, and read about the latest Villa signing. As he read his mind flicked back to the miniature camera images from Hall's he'd examined that afternoon. The contractor had given him a knowing smile as he handed it over to Proctor.

'Just love this cloak and dagger stuff, don't you,' he said.

Proctor said, 'Prefer the cloak to the dagger. Nobody twigged?'

'No, confidentiality's our watchword. Boss man at Hall's is none too pleased with CCTV - odd that, I mean it's his stuff they protect. Likes the f-word a lot, doesn't he!'

Proctor read more about the Villa signing. He got absorbed in the report and just as he was about to turn to the front-page headlines he became aware of the man standing still on his right, reading a copy of The Sun. Proctor took in the half-smiling face, pinched cheekbones and pasty complexion.

'Den, all right mate?'

'Hello, Mr P. Been a while.'

Proctor waved to a chair, 'Pull up a pew, keeping busy?'

Dennis Coyle sat down, his elbows leaning on the table top, hands crossed. He smiled with his lips compressed. Proctor guessed he still needed serious dentistry.

'I've been on the straight and narrow over a year now, Mr P.'

'Glad to hear it.'

Coyle glanced at the whisky glass as Proctor picked it up and downed it. He wiggled the glass at Coyle, 'Fancy a jar, Den.'

'Thanks, I'll have what you're having.'

Proctor threw the paper on the table in front of Coyle, 'Here, improve your education while I get a couple - pleased you've still got a good taste in booze, Den.'

'Always enjoyed a decent malt.'

Proctor looked around the pub. Early evening so only a smattering of customers around, the real rush wouldn't start until about ten or even later. Another law of unintended consequences, he thought, change the licensing laws to allow twenty-four hour drinking and what happens? Instead of regulars coming in at ten and leaving midnight, now the usual drinking time was pushed back an hour - eleven to one. But the young binge drinkers were the real beneficiaries; could get legless until three in the morning and give the coppers and hospital staff cleaning up after them a hard time.

Been over twelve months since he'd seen Den, a decent snout who'd given him some useful leads. He looked across to Coyle reading the paper and made a quick check in his wallet. If Coyle had anything on Baz Manning it would cost him fifty he guessed. He had more than enough. He ordered the drinks and noticed the barman giving him the once-over. Proctor had once visited The Grand Old Turk on a regular basis - in fact, the pub was an early haunt he shared with Ron Kydd. A long time ago; he didn't believe he was recognised as a cop - or maybe he should say a potential ex-cop. While he waited, he checked his diary and thought about the interview planned for next week with the Police Association rep to go over his case. He hesitated about getting his own brief - that went against the grain – but he realised he needed more than he currently had to mount any kind of decent defence. He needed to get to Baz Manning - and soon.

The Grand Old Turks Head was a mixed clientele bar, local born British Asians, Afro Carib blacks and working class whites - a few pseudo proles trying not to look out of place. Some small time crims too - he'd seen videos and cd players change hands in the toilets and dark corners of the car park. Nowadays mobile phones and laptops, pirated cds and dvds were the products of choice.

'Here you are, Den,' Proctor placed two glasses on the table.

Coyle leaned forward and kept his voice low. 'Saw you couple of weeks ago, Mr P.' He smirked and his piggy eyes almost closed as he enjoyed his moment of secret knowledge.

Proctor said, 'Pleased to hear it, you use Sainsbury's as well then, Den?'

Coyle cackled and tapped the side of his nose. 'Saw you taking a few holiday snaps, doing a bit of moonlighting then?'

Proctor twigged, 'At Halls? You work there, Den?'

'Twelve months now. Maintenance.'

'Half of Birmingham works there these days.'

'Expanding - that's why. Most places closing down.' Coyle sipped his malt. 'Cheers.'

'So then - now you get to sleep at night for a change.'

'Still the joker, Mr P, eh? My foreman says you're doing some work for the boss - the nicking we're having?'

'It's no big secret, Den.' Proctor raised an eyebrow, try a flyer. 'Know anything?'

Coyle licked his lips and took another drop of whisky. 'Might do?'

'Tell me something first - and you know me, Den. Anything useful and I'll be fair with you, okay?'

'Okay, but I can't stay long here with you, lot of big ears around, you know what I mean?'

'Sure.' Proctor looked around the bar that was still quiet. 'Do you remember young Baz?'

'Barry Manning, little black kid, yes.'

'Seen him around lately?'

'Can't say I have - you know what these kids are like, here, there...'

'I need to see Baz.'

'I don't think he's got anything to do with Hall's stuff being nicked.'

'That so?'

'No, course not. Never seen him round there, not his line. Clubs and that.' Coyle leaned closer, holding his drink with both hands. 'Deals, gear, you know, not a fence.'

'Do you need fences then to rip off Hall?'

Coyle held his hands up. 'Whoa, you're going too fast, Mr P.'

'When did you last see young Baz round here?'

'Oh, must be what, over six months ago.' Coyle looked across the bar to a couple of black lads wearing technicoloured woolly hats, sitting together in silence. 'If it matters, I could ask around, you know?'

'That'd be good, Dennis. Call me on the mobile, not at the nick.' Proctor tore a strip off the corner of the paper and wrote down his number. He left it on the table.

Coyle glanced around and slid his hand over it, crumpled it into his palm. He raised his eyebrows. 'Go to the bog, wait a couple of minutes.'

Proctor swallowed the remainder of his whisky and walked to the toilets where he stood alone at the urinal waiting for Coyle. The only two cubicles were empty. Proctor pulled a hundred pounds from his wallet. When Coyle walked in he waved the money. 'One other thing, Den?'

Coyle glanced at the wad. Proctor said, 'What do you think about Harry Armstrong?' He pocketed the money and started to piss.

'Armstrong?' A look of incredulity crossed Coyle's face. 'You don't think he's up to anything, do you?'

'In the family snaps I've got his mugshot. Him and another guy called Dutson, you know him? Got yours too, Den,'

Coyle pointed a finger at Proctor, 'You're winding me up, right?'

Proctor said, 'I don't do wind-ups.'

'Armstrong? Coyle said, 'He's just an arse licker to Hall. Acts as chauffeur, dogsbody. Even takes his missus shopping or picks up the kids from school. Proper little brownnose. Yeah, he's right well in there.' He blinked several times and glanced around the toilets. 'What you mean - you got my mug shot?'

'In the despatch area - middle of the night. Armstrong and Dutson were loading stuff onto a wagon.'

'You mean - you set up a camera?'

Right, thought Proctor, let's throw a curveball, Den. 'You were there, Dennis.'

'No, mate you got that all wrong. I ain't in that scam.'

'So - what scam is it you're not in?'

'Listen, not here, not now - I might be able to give you something but it's risky, dead risky.'

'Dead risky meaning expensive - don't push your luck, Den.'

'No, I'm serious Mr P. I don't know what - but something's going on there.' He leaned forward and touched Proctor's arm, 'But believe me, Mr P. I'm not into anything there.'

Proctor zipped up and washed his hands. He started the hand drier and said, 'Not looking good, Dennis, I mean, insurance job.' He pulled down his mouth, 'Not looking good.'

'You got that all wrong, Mr P.' Proctor thought he looked so worried he might be innocent, 'Listen. That lot - they're all shite. I'll tell you this - I wouldn't have minded...'

'Ah, Dennis, Dennis, they cut you out of their little scheme, that it?'

Coyle rubbed his chin hard. 'You fix them up – they deserve it, bastards.'

'You shouldn't talk about your employers like that.'

'You do believe me Mr P, don't you?'

'We'll talk again, Den. But remember Baz. I need an address, good money in it.'

The toilet door burst open and two noisy characters entered, glanced at Proctor and Coyle standing by the hand driers. Proctor remained silent while Coyle stared at the ceiling while he dried his hands under the blow drier then left without saying another word. Proctor didn't acknowledge his departure.

In the bar he took a quick look around but Coyle had vanished. Proctor smiled to himself and went to the bar where he ordered a whisky. He sipped it going over in his head what he'd gleaned from the stock figures at Hall's, linking that to what Coyle had told him and picturing again the secret surveillance shots he'd set up in the despatch warehouse. It was all beginning to come together - R K Security and Investigation might have a story and a half to tell the insurance company.

He still needed to get to Baz Manning.

Chapter 25

Sarah squealed with delight as her avatar Rhea scored a massive hit. Her expertise in combining the use of a handgun with the Uzi sub-machine gun and a clear strategy emphasising attack was working better all the time. Katie preferred the rocket launcher with hand grenade back up but their combined tactics left The Nightwatchmen devastated; The Knifethrowers were undoubtedly the tops scoring over ten thousand points and taking them to the penultimate playing level. Outthought them, outmanoeuvred them, and outfought them yet again. On her separate terminal Katie shrieked in unison with Sarah and leaped up, smashed the air with her fist.

'Be a bit quieter up there, please.' Penny's voice was plaintive and unconvincing as she tried to restore peace for Cyril to work at his school marking. That was all Katie ever remembered him doing in the evening, surrounded by scripts, portfolios, books everywhere. She put her hand over her mouth, 'Sarah, that's a million - we've got a million Linden dollars! And decimated their clan.'

Sarah's words were just audible. 'That's right, a million, they'll be hopping mad.'

'Hopping mad? Go ballistic more like.' They both stared at their screens, a fearful mood crept over them. 'I'm glad you came over, Sarah.'

Sarah went to pull back the curtains. 'Katie grabbed her arm, cried out, 'No, don't, he - someone might see you.'

'What are you so worried about. It's just a parked car, for heaven's sake.'

'With dark windows?'

'Everyone's got those these days, like a fashion accessory.'

'It's not just that'

'Weirdo's emails still coming?'

Katie said, 'Had another one today, look.'

Sarah studied her screen.

'You've got another new email'

Katie dashed to her screen and looked at the email. 'Oh, my God, it's him again.'

'Weird?'

Katie said, 'I'm going to tell him to bog off, I'll do that.' Her body was tense and she chewed her fingernails. Sarah caught hold of her arm, 'You are worried, aren't you?'

Katie withdrew her hands from her mouth and sat down on the edge of her bed, 'Sarah, I'm scared.'

Sarah sat alongside her and put her arm around her. 'It's all right.'

Katie held out her remote. 'There's something I haven't told you.'

'Not the perv - he touching you up again?'

Katie laughed, a short stifled sound. 'No, not the perv. Here, look.' She operated the remote with her thumb and opened a text message; she handed the phone to Sarah.

Sarah read for a few seconds. When she finished a hollow feeling flooded the pit of her stomach. She looked at Katie and read the words again. "Babe, I know we had some bad times but I've been thinking. I miss you, miss you real bad. How about us getting together again, I'd love that, really would. Believe me, I'm a changed man." The message was from Phil.

'What're you going to do?' Sarah asked.

Katie thought for a few seconds. She looked straight ahead, a steely expression crossed her face. 'I know what I'm going to do - I'm going to tell him to piss off, that's what!' As Katie began texting, Sarah recalled Phil's reaction when she dumped him; fear welled inside her for Katie.

Chapter 26

Proctor looked up from his computer screen as Ron Kydd entered the office.

'Ron, when you've got a chance have a look at this, will you. Marion took a call from Hall's insurers and they're getting restless. I thought an interim report might help - show them something's happening and see if they want to give any steer. What do you think?'

Kydd rubbed his close cut hair and adjusted his bright yellow bow tie. He looked over Proctor's shoulder. 'Not sure about that, Matt. Name of the game is to finger someone. The security advice is the front.' He read the text scrolling down fast. 'Mind you, this is good stuff. Professional. Might stack up all right for future contracts, more straightforward jobs.'

'I'll print it out and leave it with you, okay?'

'Right, that'll be good. What did I just say? Yoof speak - me! That will be eminently sensible, Matthew, thank you very much.'

Proctor smiled as his mobile rang. He looked at the incoming calls screen and his eyebrows came up. It was Coyle, 'Excuse me a sec Ron.'

Kydd went through to speak with Marion. Proctor acknowledged the caller.

'Mr P, re Baz - might have something for you.'

'Good man, Den, what do you have?'

'Cost me, Mr P. Had to put up front, you know?'

Proctor could see the man's mind clicking into overdrive, always a chancer was Coyle.

'Well, now you've paid up you'd better let me decide if it's worth it. Give.'

'Wasn't easy, things going on around Baz, you know.'

'I'm sure there are, got an address?'

There was a hesitation at the other end. 'You'll see me all right, Mr P, I know that. Dangerous territory here, turf gangs - crews they call themselves these days. Nasty pieces of work.'

'An address.' Proctor's tone was sharp, he knew Coyle of old and the one thing the man did not like was confrontation. Even a hint of abrasiveness could make him fold. But he was always tempted by easy pickings.

Coyle coughed, 'Aston, number 4 Cardigan Close. Baz has a room there. But you'd better be quick, Mr P, he moves fast, doesn't stop any place for long, know what I mean?'

'I'll be in touch - and Den, keep asking around, I'm keen to get to know what Baz's been up to late - who he deals with, who he's been seen around.'

Another pause. 'That's a tall order, Mr P.' Coyle paused, "Might be a tall price and all.'

Proctor closed his phone and grabbed his fleece. He went through the outer office and said to Kydd, 'Ron, I need to follow something up right away.'

'Pleased to hear it, Matt. Anything I can help with?'

'Not right now, but if this is good you never know.'

Proctor sat in the Audi and checked his A-Z, located Cardigan Close. He gunned his car along the Aston Expressway towards the address feeling a surge of adrenalin. He considered how he would approach Baz; his priority was to establish just what he'd told Romney - what his statement contained. If it came to a

155

disciplinary hearing he would have access to the material but that would be after the event; he wanted to know sooner so that he could make a pre-emptive strike - make Baz retract. And nail Romney and any other shites.

Turning into the close he wanted to close his eyes, plug his nostrils. Mattresses strewn across gardens, a discarded fridge up against a wall, uncut grass verges and sagging fencing - and the odours. Stale curry, burning rubbish, a blocked sewer spilling from a manhole all over the road. Several of the properties had their windows boarded and one four-storey maisonette had a solid steel plate secured over the front door. He looked for number four.

The front of the house was a tip, stuff scattered all over the place - he couldn't call it a garden, not even a yard. A middle-aged woman wearing a long coat poked at a pile of items of discarded furniture and clothing. A stray dog yapped and a couple of youths sat on a low wall smoking grass, watching the woman and then Proctor's car as he pulled up.

He got out and sauntered towards the house, looking back to check on his car. The woman stopped prodding and her head shot up.

'What,' she snapped.

'This place yours?'

'What's it to you?'

'No offence, seems as if someone left in a hurry.'

'Little bastard,' she waved her arm around the accumulated debris. 'He owed me four weeks rent too.'

'Baz?'

'Yeah, Baz. Barry sodding Manning. You know him?'

'A little.'

'Suspected he'd do a runner, had shifty eyes.'

'Always a giveaway.'

'You from the social? Cops?'

'No, bit like yourself, trying to get what's mine.'

She weighed up Proctor. 'Hah, debt collector, no chance mate. That little tyke will have vanished into some rat hole by now.'

'Odd he'd make such a mess of his own stuff?'

'Some of this is mine. I let it furnished.'

'Right.'

She kicked over a broken chair. 'Nah, he didn't do this, one them crews.'

'Local lot?'

'Yeah, I don't know what he keeps in the room, none of my business I say. But I think young Baz was in deep shit with those boys. Nah, they did this, ripped the stuff to bits too. Look at that sofa, will you?'

'Searching for something, were they?'

'Hah, you're a right detective, ain't you. Course they were, bloody drugs that's what they'm after. The shit as they call it. Had my way I'd bury them in shit.'

'Don't suppose you've any idea where he's gone?'

'Nah.'

Proctor looked at the door, its lock busted. 'Mind if I have a nose inside?'

She sniffed, 'Cost you a drink.'

Proctor shoved a tenner in her hands, 'Won't be long, won't nick anything I promise you.'

She gave a broad grin, her gummy mouth looking relaxed for the first time. 'Some chance, mate.'

For an instant Proctor glimpsed what once was an attractive woman. She nodded at the house, 'If you find anything of value in there then I'm Madonna's twin.'

Proctor winked at her, 'I could believe that.'

'Get on with you, my lad. His was number 4A. Lock's smashed.'

Proctor entered the room and gasped; he planted his hand over his nose and mouth. Clearly, the members of the Crew had decided to leave their trademark. And spread it over the walls. He wanted to get out fast but forced himself to search the room. In a cupboard, he came across several bills, an empty cigarette packet, a Durex pack also empty. An old copy of the Birmingham Evening Mail - he lifted it and underneath was a folded piece of paper that he opened. Bingo. A vehicle registration document, with a bit of luck for Baz's banger. He refolded it and shoved it in his pocket and made a final sweep with his eyes around the room. He wondered what the hell Baz Manning and Romney had said to convince the police hierarchy that he needed grounding.

Baz's lifestyle was pathetic, a small time drug dealer who lived a sad little life, no 'Mr Big' here. With hindsight, he wished he'd kept his mouth shut and waited until he had a strong case to nail two corrupt cops. Mr Second Chance - never again. They deserved drumming out of the service. He still needed to find Baz and it looked like forking out more cash to Coyle; and another visit to The Grand Old Turk's Head by the look of things.

He also thought it was time he spoke again with Inspector Azzra Mukherjee; he needed help. And he wanted to see her again.

Chapter 27

Sarah's hand trembled as she stirred her cappuccino. Through the coffee shop window she watched a car crawl past in slow moving traffic; the driver stared into the cafe. Her heart missed a beat - for a moment, she thought it was Phil but it was difficult to tell through the darkened windows.

Katie opened her phone and yet again read the series of text messages. 'Bastards, fucking shitty bastards.' She looked across at Sarah. 'You all right?'

Sarah said, 'I'm frightened, Katie, dead worried.'

'How'd they get our numbers? Here, let me see your messages.' Sarah handed her phone to Katie who opened up the message board. 'Swordman and The Man are from the game. Nightwatchmen clan, right?'

Sarah chewed on her lip, still stirring the cappuccino. Katie grabbed her wrist and in a high-pitched screech said, 'Will you stop doing that, you're driving me mad.'

'I'm sorry, sorry...'

'Well, I'm not going to let some sad, crazy internet nerds spook me.' She held the phone under Sarah's nose and said, 'Nor should you. I know what this is all about. They're so pissed off that we keep beating shit out of them in the game, that's what.' Katie's voice carried and a couple of women both turned and gave her a dirty look. Katie was about to spit a remark out at them when Sarah tugged her arm, 'Take it easy, Katie, no good getting angry.'

'Well, what're we supposed to do then?' Katie thumbed the mobile again and clenched her teeth. She said, 'Just listen to this. "Bitches, u n yr Knifethrower mates r ded in the wtr. Get out of our faces or we'll do you. Nightwatchmen are tops - sod off like now."

Sarah pressed her finger against her lips, 'Maybe, maybe we should report them or something.'

'Report them - to who? The police, they wouldn't want to know.'

'What if...'

'What if what?'

Sarah cupped both hands around the coffee cup to still them, her knuckles showed white. 'They've got our mobile numbers, email addresses - we didn't put them up on the internet. What if they know where we live as well?'

'They're just acting tough, couple of pimply thirteen year olds who wouldn't say boo to a goose.'

Sarah gave an unconvincing laugh, 'Yeah, yeah, you're right. I'm just being a wimp.' She chewed her fingernail, 'I wondered about telling dad.'

Katie shrugged, 'Tell you what, we'll go on the Internet tonight and hammer them, take every single bloody linden dollar they've got and if they can't that they can go stuff themselves, right?'

Sarah said, 'I wish I could feel the way you do, Katie. You've got balls I think.'

'Yeah, I know someone else who has as well.'

'Who you talking about now?'

'Pervy Hall, who do you think, silly cow. He's still coming on to me, you know.'

'Thought you'd told him where to get off.'

Katie put the spoon in her mouth and licked the cappuccino residue from it. 'He isn't bad looking, not for someone fortyish, mind you.'

'Katie, don't go there, don't even think it.'

'Got loads of dosh, could have a good time there.'

'If you do any such thing I'll never speak to you again!'

'Oh, lighten up Sarah, just winding you up.'

'Well, I hope you are, I mean, he's married, got - what - couple of kids?'

Katie giggled, 'Mandy and Candi. What a plonker calling his kids that.' She did a girlie accent. 'Mandy, Candi, and sweet little wifey Sandy.'

Sarah smiled, 'Sandy, Mandy, Candi - and Randy!'

They both burst out laughing and carried on until tears rolled down their faces. The two women across the café looked over again and gathered their shopping bags to leave. One muttered as she passed, 'Some people have no manners.'

Sarah put her forefinger across her lips as she saw Katie once more about to rise to the bait and changed the subject. 'Our Chris is coming home for Christmas?'

'That's cool, I like Chris.' Katie's eyes lit up, 'I know! We haven't had a good piss-up for ages. How about a pre Christmas clubbing session in Broad Street, get slaughtered. I can get Trees from work to come as well.'

'Karen from college is always up for a good laugh.'

'Chris as well - see if he'll bring some mates. He's got a girlfriend, Millie, she might come. Great, let's do it.'

'Mind you, Chris will probably bring the 'Geek'.'

Katie said, 'Who's the 'Geek'?'

'One of Chris's new Uni buddies. Martin something. They're doing the same course. Dad was down helping them move and he said he seemed really nerdy.'

'Gay, is he?' Katie arched an eyebrow.

'No way...well, I don't know do I? Anyway what if he is?' She read Katie's unspoken question, 'No, Chris isn't!'

'Pleased to hear it then, so when do we hit Club land?' Katie swallowed the remainder of her coffee and smacked her lips, 'And the Nightwatchmen can sod off!'

Sarah linked arms with Katie as they left the coffee shop. They made plans for the big night out thinking that as it was coming up to Christmas they would have to book in advance. They went through some mates' names but settled again on asking Karen from the college and Trees from Katie's office.

'Any fellas besides Chris?' asked Katie.

Sarah thought for a time, 'Um, not sure. We've already got the Geek pencilled in.'

Katie gave a broad grin and stopped in her tracks. 'I know, we ask the Nightwatchmen!'

'Katie!'

'Why not, that'll well throw them.'

'You're mad. Mad, mad, mad!' She pulled her cousin's arm tighter into her and a thrill somewhere between excitement and fear ran through her. 'You coming back to my place?'

'You're up for it! You want to game! I'll call Mum first to tell her.'

'Okay.'

Katie punched in the number. The night was drawing in, the shop lights were all switched on and Christmas displays in full swing. Sarah felt her heart start to pound as she thought about the night ahead. She waited until Katie finished talking to her Mum then asserted, 'We'll do the Nightwatchmen once and for all. We'll stuff them. Finish them!'

Katie grinned and raised her eyebrows, 'Wow, you're getting brave, yeah, why not. We're better than them, just one level short of top.'

'I know, as you said,' Sarah hesitated then shouted, 'Sod the Nightwatchmen.'

They swung along the road arm in arm.

'Oh, look.' Katie stopped and into a shop window displaying a range of fashion shoes. 'I need a new pair; we can get some here for clubbing.'

Sarah looked into the window and followed Katie's pointing finger as she identified a pair of fawn coloured sling backs with straps across the instep and ankle.

'Wow - I like those,' Katie said.

Sarah's arm tightened on Katie and she grasped her hand.

'What?' Katie said.

'Don't look behind you but see…in the window.'

'What?'

'That car. The reflection, see?'

'What about it?'

'I'm sure it was the one that slowed down and the driver looked in - when we were in the café.'

'You're imagining it.'

'No I'm not. It's scary.'

Katie was now tense. 'You think we're being followed.'

In the window Christmas lights flashed green, red and blue; a toy reindeer bobbed up and down dragging a sledge across the top of the shoe display. A white bearded Santa rocked, hands folded across his fat belly, mouthed ho-ho-ho.

Sarah said, 'Walk slow but don't look at the car, right?'

'Okay, okay.'

They walked along the street keeping their eyes straight ahead, arms linked. From the corner of her eye Sarah saw the car edge closer to the kerb. About ten yards behind them it slowed down and stopped.

Katie darted a glance behind.

'Don't,' Sarah said through clenched teeth.

'I think it's parked.'

'On double yellow lines? Christmas time. Wardens crawling all over the place. No way.'

'All right, all right, I get the message.'

'Come on, we'll step out, just take five minutes from here.'

Sarah released her grip on Katie's arm and strode out with Katie matching her pace. Sarah fought to stop looking behind her but Katie stopped and stared with a stony gaze at the parked vehicle. It inched forward.

'Oh, my God,' Katie said. 'It's moving again.'

'Who is in there?' Sarah said.

'Hang on,' Katie said. 'Why should we let that sod whoever he is scare us. I'm going to ask him what the hell he thinks he's doing following us.'

'Katie, no, let's just get back. We can think what to do. I've got the number.'

'You have, right…and it's grey.'

'It's a grey Volkswagen Polo and the registration number is – '

Katie gave a short laugh. 'My God, you're just the same as your dad. He'd have noticed those things.'

'There're two of them in there, not one.'

Katie swung her head around.

Sarah grabbed her arm, 'Come on, let's just get home.'

They quickened their pace, turned left into the small private estate where Sarah lived. The car still tracked them keeping about twenty yards behind. As they approached home Sarah felt her heart racing. She scrambled in her bag and found the front door key. 'Come on, hurry, we're almost there.'

They dashed the last fifty yards and Sarah fumbled to get the key in the lock. At last she flung open the door and they both dived into the hall. Sarah slammed the door shut. She ran to the living room and standing a little way from the window looked out.

'It's still there, it's stopped.'

Katie joined her and placed her hands over her mouth. 'What's that?' A sound came from upstairs.

'It's all right, it's dad.'

'Sarah, go and check, please.

Sarah stared at her. It was the first time she'd felt Katie was as frightened as she was. 'Make some coffee, I'll go upstairs.'

She stood at the bottom of the stairs, uncertain. She called out, 'Dad, dad.'

She heard the toilet flush. This time she cried out, 'Dad, dad, can you come down please.'

A muffled reply that she took for a 'yes' and Proctor emerged wiping his face with a hand towel. 'Hello, Sarah, didn't hear you come in.'

Relief flooded through her. 'Dad, I'm with Katie.'

'Good.' He threw the towel into the bathroom and started downstairs. Halfway down, he paused. 'Are you all right? Has anything happened?'

'There's a car outside. I think we've been followed.'

'What!' Proctor took the rest of the stairs two at a time until he got to the window. Sarah was behind him. 'The grey Polo with the darkened windows.'

'Right, stay here. Both of you.' He ran to the front door, yanked it open, and ran at full speed down the road in the direction of the car. It started up straight away and sped in the direction of the house and towards Proctor. He shot into the middle of the road holding out his arms towards the speeding car. It accelerated and headed straight at him.

'Dad!' Sarah cried from the door.

The car headed straight at Proctor. At the last second, he hurled himself from the road onto the pavement. The bumper cracked against his knee. He fell and banged his head and shoulder on the pavement. He pulled himself up on one elbow. The car raced away, brakes screeching as it cornered out of sight.

Proctor's vision became obscured. He put his hand to his head and felt blood run down his forehead and into his left eye. He pushed a handkerchief against the wound.

Sarah ran out and knelt beside him. Katie followed, covered her mouth.

'Dad, dad, are you all right?' Sarah's eyes were wide and frightened.

Proctor pulled himself into a seating position and inspected the handkerchief. 'I'm all right, let's get inside.'

Supported by Sarah, he hobbled to the front door. He went to the bathroom to clean himself up.

Sarah opened a first aid box and removed a plaster kit. 'Here, let me put this on,' she said. She applied the plaster, her hand shaking and smiled, 'I remember you doing this often enough, usually on my grazed knees.'

Proctor stared in the mirror. 'I do too.' He rubbed his shoulder and arm. 'Right, I'm in one piece. Now let's all sit down together. I want to know in detail what's going on here.'

Sarah exchanged glances with Katie. Proctor sat in a chair around the kitchen table with Sarah and Katie on either side. He looked at each in turn then said. 'Who's going to start?'

Sarah drew a deep breath. 'Well, about three months ago we started playing a computer game - kind of role-playing game on the internet called Hollowcost.'

Katie chimed in, 'We're really good at it, Uncle Matt, the best.'

'I'm sure you are. Tell me about the game.'

'Have you heard of Grand Theft Auto?'

'Yes, very violent, isn't it?'

'Well, Hollowcost makes GTA look like something out of CeeBeebies. It's ...illegal software.'

Proctor lowered his head to his hands. 'Go on, tell me all about it.'

Sarah explained the concept of Hollowcost, about the avatar personalities they adopted, how the game involved interactive battles, hand to hand combat, poker playing for linden dollars, theft and cheating - torture. The object was to beat all the other clans - by any means, there were no laws, no moral limits. Proctor's eyes widened in alarm.

'We don't play for real money, dad. It's all done in cyber space.'

Katie interjected, 'It's only a game.'

Proctor said, 'I'm pleased to hear that.'

Sarah explained how she and Katie, with advice from Chris set up a clan called The Knifethrowers.

Proctor groaned, 'He's not involved as well!'

Sarah said, 'We competed with several teams and beat them. We moved up the difficulty level - got to one level from the top.' She looked at Katie who stared down at the table. 'That was when we challenged The Nightwatchmen.'

Katie piped up, 'And we beat them too, Uncle Matt. They didn't fancy that.'

'How did you know they didn't like it?'

'That was when we started getting nasty emails, text messages.' Sarah bit her lip.

'Have you still got the messages?'

Sarah held up her mobile phone. 'On here.'

Proctor said, 'Show me, will you?'

While Sarah opened the messages from The Man and Swordman, Proctor went to a kitchen drawer and got a pad and pen. He sat down and winced holding his knee.

'Are you all right, dad?'

He indicated the mobile phone, 'Let's have a look.'

As Sarah scrolled through each message Proctor made notes and waited until she'd finished. 'I wish you'd told me about this sooner, Sarah,' he said.

Katie said in an upset tone, 'We weren't doing anything wrong. We thought they were some kids having a laugh.'

'Illegal software, mindless internet violence...' He glowered at both. 'Not doing anything wrong!'

'I know, dad. Sorry.' Sarah closed the mobile.

'Now then,' Proctor put down his pen. 'Today, this car, you say you first noticed it when you were in the coffee shop?'

'Yes,' Sarah screwed up her face. 'It seemed to slow down as it passed the window. I thought at first it was...'

'Go on,' Proctor said.

'The windows were dark so I can't be sure - but I thought it might be...Phil.'

'How certain are you?'

'I can't be sure - it was - the windows were so dark.'

'What about you, Katie?'

Katie squinted, 'I don't know. I wasn't paying much attention to it. Sarah saw it first and later she said we were being followed.'

Proctor looked down at his notepad. 'Why do you make a connection between the computer game, the avatars - and the car that followed you?'

Sarah and Katie exchanged puzzled looks. Sarah said, 'Well, it can't be anything else.'

Proctor said, 'Maybe...maybe someone...or two ...wanted to make a pick-up?'

Frowning, Sarah said. 'I don't think...well,' she glanced at Katie. 'I suppose it could be that, what do you think Katie?'

'I hadn't thought ...but if it had been they'd have stopped, opened the window, tried some kind of chat up line.' She hesitated, 'Well, wouldn't they?'

'Do you think that was it, dad. Some guys maybe wanting to pick us up?'

Katie said, 'Or kidnap us, some of those, what you call them, traffickers, looking for sex slaves.'

Proctor held up his hand and smiled again. 'Let's go back to the avatars thing. Set up the game on your computer. I want to see you two in action.'

Sarah smiled, 'Okay. Welcome to The Knifethrowers.' She picked up her mobile from the kitchen table. She gave a startled cry as it bleeped and dropped it.

Katie stared at the phone, 'You've got a text message.'

Sarah hesitated before picking up the phone and read the message, colour draining from her face. Biting her lips she passed the mobile to her dad.

Proctor read the message. It was from 'Swordman'. It read 'U bn wrnd no gms or els'.

His stomach tightened and an image flashed through his mind; a man stalking an unnerved woman, his mam terrified, they'd never caught the stalker. He thought of all those other Cardiff women over thirty years ago - young and old - who'd had the wits scared out of them. He looked at Sarah, his face expressionless. He thought of vigilante groups conducting a private manhunt. His mam driven to suicide, their family's world destroyed. Now his daughter and niece; was it happening all over again? He drove the thoughts from his mind and composed himself.

'Who's Swordman?' Proctor asked.

'One of The Nightwatchmen.'

'Do you think it was him following us?' Katie gasped.

Reaching across the table, he grasped Sarah and Katie's hands. 'Don't worry, no one's going to hurt you. Right?'

Sarah looked from him to the mobile phone. She bit her lip, picked up the phone, and turned it off.

Proctor repeated the text message. ' "No more games or else". They are more than annoyed with you two hammering them, aren't they?' He pulled up a chair close to the terminal, 'Now then, let's see how this works.'

'Are you sure, dad?' Sarah chewed on her lip hesitating over opening the game.

'I'm sure. But can you play another team?'

'Clan.'

'Okay, another clan, Not The Nightwatchmen, okay?'

'Yeah, right.'

He watched as Sarah and Katie set up the controls, logged on to the site and joined the game. They registered and found a clan ready to compete.

The speed and adeptness of their reactions as they controlled their avatars' actions amazed him; agile movement, anticipation, taking cover then going on the attack with an armoury of weapons. He held his breath as he watched the cyber characters explode in showers of blood and gore, the noise of gunfire and grenades popping deafening. Then a poker game, where had they learned to play poker so well? Was this a healthy thing for two young people to spend their time doing? He flinched and became still when an avatar dressed in black leathers and a balaclava leapt into view behind Katie's avatar. He tensed when he saw a piece of wire held between both hands.

Sarah screamed, 'Look out, Katie. Strangler.'

Katie attempted to swing her character out of danger while at the same time lobbing a grenade towards the leather clad figure.

But too late; he was right behind her, the garrotte was thrown around Katie's avatar's neck. The avatar pulled tightly on the wire, Katie's avatar's eyes bulged and she slipped down, the attacker still pulling hard on the wire.

'Oh, no, 'Sarah shouted. 'Special ammo, Katie, special ammo.'

Both Katie and Sarah worked their controls in a frenzy and Proctor couldn't see what each was doing such was the sped and variety of their hand movements. A loud bang came from Sarah's avatar and a screaming rocket shot out from a station above the two struggling figures. It slammed into the leather clad avatar that erupted into smithereens.

Sarah exhaled, 'Close call Katie. Let's get to safety; regroup.'

'Too right,' Katie said. In her drawn face Proctor realised how they lived this game, how the experience in cyberspace was profound and real for them; drained their emotions.

Their mood communicated to him; he leaned back in his chair, his quickened pulse racing. He waited a few more minutes until they finished, gaining a narrow points win their opponents.

Sarah pulled a face. 'Afraid that was not one of our better performances, dad.'

Proctor smiled, 'Looked pretty good to me. I don't know how you can keep up with all that action.'

'So, what do you think?' Sarah and Katie shut down the computers.

Proctor fought to control his feelings, 'Tell me, that business of strangling from behind with a wire. Is that common in these games?'

Katie said. 'That's what caught me out just there. Normally, they choose special weapons if you give up others. Some do strangling. Worst I've seen are the 'Head Drillers'. Yuk. They suck out your brains!'

Sarah spoke in a subdued voice, she looked at her dad. 'The Nightwatchmen do both.'

Proctor left the girls in the bedroom and made himself a drink downstairs. He sipped the whisky thinking about what he'd just seen. He sank into his armchair and recalled the image of Dominic Masters' dead body. That must have been how it was on the steps of the Council House in Victoria Square. A young man alone, a stealthy figure closing in on him from behind, silent, swift. The wire around his neck tightening, unable to cry out, losing the ability to breathe, his last convulsive movements to try to retain life, blackness, all over.

Sweat ran down his face. The Night watchmen clan, a cyber strangler called The Man? Swordman? Others? Body mutilators. No, this was all too bizarre. More probably a copycat murder - picked up by impressionable minds. The same modus operandi - in one case vicarious thrills using imagination and game playing avatars; very different from the real world, from real human pain and the death of a real human being. Playing a game was not the same thing as real life murder. Or was it?

Chapter 28

Proctor sat at his desk at home - he'd converted the third bedroom into an office/study since Hannah left and spent more time there than ever. He understood how people could become addicted to surfing the Net. He'd spent the past hour visiting gameplaying websites, checking out Grand Theft Auto and did some research on Wikipedia. The sites on Masters' list were variations on GTA, some he couldn't get on, password or subscription only.

He was becoming clearer about the 'cyberworld' - he thought it might be better termed the 'otherworld'. But it was the here and now; and the future. A link appeared and he was in the West Midlands police website; that didn't help; just reinforced how much he missed his work. Twenty three years he'd spent in the force since he was eighteen, near enough his whole working life - was this how it would end? Accused of taking backhanders from drug dealers. Remembered as a bent cop. A shitty ignominious finish to his career. He banged the desk and pressed his hands across his temple. The cut on his forehead had scabbed over and his bruises eased. Sarah insisted on going straight back to college and appeared to be coping - but he'd noticed she looked around the street a lot before setting off. Wire garrottes - holes in people's heads...

He needed to get into Ron Kydd's offices, one more visit to Hall's and he could wrap things up there. Question was as well as reporting to the insurers; did they report Hall to the police? He checked his watch, nine a.m.

Events surrounding Romney and Cartwright puzzled him. If, as Azzra had suggested, the skids were under them then surely that must be good news for him. He needed to know more and to find sodding Baz Manning. If he could get to him, he felt sure he could unlock just what was the state of play between Baz and those two prats. If it meant taking off the gloves with Baz then so be it. His enforced leave gnawed at him, the injustice churning bile in his stomach. He had to sort matters or he'd go into a downward spiral.

He thought of Azzra. Two weeks since they'd met at the Bistro. One phone call since. He drummed the table with his fingers for several seconds, snatched up the phone and dialled her mobile number. He continued drumming as he waited for her to pick up.

'Hi, Azzra. Is it okay to talk?'

She paused. 'Just give me a moment.' There was a delay before she spoke again; he guessed she'd moved somewhere private.

'Nice to hear from you Matt.'

'Listen - maybe we can have dinner.'

'Matt - this Masters' case, I'm working day and night.'

'Sure, sure, I've some thoughts on that.'

'Matt - you're off it! Get your own situation sorted.'

'Okay, okay...but you said you'd help.'

He heard her draw breath. 'Last time we spoke seemed you preferred going solo.'

'Yes, yes; sorry about that. Stupid thing to say.'

'Yes, it was.' She paused, 'So, what can I do?'

'Thanks. I got a lead on Baz - a dodgy room in a council estate house in Aston - but when I got there he'd vanished.'

'Done a runner?'

'Yes and no. He was under pressure from a local crew, they messed up the place and I don't know if they messed up him as well.'

'Pleased to hear he's still leading the low life.'

'I need to ask you a favour.'

'About time.'

He heard a thaw in her voice. 'I know, I know. Listen, I got a car number from a registration document - it's a long shot but could you check it out with DVLA. Might get something - anything would help.'

'Anything? Garden leave eating you up?'

'More like me eating garden leaves.'

'Feeling low?'

'What's the latest with Romney?'

Azzra lowered her voice. 'I can't talk about that right now. Later?'

'Okay, I understand, so then...are you free next night or two?'

'It's awkward...'

'Tonight's good.'

'Tonight!'

'Please. Do you fancy a balti? I can you up at, say, seven?'

'Emma's pushing us hard for a result with Masters...'

'Night off'll do you good.'

She waited a second or two before replying. 'Well, I suppose so, but make it eight.'

'Right, right, see you later.'

'And Matt, keep your chin up, eh?'

Proctor flicked shut his phone. He looked up at the ceiling above which was Sarah's room. Azzra could help him find Baz. And he could help her. Masters. Must be a link - those websites. Stalkers - my daughter's being stalked.

Proctor pressed the buzzer and Azzra's voice came over the intercom, 'Matt?'

'Yes, not too early am I?'

'No, be right down.'

He leaned his arm against the wall and tapped his feet. She appeared at the door a minute later. Her hair was swept back in a style very different from when he'd last seen her. A high bandana covered her forehead and she wore a deep red dress with a narrow white trim around the neckline. She carried a beige cardigan that she slung over her shoulder as she locked the door behind her.

'I'm parked round the corner,' he said. As he walked alongside her, he held his head high and tried not to be too obvious in glancing at her slim profile and high cheek-boned dusky coloured face. He realised he was walking too fast and forced himself to slow down. She was quiet during the short car journey to Balsall Heath in the heart of Baltiland.

Proctor relaxed as he ate the spiced balti dish from a deep pan, dipping chunks of Naan bread and sipping a pleasant Chilean red wine. Their table was against a wall, in a raised section of the restaurant. Low Pakistani music played in the background. Proctor glanced behind him, noted the adjacent table was unoccupied.

He talked about his boyhood in Cardiff, how the well designed development around the Bay had metamorphosed the city. Azzra listened and gradually released information about her parents' years growing up in Uganda. As she talked she lightened up, became more animated.

'I'd love to see it,' he said.

'Yes, it's a beautiful place,' she smiled, 'especially the countryside.' Her eyes shadowed and she said, 'It broke my mum's heart having to leave.'

'Maybe one day she can see it again.'

'Yes, yes, she'd appreciate that.'

She put down her knife and fork. 'Listen, I've got something for you.' She opened her handbag and took out an envelope. She wiggled it several times. 'I was able to get an address from DVLA, not Baz's rented address.'

'No? Where?'

'His cousin's.'

'His cousin!' Proctor slapped his head, 'I never thought to check Baz's relatives through Coyle - losing my touch.'

'The vehicle was registered in his cousin's name, Kevin Manning. And I checked some old case files. Baz has form. Apparently, when he got into a bit of bother he would use his cousin's place to lie low.'

'A bolthole?'

'Something like that. Now if Baz was on the street after the crew had done over his place, it's just possible...'

'I'll say it is. This looks promising, Azzra. But you took a bit of a chance, didn't you. What if O'Rourke found you snooping around Baz Manning's records?'

'Ah, that's something else.'

'Go on,' Proctor took the envelope and looked at the address inside. It was quite a respectable part of Birmingham in the Edgbaston area.

'Romney and Cartwright have been put on 'special duties'.

'Well, well. The old special duties allocation. So - they're in the anteroom.'

'They are in bad odour. I don't know what's going on but there's a lot of speculation. People asking the same questions as you, Matt. The mood is you've been dealt a shitty hand.'

'This is music to my ears.'

'There's a downside.'

'I thought there might be.'

'I was with ACC Merritt, going over some figures he needed for a Police Authority meeting.'

'Oh, yes.' Proctor put the address note in the envelope and pocketed it. 'Thanks for this, Azzra,' he said. 'I'll call on Kevin Manning then.'

'I shouldn't hang about.'

'I won't.'

'I say that because Merritt dropped a casual remark.'

'To do with me? Or Manning?'

'Both. I think you need to move fast.'

Proctor looked into her eyes; he read anxiety there. 'So…what did Merritt say.'

'I asked him about Romney, said I hadn't seen him around for a time. That's when he mentioned special duties. I just raised an eyebrow and then he said, 'DCI Romney is going overseas, I think.'

Proctor looked puzzled, 'Overseas?'

'I primed him, got a little more from him. What do you think?'

Proctor thought he could see the pattern. He had been kicked out, but there remained the prospect of a scandal, a clear out was called for; Merritt was shit clearing. A glimmer of hope stirred in him, 'So, maybe they don't think Romney is lily white after all?'

'Maybe. I don't know. But both he and Alan Cartwright are leaving, that's the upshot.'

'Do you know when?'

'According to Merritt end of the month. No big leaving party planned for them either.'

Proctor said, 'You know, Azzra, I can't make my mind up if this is good news or bad.'

'Whatever, now then what about this. My understanding is they're heading for the Police Service of Northern Ireland.'

'What? Belfast. Those two won't like that.'

'Have you thought perhaps they weren't given a choice? Just like you?' She shrugged and drained her wine glass.

'Thanks.' He held up his empty glass, 'Want to try another bottle?'

Azzra said, 'Why not. Let's order some food first, shall we?'

Chapter 29

Katie walked from her bus stop to work. She stepped out with a jaunty air. The morning was cold and a sharp frost the night before left white hoar on the grass verge. The sun, low in the winter sky glinted a watery yellow pallor but warmed the air. She loosened her coat collar a fraction around her neck.

Why not? The question formed in her mind and she instantly felt an aggressive, even defensive response. Why shouldn't she? You only live once and he does fancy me. The world is boring anyway, all the boyfriends I've had so far have been so pathetic, immature. Yes, I've got a good mate in Sarah and get along well with Teresa at work, even Harry Armstrong's okay and the guys in the warehouse are all up for a laugh so that's good. I want...what do I want? She struggled for an answer. Something...different; something else, new, exciting. Her mood darkened for a moment. As far as Phil's concerned forget it - he's grim; when I think how he went at Sarah, she was well rid there. Phil? That's a real no-brainer, forget him. She sucked in a deep breath and exhaled slowly.

As always, she held her back straight and her head high conscious of how her blonde hair bounced as she strode out. She looked overhead and all around, the sky was a cornflower blue with not a cloud to be seen right to the horizon. Days like these reminded her of when she was a little girl, walking in the park with her mum and dad, feeding ducks in the pond, everything fresh and optimistic then and filled with anticipation. She hardly ever saw her dad these days he was so absorbed in his work. And mum? Penny she thought was often away with the fairies, a real worry guts. She gave a quick shake of her head.

Graham. She rolled his name around her lips thinking about him. He's powerful, and experienced, he'll give me a good time. Anyway, I know how to take care of myself, it'll be a laugh. He came on to me yesterday in a big way, almost gagging for it he was. If he asks me again today I'll say yes. Why not? Add a bit of spice to my life. And of course he won't want it broadcast, too much glued to his wife and his two girls. Stupid names. But that suits me, a bit of secrecy, mystery. Sarah will hate me for it, but she'll never know. And it is my life after all, I'm a free agent, I can decide what it is I want to do. Yes, yes, why not? Be a bit of fun.

She entered the offices and Teresa was in before her as usual, busying herself with filing and taking early calls. She gave a wave to Katie who took off her coat and switched her pc on. There were some new expenses claims to enter so she started straight away on those. She frowned as she entered the figures noting how the sums were getting larger.

'Good morning, ladies.' Katie's heart gave a short thump as she heard his voice. She thought how bright and cheerful he sounded this morning.

'Good morning, Mr Hall,' Teresa murmured.

'For God's sake call me Graham,' he said. 'We're all part of the same team here. Isn't that right, Katie?' He held the back of her chair as he spoke and she felt his hands touch her back.

She flashed a warm smile. 'Good morning, Graham. You seem bright and bushy tailed this morning.'

'I am, you gorgeous thing. Just had some excellent news - big contract we've won. Against the odds but it's juicy.'

'Pleased to hear it, can Teresa and I can have a bonus then?'

He let his arm slide over her shoulder and leaned close to her ear. 'How about a bonus and something in kind as well?'

Teresa coughed and stood up gathering a bunch of despatch notes. She caught Katie's eye and mouthed 'phones' pointing to her desk. Katie mouthed back 'okay'.

'And what kind of something in kind did you have in mind then…Graham?'

He glanced around and watched the door into the factory area close behind Teresa. He reached into his back pocket and held up a pair of tickets. 'Two tickets for one of the hottest bands in town - and free drinks all night. Now is that a bonus or what?'

Katie blinked at the tickets. Arctic Monkeys and several top support acts at the NEC. 'Sounds great,' she said.

'I'll say it is - and that's not all. Afterwards we get a taxi into town and have a slap up dinner. Now isn't that a bonus and a half?'

'I'm tempted.'

'You won't regret it, be a real rave. So - is it a date?'

Katie felt an adrenalin rush, this was it, a chance to step out of the humdrum world she only knew so far, into another planet. Her chest went tight and she felt light headed. She could smell his after shave, glimpsed the blonde hairs falling over his open necked shirt, felt his hand pressing more firmly against her back, now sliding up and down in a stroking action.

'Sounds great, Graham, what time?'

'Can you get to New Street station for six? I'll collect you there.'

'Means leaving work early.'

'Don't you worry about that, have the afternoon off. Soak in a bath and I'll think about you.'

Katie laughed, 'Maybe I will too.'

He leaned over her and she felt his lips press against the top of her head. 'You'll enjoy yourself, Katie, that's what life's all about, right?

'Right.'

He glanced at the expense notes and picked up one. 'Tonight, Katie, money's no object; we'll have a great time.'

He left the office and she sat for a minute trying to stop her racing heart, she felt a buzz greater than any ecstasy pill had ever given her, she felt power.

Chapter 30

Proctor sat in his beloved Audi A3 Sportback, about fifty metres from Kevin Manning's address. The leafy avenue was quiet, few cars parked and Proctor felt conspicuous. He read a newspaper as he watched for any movement. Kevin Manning must have done all right from the appearance of his property, a detached double fronted redbrick house set in a huge garden behind a pair of wrought iron gates with a security code lock. Parked on the drive a maroon coloured BMW sparkled in the morning sun. A metal sign on the gate carried a picture of a Rottweiler with the word 'Beware' spelt out in red capital letters. Proctor felt wary; once he needed to take on a dog and he touched his left arm where the scar still showed. He glanced at his watch, seven a.m. He wondered if Baz was inside; if Kevin was an early riser. He hoped the local Neighbourhood Watch scheme sign on a lamppost nearby wasn't the most active. He didn't fancy explaining to a uniform that he was doing a spot of surveillance in order to overthrow allegations that he was a corrupt copper. That should raise a laugh.

Over an hour passed before there was any sign of life from behind the iron gates. Proctor did a quick double take as a figure inside zapped the gates with a remote and opened the car door. Hassan. Yes, that wasn't a face he was likely to forget. The Caribbean Nights casino, Hassan in the car park, an envelope being passed from him to Romney. What the hell was this about, Baz's old banger shown as registered by its owner or keeper from this expensive pad in well-heeled Edgbaston? Proctor was bemused. For a moment he thought of following Hassan but then focussed on the object of the exercise - to get to Baz Manning, to put the squeeze on him. He slid down into the driver's seat and watched the BMW purr through the gateway, the tall gates close automatically as Hassan drove away. Proctor settled down again.

Ten o'clock came and passed and Proctor began to think that perhaps any other occupants of the house were settled in for the day. But his patience was rewarded. Baz Manning emerged wearing jeans and a bomber jacket with the hood down, his head covered by a black beanie. Then a second youngish man came out and operated a remote device to open the gates. Baz nipped through pointing two trigger fingers back as he left. The other man went inside straight away.

Baz hurried along the street away from Proctor. He got out of the car and followed Baz who walked with a sideways swagger, his hands stuck into the side pockets of his jacket, arms akimbo. He took a right turn through a gateway and Proctor stepped out to keep him in view. Baz entered a small park, Proctor guessed he was using a shortcut to somewhere - he didn't see Baz as someone keen to enjoy the winter scenery nor feed the ducks. Now was as good a time as any.

Proctor skirted away from Baz's line into the trees at the edge of the park. Two young men about Baz's age came into view, walked up to him. They gave each other high fives salutes and talked for a while; Baz's hand reached across to one of them. They went through another high fives slapping routine with loud laughs. Baz's friends sauntered over the park's horizon and out of sight while he resumed walking.

Proctor moved faster to catch up with Baz, his footsteps silent on the soft grass. When he was about twenty yards away, Baz reacted and swung around. For a second he froze while Proctor launched himself flat out. Baz reacted and took off like a hundred metre sprinter. Proctor ran at full tilt until he was right behind Baz. In a rugby tackle, he grabbed him around the waist and threw him to the ground. They struggled for a short time and when Baz threw a feeble punch, Proctor's fist hit him with a solid blow to the stomach. Baz gasped and fought to get his breath.

'Hey, man, what is this?'

'I've been looking for you Baz, you're a hard man to find.'

'Hey, man I ain't done no shit on you.'

Proctor heaved him to his feet and twisted Baz's arm up behind his back; the young man cried out and bent over double in pain.

'Watcha want, watcha after?'

'Information Baz, and if you don't open up I'm gonna beat the shit out of you. How does that sound pal?' He applied more pressure on Baz's arm and this time Baz screamed in pain.

'Leave it, leave it, you'll break my bleeding arm.'

Proctor let go his arm, turned him round and sank his fist once more into Baz's stomach. This time Baz's face turned grey and he collapsed on the grass, moaning and clutching his stomach. He held up his hand, 'No more man, no more.'

'That's all right, Baz. Now I'll move upstairs.' He pulled back his fist and Baz's eyes opened wide. 'No, no, what is it. What you want?'

'You signed a statement Baz. For Romney, DCI Tony Romney, remember.'

Baz groaned again.

Proctor grabbed him by the throat. 'Remember, you little shit.' His eyes bored into Baz's who licked his lips and looked right and left in fear. 'I didn't mean no harm, they were going to stuff me, man. I was in deep shit.'

'What did you say, what was in the statement.'

'Hey, Mr Proctor, I didn't mean no harm, you believe me. Right?'

'Just tell me, Baz, because if you don't you'll think the crew's doing you over was a picnic. I'll haunt you, Baz. Now give!'

'It was - I didn't think it was a big deal.'

'What - what did you sign in the statement.'

Baz was shaking, his hands kept moving to his mouth. 'Maybe, listen, Mr Proctor if I tell you, you'll see me right, yeah?'

'Just tell me what you said.'

'I'll be in big time shit.'

Proctor shook him and threw him on the ground, putting his foot on his head. 'Listen you already are - so tell me.' He smiled and removed his foot from Baz's face. His voice softened, 'Listen, Baz, I'm not after you. There are a couple of bad guys I want to nail. Not you, not even Hassan.'

Baz looked startled. 'You know Hassan, you know my uncle?'

'Course I do, Baz, that's my job, to know things.' Well, well, Proctor thought.

'He's clean, he don't do stuff. He's a dentist.'

'Of course he is, a very good dentist too I'm told.' You're like a leaking tap, Baz. He filed away an idea; maybe I need to pay a visit to Dr Hassan - have some dental work.

'Don't worry about your uncle, all I'm interested in is what you said in your statement. And listen, I'll do all I can to make sure you don't get hammered. That's fair, isn't it? You were a good snout, I remember that. But Baz, you dropped me in the shit.'

Baz wriggled on the ground and whimpered, rubbing his gut. He crawled to his knees, he looked up through narrowed eyes. 'Okay. Okay, I'll tell you. Tony came to see me, that other cop was with him. Alan something…'

'Cartwright.'

'That's him. They said all I needed to swear was...,' he screwed up his face and gave a short gasp. 'That you were taking cash - from me - to let me do deals, you know.'

187

'Did they say why Baz?'

'Yeah. Tony said you was going to fit me up, that's what he said. But they'd protect me.' He hesitated then his voice broke. 'I didn't mean you no harm, Mr Proctor, you was always fair, They said if I didn't swear you did a deal, they'd really mess me up.'

'What did they say, Baz?'

'Break both my legs and…'

'And…'

'Cut me - cut me real bad. I couldn't take that, I…I couldn't.'

'But you were paying them off, weren't you?'

'Not me, they were dealing with Uncle Hassan. Hey, you said you knew, man.'

'Of course I do, Baz. Now listen, I need you to make another statement, to a friend of mine, the truth. I'll protect you, Baz. This time you'll be doing the right thing. You up for that?'

'Don't have much choice, do I?'

'No, you don't.'

Baz struggled to his feet; then bent over in pain. Proctor thought he'd pass out, he put an arm around his shoulder, 'Baz, you aren't a bad person, I want to help you, believe me.'

Baz said, 'You pigs don't do me no favours.'

Proctor kept his arm around his shoulders, he said, 'I'll get you out of shit, believe me.'

'Hey man, you lot, you all say that.'

'Baz, you have a choice - those guys who got you to do a deal - they're the bad guys. I'll deal with them and get you sorted. I'm the good guy. Who you going with?'

Baz wiped his hands across his face, 'Listen, they gave me some shit,' he stopped talking; across the park a couple of men appeared. Baz hopped to the cover of some trees. 'Look, I'll go with you, but piss off right now, okay.' He watched the two men keep walking until they were out of sight.

Proctor said, 'Listen, Baz. They pushed you into a bad situation. I can get you out of it. You used to be my man, right? He cupped his hands around Baz's head, 'Only way, mate.'

Baz said, 'Right, right.'

'Come with me now.'

Baz rubbed his stomach and followed Proctor out of the park to the Audi. He manoeuvred Baz into the passenger seat and entered a number into his mobile.

'Azzra?' He paused, 'Listen, I've got Baz Manning with me. He's got something he wants to tell you. I'm bringing him to the station.'

There was a pause then Azzra said. 'Not a good idea, Matt. I'll come to you. Caution him. Okay?'

Proctor gave her his location. 'I'm still in bad odour then.'

'Been more developments. I'll fill you in. See you in about half an hour.'

'Right.'

Baz Manning crouched low in the car seat kneading his stomach, blowing short whimpers.

Proctor glanced at Baz and thought about him and the rest of the Baz's of the world. He thought about his son Chris and his daughter Sarah. A rabbit ran out from a hedge bordering one of leafy Edgbaston's parks and darted across the road and through a gap in the hedge on the opposite side. Safe. Not everyone made it to safety.

What had happened to Baz along the way - he had a strange sympathy for the little tyke, he was always going to be a loser, a bit player, where had Baz gone wrong? Proctor recalled the punches he'd laid into him, they were hard, punishing. He tightened his grip on the steering wheel. 'Shit,' he said out loud.

Marion Kalkowski winced as Proctor limped through the door of RK Security. She went to him and placed her finger on the wound on his forehead. 'You should have that stitched, you know.'

'Yes, probably. Ron in yet?'

'In and out, you know what he's like, busy, busy, busy.' She looked again at the cut on his forehead. 'Want to tell what happened?'

'Long story, Marion - though nothing to do with Ron's job at Hall's.'

'Good, he needs these insurance contracts. Business isn't as good as he makes out.'

'No? Maybe I shouldn't be...'

'He wants to help - anyway, you're self-financing.' She held her arms out wide. 'He wants to help you - you're his friend,' she shrugged.

'Am I? That's good to know.'

'So?' She folded her arms across her chest in a matronly pose.

Proctor smiled. 'Ron's told you about my situation?'

'There are no secrets between Ron and me.'

'I'll bet!'

She chortled and said, 'I'll make some coffee. Of course there are secrets.' She kept her back to him and said. 'Do you think I tell him everything?'

Proctor laughed, 'I think you have a dark past, Marion.'

'We all have pasts,' she shrugged and said, 'Dark? Who knows. But you - are you getting anywhere with proving your innocence?'

'Some straws in the wind. But I need to make things happen myself.'

'You know Ron will help as much as he can.' She studied Proctor's face for a few seconds. 'When you were in trouble, he got a phone call. I've never seen him so angry.'

'No?'

'Matt, let me tell you something. He is a good friend. Let a good friend help you.'

Proctor looked at this middle aged woman whose penetrating eyes he felt bored into his soul, as if his innermost thoughts were tattooed across his forehead.

'Does Ron still use the Caribbean Nights casino much?'

'Yes, he enjoys a game of blackjack. I do as well. But he's a controlled gambler.'

'I think I'll take your advice, get Ron to check someone out.'

'Do that - he wants to help. I know you and he went through some good - and not so good - times together, yes?'

'Yes, Ron looked after me when I was rookie and wet behind the ears.' Proctor recalled a few dodgy arrests made by Ron but which sent serious villains down. Never get away with that nowadays, he thought.

'He taught me a lot did Ron.' He thought about how he'd dealt with Baz - got a result. 'Yes, Ron showed me a few tricks of the trade.'

Marion put the coffee cup in his hands and said, 'Let your friends help, sometimes we can be too proud.' Her black eyes bored into him.

'When's he due back?'

'About an hour's time.'

'I'll wait. I need to write up some notes.'

He heard Ron's distinctive voice as soon he entered the office. There was a short silence and whispering before Marion lifted her voice and told him Proctor was waiting for him. Proctor smiled, it was good to see Ron enjoying life again; he remembered how devastated he'd been when Helen died from breast cancer.

'Morning, Matt. How's it going?'

'I've got some stuff on Hall, I'm sure he's got an insurance scam going. I need a bit more to hang him though.'

Ron beamed. 'That's great news, my esteemed colleague. Just what the doctor ordered. Do us a world of good with the insurers, sure to get more work there.'

'You're a good investigator, Matt. I was confident you'd get us a result.' He looked Proctor up and down and tossed a thumb in the direction of Marion's office, 'Her Ladyship warned me you've been in the wars.'

'I've been to your club.'

'The Caribbean Nights?'

'Met a few old detective friends there.'

'Go on, tell me I should ask how they look!'

Proctor touched his forehead, 'I didn't get this from them.'

'What happened then?'

'Pavement leaped up and hit me.'

'I trust you weren't over imbibing?'

'No such luck - tell you about it later. But I got a whack on the back of the head for upsetting Tony Romney. I came off worst, no doubt about that. But I've got a lead on Baz Manning.'

'Umm, getting injury prone.' His face expressed worry. 'Those two are bastards. Hope you haven't dug yourself in too deep, Matt.'

'I need to know more about a guy I met there. He seemed to know the club well - might be a member.'

Ron's face lit up. 'I can check him out. What's he look like? Got a name?'

'I hoped you'd say that. British Asian, Hassan, think he's a dentist in Edgbaston.'

Ron pulled out a notebook and scribbled in it. 'Done, get on it right away.'

'Thanks Ron - appreciated.'

Ron squeezed his shoulder, 'Anything, my friend, just ask.'

Chapter 31

Katie swayed to the music that pounded through her body; she let her head rock from side to side to the beat; her hair falling across her face. She fought to keep Graham Hall opposite her still in her sight, occasionally reaching over and holding him to steady herself. He pulled her close squeezing his body against her and nuzzling her head. His green shirt, changing colour with the strobe lights, disorientated her. She wanted this moment, this sensation to go on forever. Hall put his arm around her waist, his hand across her backside and led her back to their table. He pushed her glass across the table and poured two more large measures of bubbly.

'You can't beat champers, Katie. Only the best.'

She leaned forward and holding her glass with both hands slid it below her mouth and sipped a drink. She spluttered as some bubbles went up her nose. She giggled and said, 'Only the best for the best.'

'That's absolutely right, the best for the best.' He looked around the club then at his watch. 'Tell you what, time's getting on. I think we should get off now, place is thinning out.'

Katie laughed out loud as she struggled to her feet. Hall guided her movements with his arm around her back. 'There you go, Katie, that's it. Just hold onto me, okay.' He gathered her bag from the floor and tucked it under his arm, slinging his jacket across her shoulders. 'Be a bit on the nippy side once we're outside, car's nearby though.'

'Train, I need to catch train.' She blinked several times and launched into a sneezing fit as the cold night air hit her. Her vision blurred and she felt her head spin; the headlights from passing traffic became fused into long continuous beams of light. She fought to clear her head. Slowly, Hall guided her up a flight of stairs and through the multi-storey car park. She thought how gloomy the lights were and said, 'I think I'll have a sleep now.'

'Soon, Katie, soon, just keep concentrating, one step at a time, not far now.' She tipped over sideways a couple of times in her high-heeled shoes and winced as she felt a sharp pain. She bent over and rubbed her ankle.

'Shoes,' she muttered.

'What?'

'Get off...shoes.'

'Ah - right,' He held her as she struggled to remove first one shoe then the other, dropping one in the process. He sat her down on the car park floor while he collected the shoes, struggling to keep hold of the handbag. 'Shit,' he muttered.

Katie giggled, 'Naughty, no swearing, no...' she hiccupped 'bad language'. The cold concrete numbed her backside. She scrambled to her feet while Hall fumbled with the remote, dragging open the Porsche's doors. She collapsed into the passenger seat. He slung her shoes, bag on the back seat, and sat for a few seconds in the driving seat glancing around the deserted car park. He smiled at Katie who leaned her head on his shoulder. She shivered and he switched on the car engine, setting the climate control to hot.

'It's all right, you'll soon get warm.'

He put his arm across her shoulder; let his hand rest on her breast. She felt his body warmth against her. She raised her mouth to his and his long hair tickled her cheek as their lips met. The car seat slid back and she sank down until horizontal, feeling Hall's body ride on top of her.

Katie's head throbbed as she lay alone in bed. She closed her eyes and tried to recall the events of the night before. Great meal, champagne, the nightclub, dancing, dancing…she sat bolt upright. Where was she? On the bedside was a radio clock, she leaned over to read the time. A stabbing pain jabbed behind her eyes and she lay back closing them, rolled on her side emitting low moans. Again, she pulled herself up and focused on her surroundings. She tried to make some kind of sense of the images that floated in her memory. The car park, Graham Hall in the car, sex Then what? Yes, he'd driven here and what, what, a lobby, booking into the hotel. This was it, she was in a hotel room; out all night - she'd have to invent a story for her parents. Sarah, she'd get Sarah to cover for her. She closed her eyes and thought hard. She couldn't be sure, Katie crawled from the bed and went to the bathroom where she retched for a minute. She drank a long glass of water. She fumbled in her handbag and with a cry of frustration tipped the contents onto the bed. She found what she wanted. She returned to the bathroom and filled another glass of water, swallowed the morning after pill and gulped down the rest of the water. She got back into the bed and sat up with her arms clasped around her torso, fighting an urge to gag. She looked at the clock, ten. Alongside it was an envelope. She opened and read the note.

"Katie, great night. No worries. No need to rush back. Forget work, Graham. PS - get taxi home, paid for see reception." He'd put three kiss crosses at the bottom.

Katie lay back and groaned, rubbing her head. She lay still for a short time then fell asleep again for about an hour. When she awoke, she felt a lot better. She showered and put on makeover.

She collected her clothes that lay scattered over the floor. Stumbling as she dressed, a part of her felt soiled.

She sat in front of the dressing table mirror taking deep breaths and began to feel more human. She re-read his note; a small smile creased her face for the first time that morning. She picked up the phone and dialled reception, 'I've a taxi ordered, can you call it now?'

A woman's voice answered, 'It'll be a few minutes.'

'I want it now.'

A short pause, 'Of course, madam, straight away.'

Chapter 32

Proctor worked on his report for the insurers detailing what he'd discovered at Hall's Steel Stockholders. He talked through his findings with Ron. The scam was obvious and showed the naivety and at the same time the arrogance of Hall in thinking that he could get away with it more than once. A single hit and in all likelihood he'd have made a successful claim. But by being greedy and lodging three claims in the space of six months, he'd raised the insurers' suspicions.

'How'd he shift the materials? Fences?' Ron asked.

'I'll come to that.'

'So the reprobate Dennis Collins put the proverbial finger on the culprits.'

'All three.'

'It's Collin's word against them then?'

'No - look at this, Ron.'

Proctor removed the micro cassette from the miniature camera, inserted it in a drive in the camcorder and passed it to Ron. 'Happy viewing.'

Ron gave a low whistle, 'Clear as the brightest day.'

Proctor thought back to his meeting with Collins at the Grand Old Turk's Head, when Collins revealed that Phil Dutson was part of the operation; he'd given a sigh of relief that neither Sarah or Katie were now involved with him.

Ron studied the recording. 'So Dutson and Armstrong loaded the truck in the middle of the night.'

'Empty warehouse. Dutson drove off with his load.'

'You followed him?'

'Of course.'

'Of course!'

'Dutson took the materials to a lock-up in the Newtown area of Birmingham. Hall reported the 'theft', insurance claim was lodged and bingo.'

'Umm, hardly get full market value for the stuff,' Ron said.

'True,' Proctor said. 'They got nothing for it.'

'I can see you are playing the enigmatic sleuth, mon amigo.'

Proctor said, 'Okay, the 'stolen' metals were kept in the lockup for a month or so, false invoices raised and the same stuff was retrieved and returned to the plant.'

Ron listened now and again shaking his head in disbelief. 'How did he think he'd get away with it? One hit maybe.'

Proctor said, 'I think he saw other firms in the locality being burgled.'

'And thought they'd believe his warehouse was just as likely to be targeted? One aspect puzzles me, Matt.'

'What's that?'

'Why was Collins so ready to spill the beans on Hall and Dutson? If that gets out he could be in deep doo doo.'

'Collins was pissed off with both Hall and Dutson - and Armstrong who was in it as well.'

'Why?'

'Simple. He wanted to be part of the action. They froze him out even though in the past he'd done some minor stuff for Hall, a bit of fencing of dodgy steel. He could see them making a killing and he felt really narked by that.'

'So when Mr Proctor came asking questions...'

'He was more than happy to drop them in it.'

'The eternal myth of honour among thieves.' Ron put down the camcorder and sat back rubbing his lower back.

'Mind you,' Proctor said, 'It cost me a few hundred quid as well!'

'A bargain, my friend, a bargain.' Ron looked at Proctor with a quizzical smile. 'You are going to feed this to the police? Insurers certainly will.'

'I might drop it in passing to someone I can trust.'

'Win some kudos, that it Matt?'

'Just someone I owe a favour.'

Chapter 33

Katie entered data on to the computer, a slight smile playing around her mouth. She sang, tossed her head from side to side. What a week, she thought. She'd stayed off work the previous Wednesday after returning home in the taxi, but made sure she got out well before her parents' house. Her parents swallowed the story that she'd spent the night at Sarah's.

'Why didn't you phone?' Penny asked.

'Sorry - got a bit tiddly.'

'Katie!' her mum said; that was it.

She'd gone out with Hall again on the Friday night and this time she remembered everything. She guessed it was really good sex they'd had; she made a lot of noise and he seemed satisfied afterwards. He'd driven her south along the M5 motorway to Worcester. They'd stopped at a block of apartments and stayed there all evening coming back just before midnight. Hall told her this was one of several properties he let but this one was vacant awaiting the next lot of short term tenants. He'd laughed and said, 'Perhaps I might leave it empty.' She'd walked around the two bed roomed apartment, one room en-suite, fingered the luxury furnishings, lolled in the largest sofa she'd ever seen; later luxuriated in a huge bath with what looked like gold plated taps. Since then he'd been more than attentive than ever and she thought she'd better watch it because Trees kept giving her odd looks.

'Cat's got the cream then?' Teresa cupped her chin on her hands, her elbows resting on the desk.

'What?'

'You're bright and cheerful this morning.'

'Why shouldn't I be?'

'No reason - must be something though.'

'Nothing special - anyway I'm always cheerful, aren't I?'

Teresa sighed. 'Suppose you are, wish I could be more like you Katie.'

'Just get out more, that's all. Anyway, we'll have a great night next week in Brum at the club.'

'Yeah, I'm looking forward to that, should be a laugh.'

Both were startled when Graham Hall entered carrying a large box that he placed on Teresa's desk. He gave a conspiratorial wink.

'Look what I've got,' he said. He lifted the lid and pulled out two wrapped presents that he handed to Teresa and Katie, 'Christmas has come early for my two favourite staff. Don't open them now, for Christmas morning.' He then tipped the box on its side and Christmas decorations tumbled out. 'Right, you two, I want you to get busy and put these up. The festive season starts now.'

Teresa put her hand over her mouth, 'Mr Hall, we've never put up decorations in Reception before. You said -

'Never mind the past, Teresa, we want to get upbeat around here and we're all going to jolly. Aren't we, Katie?'

'If you say so.'

'I do say so.'

Katie gave him a slow smile, 'Well, I'm up for jolly.'

Hall picked out a sprig of mistletoe and held it over Teresa's head. She giggled and said, 'Mr Hall...'

He brought the mistletoe and held it over Katie's head. 'Umm', she said. Teresa began rummaging through the decorations pulling out tinsel, streamers, baubles then a folded artificial Christmas tree. 'Oh, Mr Hall, can we put it up today?'

'Sure.'

She pointed to the reception point and said, 'Over there by the door. Visitors will see it straight away.' She picked up the tree, ran through the office door to the reception foyer, and tried different positions to site it.

Hall leaned over Katie and whispered in her ear, 'And how's the sexiest lady in town this morning?'

Katie leaned her head back against his stomach, 'Just say when and I'll show you how much I am.'

'Great. I think we have a good thing going here.'

'I do too.'

Hall glanced over to where Teresa was on her knees bent over the Christmas tree. He spoke quietly, 'One thing, Katie, we are both having a good time, right?'

'Yes,' Katie looked up at him, her eyes glinting. 'You can say that again.'

'Just one thing though, we must be careful. Our secret, right?'

'Yeah, sure, no problem with that.'

'Good girl,' he said. 'By the way the insurance guy Proctor is coming in on Friday morning. He wants to look at our staffing details again. I'll get Harry to join you so he doesn't start snooping where he shouldn't. Okay?'

'Right.'

He looked over again to Teresa who was absorbed with decorating the tree. Hall touched Katie's shoulder, 'Yes, just between us, right. Going to be a helluva Christmas.' He walked away and stopped to have a word with Teresa, looked back and waved to Katie before he left the reception office.

Katie watched him go; she put her thumb in her mouth and chewed on it. She regretted being so open with Uncle Matt last time he visited the offices. She now understood better the special accounts file that Graham Hall kept. She thought it was to do with tax. Harry Armstrong accessed the file a couple of times a week, sometimes making entries. She knew he was cleverer than he made out. She didn't want to ask too many questions but a part of her felt nervous as to exactly what the account was all about. She bit hard on her thumb and a thrill ran through her, 'I'm having an affair. He has loads of money. Runs a big business. He fancies me.' She smiled, 'I quite fancy him' she thought. She closed her eyes and recalled the overpowering smell of leather from the seats of the Porsche, felt again the power as the car accelerated along the motorway pushing her back against the seat like a powerful hand. She reached across and touched the wrapping on the present wondering what might be inside, how different her present would be from Teresa's. Yes, she would keep their secret, that was best all round. But the future...a mood of anticipation swept through her and she wrapped her arms across her body shuddering with pleasure. She leaped up and joined Teresa to help with the Christmas tree decorating. Yes, it looked as if this Christmas was going to be something special; and then there was next year to look forward to.

Chapter 34

Proctor washed and shaved early in the morning. He looked forward to seeing Chris for a few days break. He wanted to tap his brains on the computer gameplaying - and if necessary do some hacking. Stevie Cole was doing just that in relation to the Masters' murder, although he knew Azzra would have a fit if she realised Cole was doing his bidding.

He closed his eyes and repeated the password for Katie's computer. She'd never have realised he'd clocked that over her shoulder; but that sort of thing was all part of your training - like reading numbers and text upside down from across a desk or rehearsing the model, colour and registration number of a car when something aroused your suspicions. Mentally noting if people had round faces, oval faces, hazel, blue or brown eyes, tattooed or arthritic hands. Observation training, after a time it became second nature. Like Ron Kydd wearing the brightest and biggest bow tie he'd ever seen yesterday - and he'd spotted him passing a small gift to Marion. Old dogs and old tricks.

He'd left his report with Ron to top and tail. Ron had grunted, 'You still hunting Romney, etc.?'

'Something like that.' Proctor said. 'I'm also paying a dentist a visit, though.'

'Well, good luck, just thinking about those drills whirring inside my mouth makes me break into a sweat.' Ron looked up, 'Not that pillar of society, the revered Dr Hassan by any chance, dear boy?'

The receptionist at The Old Abbey Dental Practice, located a short distance from the Five Ways island, sounded as if she were talking not with a plum in her mouth but a bagful. Proctor had made an appointment saying he was enquiring about registering with the practice as a private patient; but right now, he needed emergency treatment for a raging toothache. He said that Dr Hassan was personally recommended to him by one of his patients, a police colleague - was he available? A brief pause, some consultation on the other end and she replied, 'Yes, Dr Hassan can see you later this afternoon, four o'clock, can you accommodate that?' Proctor said he could accommodate that with pleasure.

He parked up in the dental surgery car park at quarter to four. From the models of cars parked there, he judged Hassan and his practice colleagues had clients with deep pockets.

The waiting area was furnished with the plushest chairs and sofas he'd ever seen in a dentist's surgery. No dog-eared copies of ancient editions of magazines and old Sunday papers supplements. No, The latest issue of The Lady, several copies of the Guardian, Telegraph and Times, and an array of glossy magazines with horses, hounds, guns and elegant young women dressed to kill on their covers. A booklet titled 'Shakespeare's Warwickshire' rested on top of today's Birmingham Post. The headline read 'Poll lead for Bullivant.'

Proctor gave his name to the receptionist who flashed TV celebrity whitened teeth and asked him to take a seat. At precisely four o'clock she approached him and said, 'Mr Proctor, Dr Hassan will see you now.'

Wearing a spotless white coat Hassan greeted Proctor with a broad smile that soon vanished, replaced by a tightening of his lips and a deep frown. His hygienist busied herself behind him arranging dental instruments. Proctor closed the door behind him and walked up beside Hassan. He pitched his voice loud enough for her to hear. 'I think I have a medical problem I need to discuss with you in private before treatment. It might help if you asked your assistant to leave for a short time. Would you mind?' Proctor smiled.

Hassan hesitated then said, 'Sophie, just give me a few minutes alone with Mr Proctor, please?' She looked surprised , pulled a face and left the surgery. Hassan removed his surgical gloves; Proctor stared at the double banded gold ring on his finger.

'I'm glad you recognised me, Dr Hassan.'

'I don't think we've met before.'

'Oh, yes we have. I think the last time I saw you was in the car park of the Caribbean Nights casino on the Hagley Road. Nice ring you have there by the way. Most unusual.'

'What?' Hassan pulled his head back. 'Now look, I'm very busy. What is this medical condition you...'

Proctor pointed to the dental chair, 'Have you had to stitch up many gums, Dr Hassan?'

'What? it's unusual but sometimes root work -'

'It's a procedure I'm familiar with. Being stitched up.'

'I'm not sure I understand - '

'No?' Proctor looked around the room. 'You have a well appointed surgery here. And I suspect very well appointed patients.'

'Now look here, I don't think your behaviour is -'

'Appropriate?'

'Quite!' Hassan began to stride towards the door when Proctor stepped into his path. 'I think you do know who I am – and why I'm here.'

'You're a - I don't know what you're trying to say. Look here, I have a busy patient schedule today so ... ' Fear showed in his voice.

'So the sooner you listen to what I have to say the sooner you can see your patients.' Proctor sat down slowly in the dentist's swivel chair and crossed his hands over his stomach. 'Tell me, Dr Hassan, do you enjoy this life,' he waved his hand around the surgery in an expansive gesture.

Hassan licked his lips, his voice lowered. 'Of course I do. What is this? What do you want?'

'I want you to continue to enjoy this life, Dr Hassan, and the fruits of your hard work. Nice home in leafy Edgbaston, a loving family, pillar of the community - and time to enjoy an occasional flutter or two at the casino. Or is it a bit more than occasional? You enjoy all those things, a very satisfactory lifestyle. Yes?'

'Look here...' Hassan seemed to find a grain of stomach. His voice shook, 'I'm going to call the police.' He headed for the door.

'You do know I am the police?'

'Not...'

'Not, not what? How would you like me to put it, not in 'active service?'

Hassan looked drawn. His brow furrowed, 'What's this about?'

'When I saw you last at The Caribbean Nights I think you were engaged in a transaction – with Detective Chief Inspector Tony Romney?'

'I don't know what you're talking about, I'm going to...' He placed his hand on the door handle.

'Don't! Your patients, let alone your colleagues, might find it embarrassing.'

'Find what embarrassing?'

'To hear their dentist - business partner - deals in Class A drugs.'

'I...no, that's not...?'

'You heard.' Proctor pulled himself out of the chair and stood over Hassan. 'I know all about your arrangement with Romney, Cartwright - and others.' He waited for a reaction; Hassan took several quick breaths. So, there might well be others. 'They keep off your back - you pay them a price, right?'

Hassan took his hand off the door handle.

'Did you know that your police officer friends are in a spot of deep doo doo? You know - the stuff that once it starts flying lands in all sorts of places - and people. Including respected dentists who gamble too much. Need that extra funding to feed the croupiers?'

Hassan wilted; he held onto the side of the chair and his face crumpled. 'I don't believe you,' he choked on the words.'

'Up to you, but I can help you - if you want help?'

Hanson's eyes narrowed as he studied Proctor's face. 'Go on,' he whispered.

'Romney and Cartwright are under investigation. You are a known associate of theirs and suspected of paying them to ignore your 'extra-curricular' activities. The reason nothing has happened yet is because certain powerful people in the police want the heads of certain other powerful people masterminding drugs circulation in this city. Do you follow?'

Hassan's colour changed from deep olive to grey. His jaw muscles tightened and he clenched his hands to stop them trembling. He staggered into a chair and covered his head with both hands.

'Tell me, Hassan, did you get into debt - gambling?'

Hassan rolled his head from side to side. He lowered his hands, 'I got into this...'

'You needed money?'

'Yes, yes, now this...' he waved a hand around the surgery.

'From what I've heard you're a good dentist, well thought of, right?'

Hassan rubbed his hands together, glancing around with a wild look in his eyes. Proctor thought he was going to lose it. He reached over and held Hassan's arm. 'Listen I can help you - if you help me.'

Hassan calmed a little. His voice broke, he said, 'My parents were from Delhi. They came to England with nothing. They built a thriving corner shop. I was their only child. They struggled - but got me to university, medical school. I was - still am - the centre of their lives. They are - proud, very proud of me.'

'So they should be, you did well.'

'They are both old now. If they found out about my - 'he waved a hand around in the air - 'it would break their hearts.' He rubbed his forehead as if trying to remove a smear.

'And my wife. She would not survive my...destruction.' He looked down at the polished tiled floor of the surgery.

Proctor tightened his grip on Hassan's arm. 'Listen, there's a way out. A way to stop your parents - your wife's lives turning to misery.'

'You think so?' Desperate hope showed in his eyes.

'I do. If you co-operate, there is way out. I want you to phone this number.' Proctor tore a page from his notebook and wrote Azzra's details then handed it to Hassan

Hassan dropped his head. 'I always knew one day this would happen. That someone would come to me and I would have to face the consequences. You know - you might find this hard to believe - but I detest drugs, what they do to people, how they ruin lives. But I am weak; I have a compulsion, as bad as any alcoholic's.' He rubbed his hands across his forehead. 'You know; this is a relief. I wanted out from their clutches but I had to deal - I had to have money. More and more money.

210

Proctor pressed him, 'See my colleague, talk to her. It's the only way.' Although Hassan's eyes were moist, he turned wary. 'Why do I have to see your colleague, can't you deal with it?'

'She's the senior investigating officer. Works better that way, if need be she can organise witness protection. Speak to her - do it today.'

Hassan said, 'Yes,' he said, 'I have no choice.'

Proctor said, 'I'll ask Sophie to come through in a minute, tell her I need to make another appointment, okay.'

Hassan sniffed and fetched out a handkerchief and blew his nose. 'Yes, please do that, will you.'

Proctor left the surgery thinking Hassan would be polite even to the devil as he was steered through the gates of Hell. But do weak people go there with the evil ones?

Chapter 35

Proctor shouted goodbye to Ron Kydd as he descended the stairs two at a time on his way to Hall's Stockholders. Hall had sounded far from happy when Proctor said he needed more information; Katie could provide what he wanted.

'I didn't say you could put in that camera,' Hall snapped.

'It's just a trial - at our expense. But I think you'll find the insurers will insist.'

Hall went on a swearing rant and left Proctor in no doubt that he wanted neither CCTV nor Hall anywhere near his premises. Proctor hoped to avoid him otherwise there'd be a shouting match if not a punch-up.

There was a nip in the air, the winter sky cloudless. Proctor drove past early morning commuters in smart suits and best dresses in anticipation of their office Christmas lunches. An abundance of festive spirit struck Proctor when he entered Hall's reception foyer. A Christmas tree, swamped with decorations took centre stage and the flickering red, blue and orange lights warranted a health warning for anyone prone to epilepsy. Silver and gold coloured trimmings floated over the ceiling and walls.

'Good morning, Mr Proctor, compliments of the season.' Teresa beamed the broadest smile he had ever seen her wear. She wore a red Santa hat with a white fur trim around the edge.

'And to you Teresa. You've got the seasonal spirit going around here.'

She pointed to the inner office where he could see Katie beavering away on her computer, 'Go straight through, Katie's expecting you.'

'Thanks,' Proctor said, 'By the way, is Mr Hall around today by any chance?'

'He went to a meeting early this morning but I understand he'll be back late morning. Did you want to see him?'

'Only to say hello - but you needn't trouble him.'

Teresa smiled again then pulled out a twirly whistle and blew it, her cheeks bulging as it unfurled then retracted.

Proctor said, 'Yes, very good.'

Katie looked up as he entered and seemed preoccupied. She indicated the screen and said, 'Wait a minute, just need to finish off this.' She gave a final tap on the keyboard with a flourish and closed the menu. 'There, done. So, what do you want?'

Proctor was puzzled. Katie normally gave people her instant attention, especially her 'Uncle Matt' ever since she was a child. Why so curt? Was something troubling her?

'Keeping well, Katie? I gather from Sarah there haven't been any more nasty text messages.'

'No, no, beginning to think you were right. Those guys in the car were probably looking for a pick up - then got shit scared - excuse my French - when they saw you come charging at them.'

She opened the menu on screen and said, 'I've updated the staffing records. Graham – Mr Hall said you'd like to see them again, yeah?'

'That's right.'

She opened the file and sat back. 'Do you want to sit here?'

'Thanks. That'd be good.' Katie got out of her seat and stood up.

'Will you be long?'

Proctor sat at the computer and worked the mouse over the list of names. 'No, no, I don't think so? Is there a problem, Katie?'

'Would you like some coffee?'

'Yes, please.'

'Milk, one sugar, right?'

'Spot on.'

She left and Proctor frowned as he studied the screen. What was it? She seemed brittle, preoccupied. Probably the cumulative effects of the last few weeks, weird e-mails, text messages, apprehension over the car, the stalking. Anyway, now was his opportunity.

He glanced through the dividing window. Katie was in the small kitchen adjacent to reception making coffee; Teresa was focussed on her screen monitor as she listened to someone on the phone. Proctor reached into his pocket and removed a USB memory stick; he slipped it into the drive. He minimised the staffing file and opened the main file menu scrolling through until he came to it. 'Expenses'. He looked around again and tried to open the file. It failed, message was 'password needed'. He recalled the five digits Katie had used. He re-entered using 'K' as the sixth digit. Bingo first time – the file opened. For several minutes he absorbed the information, then copied the file to the memory stick in the drive. He ejected the memory stick and dropped it into his jacket pocket. He heard a slight cough behind him and froze before closing the file and reopening the staffing file. He turned casually to see Harry Armstrong looking over his shoulder, his face expressionless.

'Good morning, Harry, how are you?' Proctor smiled.

'What was that file you were looking at?'

'Just updating my staffing list.'

'That was a finance file,' Armstrong's tone was accusing.

'Don't think so, Harry, look.' Proctor pointed at the screen.

Armstrong re-examined the open file, looked at Proctor for a few seconds then said, 'Ask Katie to lock up when you're done.' He left without another word.

Proctor went into the small stockroom from which Armstrong had emerged. All he could see were piles of boxes and stacked files.

'Shit,' he muttered. The room not much larger than a broom cupboard but was filled from floor to ceiling with stored files, paperwork tied in bundles.

'Shit, shit,' Proctor muttered again. He returned to the computer and began making notes from the staffing file.

Katie entered carrying his coffee. 'Nearly finished yet?'

'Shouldn't be more than half an hour. Do you need to use this terminal?'

'I have a lot on. I'll give Teresa a hand.' She went to leave when Proctor said, 'I didn't know Harry was in the cupboard', he laughed.

'No,' Katie smiled. 'He spends a lot of time to-ing and fro-ing there. I haven't a clue what's in there. Old files and that I think.'

'He asked me to get you to lock up.'

'That doesn't surprise me. He's such a worry guts.' She went to her desk and opened a drawer and took out a bunch of keys. She selected one and locked the door to the storeroom, tossing the bunch of keys back in the drawer. 'Right, I'll leave you to it.'

Proctor drummed the desk; how much had Armstrong seen on the screen? Would he tell Hall he'd seen him viewing the 'Expenses' file? He swore under his breath and closed down the computer. There was no sign of Katie so he said goodbye to Teresa and asked her to thank Katie. Leaving the car park he couldn't shake off a mood of foreboding. The morning's blue sky had turned a bleak shade of grey.

Chapter 36

The flickering Christmas tree lights irritated Katie when she returned to her desk. She grunted when Teresa passed on Proctor's thanks.

She sat at her desk and chewed at a rag nail on her finger. Since going out with Hall, she was getting worried about how much information Matt Proctor was gathering and why. If it might cause problems for Graham Hall. She felt torn; she wanted the good times to continue with Hall.

Teresa looked up startled when the reception door flung wide open. Hall, his face furious and trailed by a pale-faced Armstrong, stormed into the room. He pointed at Teresa, 'You, out.. Now!' A vein on his neck pulsed and his face was flushed. She jumped up straight away and scurried out of the office.

Armstrong pushed the door shut behind her. They charged into Katie's office. Her mouth fell open as she took in Hall's expression.

'What the fuck do you think you're doing?' he yelled.

Katie's mouth opened and shut but no words came. Hall bent over the computer and spoke with vehemence, 'Open the Expenses file.' He watched her tap in the password and open the file. He scanned the list of details and closed his fists. Katie's pulse raced and she felt her stomach hollow.

'What...what is it?' she said.

'What is it, what is it?' He put his face up against hers and she smelt his strong after shave. The smell made her feel sick.

'You little bitch,' he spat the words.'

'What?'

'You've been spying on me, haven't you?'

'No. I don't know what you mean.'

'Proctor was seen looking at that file. How? I told you the staffing file was all he could see. You have the password for the 'Expenses' file, right.'

'Yes, but -

'I told you that file was highly confidential. Right?'

'Yes, but I didn't tell him -

'No? He guessed it, did he?'

'I - I don't know.'

Hall's temper spilt over. He brought both fists down hard on the desk. 'Right, that's it. Collect your stuff, clear your desk. You're fired. Harry, stay here and watch her. I want her off the premises in five minutes.' His face was bright red and droplets of spittle frothed at the corners of his mouth. His eyes slit as he said under his breath, 'Fucking little whore.'

Hall pulled open her desk drawer and began rifling through it. He flung a nail file and a pair of scissors on the desk.

Tears welled in Katie's eyes; she said, 'Please, Graham, don't do this. I haven't done anything, believe me, please.'

'Liar,' he shouted.

'I'm not lying; it's the truth, please.'

'No way could Proctor have opened that file without the password.'

'I don't know how he found out. I'll ask him, I'll get him to tell you.'

'You must be joking.'

She clawed at his arm, 'But - but we…we've had a good time. I like you - I do, Graham!'

He threw off her hand. Armstrong removed a makeup bag and threw it on the desk.

She lunged forward and grabbed her bag. 'Leave that alone,' she screamed at Armstrong. 'Don't touch my things.' Something snapped in her and white-faced she turned on Hall, 'You bastard, you can't do this.'

'I can, bitch. Now get out.'

Armstrong unplugged the computer and disconnected the UBS link to the printer; rolled up the mains lead.

Katie faced Hall and bile rose in her mouth. She clenched her hands to her sides and said, 'You won't get away with this. I'll tell your fucking wife what's happened.'

Armstrong froze; he looked with dread at Hall.

Katie gasped as she felt Hall's fingers dig into her arm; he shoved his face close up against hers. 'Listen, you little bitch. Don't even think of that. Try anything like that and you'll regret it. Believe me, I'll kill you. Got it?'

He flung her away and she hit the floor, her head hammering down, her elbows whacking the hard surfaces. The pain stung; she cried out. She flooded into tears.

White-faced and with his hands clenched, Hall said, 'Now get the fuck out of here.'

Katie stumbled through the car park, her mind in a whirl. She clutched her makeup bag and clamped on to a carrier containing her belongings. Mascara smudged her eyes and face. She sobbed, rummaged for a tissue. She blew her nose; her hands trembled. She heard running footsteps behind her, some warning instinct drove her to start running.

'Katie, Katie, wait.'

She turned to see Teresa, her heart thumping.

'Oh my God, are you all right, Katie. What's happened?'

Katie dropped the bag and felt what little strength she had drain from her. She slumped to the ground.

Teresa bent over her, 'My God, I've never seen Mr Hall so angry. He kept shouting, it was terrible. I was shaking all over.'

'He sacked me.'

'What? Why?'

'He thinks I give away...stuff.'

'To Proctor, the insurance guy?'

Katie said, 'I don't know.'

'It's terrible. Sacked you.' Teresa knelt down beside Katie and held her head. She struggled to pull Katie to her feet, 'I'll get you home. I'll drive you.'

Katie hung onto her.

'Come on,' Teresa half -dragged half-carried her to the car park.

They got into Teresa's small Ka motor. She started the engine, 'I can't believe this.'

Katie's shoulders shuddered as Teresa drove off. After a minute, with her voice breaking she said, 'We were shagging, you know.'

Teresa braked to a stop, staring straight ahead. She said, 'Oh, my God.'

'I'm going to drop him in it - tell his wife.'

Teresa placed her hand across her mouth, 'Oh, my God.'

Chapter 37

Proctor turned on the radio; after hearing the headlines about more financial travails in the banking world, Afghanistan still claiming young soldier's lives, a fresh round of allegations of corruption and sleaze in Parliament, he switched off and started to prepare dinner for Sarah and him. He heard her laugh on the phone upstairs. Then she was quiet except for an occasional "yes" or "um". Normally, she gave as good as she got when it came to talking and listening.

He cooked spaghetti carbonara, a dish they both liked. He got out a few rashers of bacon, spaghetti, eggs and cream then listened at the kitchen door but no sound from Sarah's room. He frowned and decided to check out the dish with her. He climbed the stairs, rapped on her door, 'Sarah, can I come in?' He heard a distant 'yes' and stepped through.

Sarah sat on the edge of the bed with her mobile phone clamped to her ear. She leaned forward and her arms were closed across her body, her demeanour sombre. Proctor thought how frail she looked. He waited to get her attention but she didn't look up. He moved into her line of vision and squatted down on his hunkers waving a hand across her eye line. She blinked then said, 'Hold on, Katie.'

'Spaghetti carbonara all right?'

Her eyes were glazed as she looked at him for a few seconds then said, 'Yes, yes, fine.'

Proctor stood up to leave and stepped on a couple of crumpled tissues on the floor. He studied Sarah more closely and noticed her red rimmed eyes. He bent down again, 'Sarah, is anything the matter?'

She looked at him and couldn't find any words, 'Dad's here now, Katie. Do you want to speak to him?' She handed the phone to Proctor and pulled another tissue from the box, wiped her eyes then blew her nose.

Proctor took the phone. 'Katie?'

He listened in silence trying to calm his rising anger. He could feel the emotion in her voice as she recounted what had happened after he left Hall's. 'I'm sorry, Katie, this is my fault.'

'No, no, it's not just the stuff on the computer... something else'

'What?'

'It's - well, personal stuff. Please, please, I need to think.'

'Okay, okay. Katie, have you talked to your mum and dad yet?'

'I can't, it's...complicated.'

'You can appeal against the sacking.'

'No, no, there's no way I'm going back there.'

'I see. Anything I can do...to help?' Proctor felt the hollowness of his words. What could he do? He hadn't been able to help himself when told he was out for something he'd never done. Hardly the prime candidate for employment counselling. He wanted Hall's smarmy face twelve inches away so he could put a fistful of fives in it.

Katie sniffed, 'Thanks, Uncle Matt anyway. Can I speak to Sarah again, please?'

He handed the phone back to Sarah. He indicated he was going downstairs and left the bedroom.

In the kitchen, he prepared the meal thinking about the short time from when Armstrong emerged from the storeroom to stand behind his shoulder. What he'd seen had sent him running to his boss and tell all. Proctor lifted the spatula he'd been stirring the pasta and cream with, slammed it down on the kitchen worktop. Shit, how could he have been so careless! Sloppy, incompetent. What next?

The shit would hit the fan.

He served the spaghetti carbonara on two plates. Listening, he could hear Sarah speaking upstairs on the phone sounding more composed. He scraped his plate into the waste bin; put the other in the warm oven. He grabbed a pen and wrote a note saying 'Dinner in the oven, got to go out.'

Chapter 38

Proctor opened his mobile in the Grand Old Turk's Headf, he punched in Ron Kydd's number. When Ron answered, he explained that the he'd been rumbled by Hall. How they needed to conclude everything right away and report on the frauds to the insurers before counter allegations and attempts to destroy evidence were made. At least he held the memory stick and the concealed camera pictures.

'Can we meet you tonight at your office?' He knew Ron would understand the urgency; he agreed.

Proctor then made a second call to Azzra Mukherjee. When she answered he said, 'Azzra, listen, I need your help.'

'Nice to hear from you.' She sounded aloof.

'Listen, Hassan's going to call you. He's a poor crushed sod. But he'll tell all about Romney.'

'Matt, that's good.' Her voice lifted.

'I've got a lot of stuff on Graham Hall, it's an insurance scam. He's into organised thieving, thieving his own materials, reclaiming it against insurance. At least two accomplices. All this is about to be passed on the insurers - but just now it's got personal. I want to nail him, Azzra. Will you help?'

A short pause at the other end. 'I said I wanted to help you, didn't I?'

'You did. Another thing - Masters' murder - I think there's Internet stuff that needs investigating...'

'Matt - I know what Stevie Cole's been up to. Get your mitts off my fucking case.'

Chapter 39

Proctor placed four coffee mugs on the kitchen unit.

He looked over to the kitchen table. Sarah clamped her hands together; Katie, sat opposite, wouldn't catch her eye. Chris stood by the window staring down the garden.

Proctor fought hard to stay calm but it was proving difficult; palpable tensions filled the room. Unlike many investigations he'd undertaken this was much too close to home - it was home. He forced his mind to become dispassionate, to work through in a logical manner what had happened over the last few weeks.

Sarah looked up and gave him a quick smile. She rose and got a tray from a kitchen cupboard and placed the coffee cups on it, spooned instant coffee in and got milk from the fridge. She carried the tray to the table. Barney sauntered through and stuck his nose in his bowl, swallowed a long drink of water, saw no goodies on offer and went back through to his favourite rug in the living room.

Proctor said 'Thank you Sarah, forgot about that'. He sat at the table and waited until everyone had a cup of coffee in front of them.

'We need to go over together what's been happening.' He reached into his back pocket and pulled out a notebook, laid it on the table. He took a pencil from the spine and placed that alongside the notebook.

'Where's Martin,' he said looking at Chris.

'Upstairs, on his laptop. He won't disturb us.'

Looking at each in turn, then finally at Sarah he said, 'A week ago Sarah was nearly killed. I'm not exaggerating - this was an attempt on her life. Now - I need to ask you all one thing. I want you to be totally honest with me - and with each other. Sarah, you and Katie have had threats over internet gameplaying. Now, Chris is studying advanced IT at Uni - he wants to make a career in it. He's the most computer literate person among us. I think he can help get to the bottom of what is going on here.'

Katie and Sarah exchanged glances. Katie picked up her coffee and the cup trembled in her hand. She thought about taking a sip but shaking, she put the cup back on the table, holding her hand across her mouth. She was so pale Proctor thought she was going to be sick.

'Is that alright with you two - Chris being here?'

Both indicated their agreement.

'Right,' Proctor looked at his notebook. 'Sarah, when did you and Katie start playing Hollowcost?'

'I suppose - about six months ago. Katie?'

'What - yes, yes, I suppose it was.'

'Tell me about what went on, who you played, what happened?'

'Well,' Sarah puffed her cheeks and her hand went to her neck where a red burn mark still showed. She wore an elastic support bandage on her elbow. 'I showed you how the game works. People join a gang - a clan - and take on cyber personalities. Katie and I played as a team called The Knifethrowers. In each game, we won points by a combination of tactics and I suppose you'd call it blast them'.

'Tell me about the 'tactics'?'

'Well,' Sarah said. 'You could challenge a team to a game of poker, chess, sudoki, almost anything.'

'Texas Hold 'em?' Chris asked.

'Yes,' Sarah said. 'And if your avatars win Linden dollars you could then negotiate land and building purchases - businesses and allies.'

'So it required both brains and brawn to win?' Proctor said.

'Well, yes, for poker and negotiations yes, you needed to have your wits about you. But the rest was, well, quick reactions...'

'Those two have the fastest thumbs in the west.' Chris flicked his thumbs back and forth and for the first time since they'd sat down Katie smiled. She wiggled her thumbs in return.

'And you progressed - what, moved up some kind of league?' said Proctor.

'Sort of.' Sarah said, 'But it was more a question of gaining the highest points score, converting those to linden dollars and adding that to the value of your asset holdings.'

Proctor said, 'I think Bill Gates missed out on you two. You got to be top team, right?'

'Yes, we did.'

'And that's when things got nasty?'

'Yes, we got text messages, e-mails telling us to get out of the game.'

'Have you deleted any?' Chris asked.

Sarah and Katie both shook their heads.

'And then there was the car that followed you from the café?'

'What was that, dad?' Chris looked surprised.

'No, you wouldn't know about that. A car with smoked glass windows followed them. Nearly ran me over when I went to check it out.'

'Followed them to here? Stalked them?'

'Yes - but I thought it could just have been a bit of bravado - or a would be pick up perhaps.'

'But happening so soon after those messages, dad...?' Sarah said.

'I know, I know.' Proctor said, 'Katie, you had a run-in with Phil Dutson on the way home from work, didn't you?'

'I didn't know you told...'

She looked across at Sarah who spread her hands and said, 'Sorry, Katie.'

Katie's anger flared in her flushed face. 'That was in confidence. I thought I could trust you.'

'You can, Katie. Believe me, you can. That's what this is all about. No secrets, nothing hidden. Everything out so we can sort it. Before something really bad happens.'

Chris said, 'Dad, do you think Phil has something to do with - Sarah's attack?'

Proctor said, 'I don't know. Maybe Phil - or this Internet clan thing. Sarah, when you broke with Phil he was angry, right?'

'Yes,' Sarah said.

'I'll say he was,' Katie said.

'Was he angry with you, Katie?'

'He got nasty more than once.'

'Physically?'

Katie bit her lip. In a subdued voice she said, 'Yes, he slapped, no, punched me, knocked me about. That's why I warned Sarah off him.'

Proctor restrained himself, 'Did you tell anyone about that?'

'No, no,' Katie reddened and said, 'No, I didn't even tell Sarah.'

'Were you frightened about what Phil might do if you'd spoke out?' Proctor softened his voice as he studied his niece's face, thought about her ordeal from Graham Hall.

Katie lowered her head, 'No, not that. I was...ashamed, thought it was my fault...I mean Phil slapping me.'

Proctor reached out and held Katie's arm. 'That was difficult for you. Thanks. Sarah, anything you can tell us that might help us understand what's going on?'

She thought for a few seconds then said, 'When I dumped Phil he frightened me, I've never seen anyone look so evil.' She held Proctor's eyes for a time then said. 'But I don't think it was Phil or his mates who followed us - I think it was people from The Nightwatchmen clan who followed me, attacked us.'

Katie chewed her knuckles. 'There's something else...you should know.' Her voice choked as she looked down at the table. 'I've been with...someone from work...'

Proctor caught his breath, 'Go on?'

She snatched an intake of breath, 'I told Teresa at work about it.' She wiped the back of her hand across her eyes. 'I told her - because he dumped me – that I'd...tell his wife...'

'And Teresa told this guy that?' Proctor dropped his pencil.

'No, no.' She placed both hands against the sides of her head. 'I told him myself.' She kept her eyes focused down on the table, her voice quiet. 'He went berserk.'

'Who?' Proctor knew the answer.

Sarah slapped her hands down on the table, 'Hall. Bloody Graham Hall, that's who.'

Chapter 40

Proctor sat back in an armchair watching Chris working the computer keyboard and mouse. He felt good seeing him back in the house. He listened to the persistent clicking of the keystrokes, each like a tiny probe in an archaeological dig exposing a fragment more knowledge. The girls were upstairs listening to music. He couldn't stop thinking about Sarah's attack at the bus shelter; the stalkers in the car following Sarah and Katie from the coffee shop. He closed his eyes, tried to squeeze out his imaginings. He picked up his notebook and flicked through the pages, tapping his fingers on the hardcover back as he read his notes.

He looked up and watched Chris replace the simcards from Chris and Sarah's mobile phones.

'Any joy?'

Chris didn't reply for a time. 'Getting there.' He resumed working on the computer, his hand across his mouth. 'I need to do something illegal, dad.'

'What's that?'

'Hacking.'

'Do what you have to do. I want these sods stuffed.'

'Do me a favour?'

'What?'

'Leave me alone. I find you sitting there willing a result distracting.''

230

Proctor heaved himself to his feet, 'I can understand that. I'll leave you in peace.'

He went to the kitchen and planned three phone calls. The first was to Ron Kydd. Marion answered; said Ron was out of the office.

'Any feedback from Hall's insurers yet, Marion?'

'Ron had a short conversation over the phone. They're pleased with your report – and the back up evidence, especially the camera pictures.'

'Good, so they won't accept the claims?'

'No, they won't. They've called in the police. I suppose that's a strange thing to have someone say to you of all people.'

Proctor smiled, said 'Yes, yes it is. I want to see Mister Graham Hall well shafted.'

'That sounds personal?'

'It is, very much so.' Proctor exhaled a long sigh, 'Can you ask Ron to call me, please.?'

'Something's wrong, Matt, isn't that so?'

'How…?'

'In your voice?'

'I see - the Mystic Meg act again.'

'If you like. What's happened?'

'Quite a lot, Marion, quite a lot. I'm beginning to think there's some kind of bad karma around me and my family.'

'I heard about your daughter's attack from Ron. Nasty.'

'You're not wrong there. '

'Be careful, Matt.'

Proctor said, 'What do you mean, be careful?'

'I mean take care - of your daughter.'

'I will, I bloody well will.'

'You're a good man, Matt.' Marion rang off before Proctor could say any more.

Proctor's second call was to Ranjit Hassan. He thought it was time to 'close the sale' so to speak.

He then made his third call to Azzra Mukherjee. Before she picked up, he cancelled. He thought for a few seconds then went upstairs and knocked on Sarah's bedroom door. He rapped the door. 'You two decent?'

Sarah opened the door and he entered the bedroom. The girls were sprawled across the bed.

'Listen, I'm sorry to have put you through that.'

'It's okay, dad, it's for the best.'

'You all right, Katie?'

She lowered her eyes and looked away. Proctor was aware of her embarrassment. He said, 'What happened between you and Graham Hall is your business, Katie. But if he threatens you that's another matter.'

'I don't think that'll happen. I've had a talk with Sarah. It's over and I won't say anything to his wife. He's just a jerk.'

Proctor sat on the edge of the bed, 'I'll tell you who does worry me, that's Phil Dutson.'

Sarah went to the window and looked out. 'I think you're right, dad.'

'If he tries to get in touch with either of you - by any means - let me know right away.'

'He's bad news.' He waited for his comment to sink in, 'I think you're better off well away from Hall's, Katie. I can't say you too much at the moment but believe me there's going to be a reckoning.'

Sarah scrutinised him, 'Hall's in some sort of trouble with the police, is that it?'

'The less you know the better; it'll all come out in the wash.' His words echoed in his head, shit. 'Yes, he is.'

Katie looked wan, she said, 'I hope I don't get into trouble with…'

'Don't worry, Katie,' Proctor said, 'He used you - in more ways than one'

'I didn't understand any of it.'

'I know, don't worry.'

She gripped her hands together;' I've been a right prat, haven't I?'

'We all make mistakes. Don't beat yourself up.'

'Thanks,' she said.

Sarah moved around the bedroom with a sense of purpose clearing away loose clothes, realigning cushions, her lips compressed. 'I'll tell you what, dad. Phil Dutson, Graham Hall, sodding Nightwatchmen. We're not going to let any of that lot get us down, are we Katie?'

Katie looked at Sarah, 'We're not?'

'No, we're not. We're going clubbing in Brum as we've planned, that's what we're doing. Christmas Eve, right?'

'Yeah, yeah, great,' Katie's expression lightened, her eyes brightened for the first time that evening.

Proctor looked from one to the other, 'Who's going?'

Sarah said, 'Katie and me, Teresa, Karen - Chris and his uni pal Martin.' She added 'Millie', waiting for a reaction from Proctor.

'Good, good,' Proctor made to leave the room. 'I'll say goodnight then.'

He stood outside the bedroom for some time. He didn't like it but Sarah was right. Life had to go on.

Chapter 41

No night is a good night to die. But a rain-sheeted, filthy Christmas Eve night in the heart of the second city was one evil night to get murdered.

For such a big night, Broad Street was relatively deserted. Despite the bright, winking Christmas lights - reds, blues, greens, yellows - suspended across the street and on the Victorian facades of shops, pubs and clubs; nobody lingered. Taxis came and went, ferrying scantily clad girls and well-gelled young men between venues. The occupants scurried from the vehicles into the shelter of warm, dry and noisy establishments. The awful weather had prevailed for the best part of a week. And still the rain sheeted down.

The floods had hit the West Midlands earlier that day. Hour after hour, the rains surged into already saturated ground driving up the water table. Homeowners in Shrewsbury watched the Severn rise and further downstream in Bewdley and Worcester the Environment Agency's fluorescent-jacketed staff erected flood barriers. Their restraining force fought against angry brown water that tumbled down its long journey from Plynlimon in Wales' Cambrian mountains to disgorge two hundred and twenty miles later into the swollen Bristol Channel.

In Broad Street's clubland there was no place for the water to escape. The black tarmac rippled like a lake as rain spat its fury into the night. Clubbers scurried into doorways some holding newspapers over their heads to protect the work of hours and small fortunes spent on hairdressing. Four young men well loaded with Beck's and Carling Black Label lager danced in a street pool, their shouts and laughter snatched away by the slashing wind and drumming rainfall.

Outside Symphony Hall, a parked police car kept its engine running. The windscreen wipers swished back and forth at speed like demented tennis watchers. Two officers sat low in their seats willing an end to their shift.

Further along Broad Street a Ford Astra slid past the Cineworld complex advertising the latest James Bond film with a large poster of Daniel Craig firing a Walther P99 semi-automatic pistol through the 'O' in Bond. The Astra eased to a stop and the driver, hidden behind darkened windows cut the engine. The car lights switched off. Only the wipers moved in intermittent mode offering occasional glimpses of the street scene.

The girl was in her late teens. She staggered along the sodden pavement, her soaked hair sticking across her face. Her skimpy top and skirt clung to her slim frame, her black bra and pants visible through her saturated clothes. A solitary piercing in her midriff sparkled as it caught the street lights reflected from the watery pavement. Her foot caught an uneven paving block and she wheeled to the curb edge, grabbed a lamppost with both arms and propped her body against it like a rag doll.

Dizzy, so dizzy. Shook her head. Blinked to clear her blurred vision, pushed her hair from her eyes. Closed her eyes, blinked several times, opened them again, squinted first through her left then her right eye. Saw better looking through one eye only. The lamppost pressing into her breast lost its twin; the light overhead ceased to shower like a silver firework; the dark car parked twenty yards away fused into a single black blob. She felt a slight alarm. She was alone. Where had he gone? The boy from the club - what was his name? What was it? Think, think. Baz, yes Baz. Baz who?

Didn't say. He was nice. But where's he gone, where's Baz gone? She peered around, one arm still anchored to the lamppost, her hair plastered to her cheeks. She mouthed 'Baz'. She tried again; her slurred words seemed to come from behind her eyes and not from her mouth. 'Baz, where are you?'

She blinked again, startled, as a car door nearby slammed shut. The black blob was alongside her lamppost.

Chapter 42

Inside the Roadrunner club, the party atmosphere hit a crescendo, the place buzzed, the music got louder, matched by shouting and laughter. Sarah screamed at the top of her voice to get through with her tray of drinks, 'Excuse me, excuse me.'

'Where's Katie?' She held the tray of drinks, two J2Os for herself and Teresa, a spritzer for Millie, a vodka and orange for Karen. Chris and Martin were looking after their own drinks. Karen barked her short shrill laugh and leaped up, grabbed her drink, 'You been ages. What took so long?'

'It's manic at that bar. This place is rammed.' She said to Martin, 'Chris not got your beers yet?'

Martin shrugged.

Sarah placed the rest of the drinks on the table, pulling a face as she felt the glasses slide on table spills. 'It's like shit here.'

Millie wrinkled her nose in sympathy. 'You want to see what it's like outside. Pissing down. Maybe we should call a taxi now - be bedlam later.'

The club lights flickered and then cut out leaving them in darkness. Several people screamed

Sarah said, 'Sod it, that's all we need.' She felt for her chair. The lights sputtered back on and a huge cheer went up as the emergency generator kicked in.

'Thank God for that. What was that?'

Martin said, 'Outage.'

'What?'

'Power cut, generator running until they get it back.'

'Where's Katie?' Sarah repeated.

Karen shrieked a loud laugh, 'Gone for a quick shag,' She lost her balance and fell back into her chair. 'Oh, …feel dizzy.'

Sarah looked at Millie, 'Is she pissed again? Where's Katie?'

Millie shrugged her shoulders, 'Gone to the loo?'

'No, she won't have. We always go together.'

Karen giggled, 'I told you. She went off with that black boy. Baz. Is he gorgeous or what?'

'What you mean - went off where?' Sarah leaned over Karen, frowning. 'When was this?'

Karen glanced at her watch. 'Soon after you went to get served. Fifteen minutes maybe.'

'I haven't been away that long!'

'Well, whatever…I'm just saying.'

'Did she go outside? With this Baz? Millie, Teresa, you should have stayed with her. She's had a skinful.'

Millie said, 'I didn't see her go off with anyone.'

'S'all right, Sarah,' Karen staggered to her feet. 'Keep your knickers on.'

'Who is he? This Baz? You know him?' Sarah thumbed Katie's number into her mobile, willed an answer; none came.

Karen looked vague, 'Think Katie said something about going out to look at mobile phones.'

'Oh, sod it. I'm going to look for her.' Sarah pulled her jacket off the back of the chair and draped it over her shoulders. She headed for the Ladies.

'Stupid cow,' Karen muttered. 'Who does she think she is? Our bloody minder.'

'She's Katie's best mate, you know, they're cousins,' Millie said.

'Too stuck up, that's her trouble.'

238

'Karen, just shut up, will you?' Millie said.

'I won't shut up,' she shouted.'

'All right, all right,' Millie guided Karen back down onto her chair.

Teresa said, 'I think I'll phone that taxi, Millie. Time we were getting back anyway.' She took her mobile from her bag and called.

Karen stumbled to her feet, 'I'm getting another drink, not one for that stuck up cow. You want anything?'

Millie said, 'You've had enough.'

Karen gave her a middle finger salute.

Sarah pushed her way through to the toilets. Inside she knocked on occupied cubicles calling Katie's name. 'No Katie in here' was the politest response she got. She moved as fast as she could around the club, her eyes scanning faces, nudging past packed groups, peering into dark corners. Shouldn't have left her. You'd think those two would show more sense. Where was Chris? Baz. Who was this Baz?

'I can't see her anywhere,' Sarah's words were met with a blank stare from Karen. Teresa and Millie looked anxious.

'I've…I've phoned a taxi,' Teresa held up her phone.

'I'm going to look outside.'

'It's pouring outside, Sarah,' Millie said.

'I must find her,' Sarah grabbed her bag and pushed her way towards the club door.

Millie jumped up, 'Wait, I'll come with you.

The doorman listened as Sarah described Katie and asked if he'd seen her leave with a black boy - Baz. He grinned displaying whitened teeth, his shaved ebony head glistening from the flashing strobe lights.

He fingered his black bow tie, 'Hey, I know her, I saw her leave. With a black guy called Baz? Maybe. But you know how it is - we all look alike, don't we?' Sarah's face tightened and he held up his hands.

Millie said, 'Watch it, brother.'

The bouncer looked chastened, 'Okay, I can see you're worried about her.'

'I'll look outside,' Sarah stepped to the door.

He pursed his lips as he took in her skimpy outfit and looked out at the driving rain, 'You want to go out in this?'

'Yes, yes, we've got to find her.'

He reached behind the door and held up a large golf umbrella, 'This might help - but make sure you don't take off with it - or it doesn't take off with you.' He laughed at his own joke.

'Thanks,' Sarah and Millie huddled beneath the umbrella and stepped into the street. The cold wind pierced through their thin clothing. They tilted the umbrella forward and pushed against the rain lashing along Broad Street.

A crowd of youths spilt out of O'Neill's bar chanting football songs, oblivious to the soaking they were taking. One pulled off his shirt and twirled it above his head screaming 'Albion, Boing boing'. They didn't hang about; all dashed across the road and into another bar. Near Symphony Hall the police car's lights were turned from sidelights to dipped.

Sarah struggled against the force of the wind, unable to see more than a few yards ahead. She squinted up and down the street, now almost deserted. The umbrella nearly took off, Millie made a grab and her foot hit into something.

'Oh, my God,' she screamed.

Sarah froze. A body lay slumped on the edge of the pavement. A sudden gust turned the umbrella inside out; sent it across the road. Sarah bent over the crumpled figure of a girl, her skirt high up her thighs, top clinging to her body and her hair a tousle of rattails.

'No, no.' She slumped down alongside Katie and made to pull back her drenched hair from her face. The matted hair was soaked in blood. Sarah pulled her hand away and watched the rain spill over it washing away blood. She stood up shaking, her hands to her mouth. She screamed at the top of her voice.

Millie yelled to the club bouncer, waving her hands. He stepped out from the club entrance, his hand held above his eyes as he tried to see. Sarah kept screaming, her arms clenched across her bare midriff. The bouncer bolted from the doorway towards them.

Reaching the prostrate body the bouncer felt for a pulse. Rivulets of rain poured off his head and face. He said, 'Call an ambulance. I'll get help,' and sprinted down the street to the parked police car. He threw frantic waves at the car that eased along the street towards him and stopped. An officer jumped out and ran to him.

The bouncer pointed and they both raced to Katie's body.

After a brief examination, the police officer stood up and spoke into his intercom. 'Call an ambulance, Dave; we've got a fatality here. Bloody horrendous injuries, strangled, huge hole cut in her head.'

Sarah and Teresa clung to each other, their faces pale and blank. Through the rain, Karen emerged like an apparition.

'What's happened?'

Karen saw the limp body of Katie and went to go to her, the policeman held up a hand, shouted, 'Keep back please.'

'Did you see...' Karen stopped.

'What?'

'A boy...'

The police officer said, 'What did you see?'

'I saw a black kid - he ran off,' she pointed along Broad Street in the direction of the Five Ways.

Millie screamed at her, 'You saw nothing, you were inside getting pissed.'

Proctor phoned in and spoke to Ron Kydd. 'I'm not coming in today, Ron.'

His tone transmitted to Ron who stayed silent.

'Bad news. My niece young Katie…' Proctor sucked a draught of air. 'She was in Brum last night - Broad Street, oh, shit Ron. The poor kid was murdered. Murdered. Fuck! Horrendous, Ron, horrendous.'

Ron spoke, 'Sorry, Matt, so sorry, can I…can I come round?'

Before Proctor could answer Marion Kalkowski had grabbed the phone and said, 'I'm sorry, Matt, Coming over to see you.' She put down the phone before he could answer.

Ron and Marion arrived together. As soon as he opened the door, she threw her arms around Proctor. He felt his eyes sting. She led him inside and sat him on a sofa, put a kettle on.

'How're Penny, Cyril?'

Proctor placed his hand over his eyes. 'Devastated, just devastated.' He said, 'There's nothing - no words you can say. I've just left them.'

Ron grimaced, 'Rest of them?'

Proctor looked upwards. 'Traumatised, all of them. Chris and Martin are back at their house in Brum. Young Millie - Chris's girlfriend, is proving a big help. Doing the practical things. Sarah's upstairs - hardly slept. She's catching up.'

Ron touched Proctor's shoulder. 'I'll see how the tea's doing.'

Marion came in with a tray, she sat beside Proctor. Ron stood in the doorway, stroking his purple coloured bow tie.

Marion said, 'I want you to talk to me,' she said.

Proctor looked surprised, didn't know what to say.

'I know the area you're looking at.'

'What?'

Ron threw his arms up in the air. 'She has Eastern European attributes, Matthew. A Transylvanian mentality methinks. Listen to her soliloquies sometimes - they ring like music.'

Marion's chastening glance stilled his runaway tongue.

She took Proctor's hands in hers and said, 'Matt, I know this is a bad time. But you must get strong, stay strong.'

Proctor flashed a look at Ron who stared at his shoes, his lips tight.

'Don't worry,' there was an edge to Proctor's voice. 'I am strong.'

Marion's grip tightened. Proctor was shocked that her thin hands could exert such force. She stared deep into his eyes, he felt almost hypnotised. She said, 'When I say get strong, I mean get fierce.'

Chapter 43

'I feel like absolute shit.' Proctor twiddled his wine glass watching the ruby liquid swirl around the rim of the glass. Azzra leaned across the table in Luciano's Italian restaurant. It was lunchtime and the place was almost deserted, the waiting staff huddled together at the far end of the restaurant, heads close together as they shared a savoury bit of gossip.

'I wish you would stop doing that,' she smiled. 'I can see an accident happening any moment.'

He stopped and put down his glass, picked it up again and took a sip, looked at the label on the bottle. 'Italian rubbish - nothing like a fine Chilean.'

'Just drink the stuff - forget the geography lesson.'

Proctor said, 'I was careless, should have checked the office out before copying the damned file.'

'Don't blame yourself. Anyway, we've got him in for questioning.'

Proctor glanced at her. 'I don't think he killed Katie.'

Azzra put her fingers to her lips, 'Please, Matt, not the Internet stuff again. In the Masters' case, Stevie's checked out all the websites on his list. Nothing relevant there.'

'Hollowcost?'

'He couldn't get on that. Tried but then Emma charged in - bollocked all of us. Told us we were being fanciful - 'drag in known violent offenders' - 'more house to house' - 'get it sorted'. She really let rip, Matt.'

'Chris and Sarah - and Katie...' he slapped his hand on the table. 'They got on that website easy enough. Chris did some hacking.'

Azzra let a forkful of spaghetti fall on to her plate, 'Should you be telling me this?'

Proctor threw his napkin on the plate, 'Oh, for Christ's sake Azzra, this is not some kind of lone nutter on the loose. This clan, The Nightwatchmen -'

Azzra put her hands over her ears. 'I don't need this Matt. I've got my steer from Emma.'

'You should think for yourself, she won't commit resources to a proper computer forensic examination.'

'Who the hell do you think you are? Think for myself! Maybe if you'd done a bit more thinking instead of mouthing off at Romney and Cartwright you wouldn't be in the pickle you are.'

He glowered at her for several seconds, then held up his hands. 'Okay, okay.'

They were both quiet, composing their thoughts.

'I've got charge of the case,' Azzra poked the fork at the spaghetti bolognese.

Proctor stared at her for a while as he took it in. Katie in a morgue, his sister Penny sobbing her life away, Sarah hiding away all the time in her bedroom. And now....

'What?'

'I'm the senior investigating officer.'

'Into Katie's murder?'

Azzra said, 'Afraid so.' She glanced around the quiet restaurant. 'We shouldn't be talking about that here.'

Proctor rubbed his hand across his forehead, 'Jesus. My niece was murdered.' He slumped down into his chair.

'Okay, any idea who might have done it?' Azzra asked.'

Proctor spoke with feeling, 'Yes!'

'The 'clan' thing again! Try playing another tune, Matt, please.'

'Okay, Katie was recently harassed by an ex boyfriend - same guy Sarah went out with too.'

'Not very good taste in men then.'

'No, probably not. Does any woman?'

'I'm here with you, aren't I?'

'I thought this was official business.'

Azzra smiled, 'Combining business with pleasure. Right.'

Proctor relaxed a little, held up his wine glass, 'Cheers.'

'So, Sarah went out with this Phil...'

'Phil Dutson.'

'He used to be with Katie, she gave him the big E.' he paused, 'Sarah's next.'

'What about Sarah?'

Proctor's mouth puckered, he said. 'I'm serious, I think Sarah's life's in danger. They're out for revenge.'

'Oh come on, Matt, let's stick with the real world. Now, Phil knew them both, did he threaten Katie?'

'Well, not that I know. She told Sarah they had a big row when she dumped him, though. Nor would she go back to him when he tackled her.'

Azzra stared at Proctor, then said, 'Although Katie was your niece, Matt - there were things going on in her life you didn't know about.'

'Like what?'

Azzra shifted in her seat.

Proctor said, 'For Christ's sake. Azzra, this is a family tragedy, what do you mean?'

'Katie was having an affair with... someone.'.

'Well. Well, you have been busy.'

'From Hall's Stockholders.'

'A certain Graham Hall?'

Azzra pursed her lips and said, 'You knew?'

'Not long,' Proctor said. 'Katie told me - us. Talk about remorse.'

Azzra said, "It took a while for us to get him to admit it - but once he realised why we were pushing him, he opened up.' She frowned, 'You could have saved us time and trouble there.'

'Right, right.' He drew a deep breath, 'Sorry, so you have Hall in the frame for Katie's murder?.'

'Maybe. And a young black lad who scarpered after taking Katie out of the club.'

'Known?'

'You know him.'

'I do.'

She leaned closer to Proctor and lowered her voice to little more than a whisper, 'Sweet little Baz Manning.'

Proctor stood up and walked a short distance away, his hands stuffed into his trouser pockets. When he came back his features were determined.

'Hall did not kill Katie. Too much to lose. Nor did Baz Manning - wouldn't have the balls to do anything so horrific.'

'Matt, think for heaven's sake. Opportunity and motive. Hall was heard by Teresa to threaten Katie when she said she'd tell his wife about their affair. And Baz left the club with Katie; he was seen running off up Broad Street - and the next thing is your Sarah stumbles over Katie's dead body. We couldn't have two clearer suspects!

'I still think there's a link to that internet stuff.'

'Forget the internet stuff - it's Broad Street, that's where it happened, not in bloody cyberspace.'

Proctor closed his hands together, 'Listen Azzra, I've had a heavy couple of days, I need to get away from this for a bit.'

She leaned forward and stared hard into his eyes, 'Matt, I don't want to do this - but I have to ask you some questions.'

There was silence as they looked straight at each other.

'Matt, I'm leading this investigation, I need to ask you.'

'I know.'

She drew a deep breath, 'Where were you between eleven pm and midnight on Christmas Eve?'

'At home, drinking.'

'On your own?'

'Yes, yes, I was on my own.'

'Thank you. I need to speak to Sarah again. Will you bring her to the station please?'

'Dad, I'm nervous about this.'

Proctor put his arm around Sarah. 'I know', he said, 'I know'.

'Can you come in with me - when they ask all these questions?'

'Yes, of course.'

They waited in Brasshouse Lane police station. The journey in had been horrendous. Proctor believed the traffic problems of Birmingham were getting as bad as London's. They arrived late for the appointment with Azzra and Stevie Cole.

Proctor fought to control his temper. He knew he was being stupid. Azzra was the Senior Investigating Officer in the case, the top guy in the enquiry. She had her team around her, good people, good detectives. And she'd been generous with information, keeping him informed about developments she didn't have to tell him. He appreciated that, but he was still angry. He now listened to her as she filled in the gaps for him.

Sarah's information had been put through to the HOLMES Receiver, documented, logged. CCTV film of vehicles on Broad Street on Christmas Eve were examined, connections made. Hall's car was caught on camera; he was recorded having a brief exchange with a very drunk Katie near where her body was found. Under caution he explained what he was doing there - looking for a prostitute. The trophy wife was none too pleased. Apparently he was unable to get into his own house - all the locks had been changed.

Baz was also captured earlier on camera but nothing showing the actual attack on Katie. The power outage on Broad Street left gaps in the camera recording.

Azzra and the investigating team were now pursuing a single line of enquiry. Emma O'Rourke had put it the simplest terms. According to Azzra she said the straightforward job was find and apprehend Baz Manning, 'Get the nasty little shit off the street and locked up'. That had come from the very top. An early arrest was what the public wanted - the pre election polls all showed that.

Proctor knew in his heart of hearts it was wrong. No way did Baz Manning kill Katie. No way.

He drove Sarah home; she was quiet. He reached over and squeezed her hand, she gave a little smile and said, 'Don't worry, dad, I'll be all right.'

Chapter 44

Proctor swallowed another drop of Scotch in The Old Joint Stock while Ron sipped his own poison, London Pride beer. Proctor was getting maudlin. As he listened to Ron he thought about the vicissitudes of life. One moment you're up. Then you're down. There was no pattern to it, no sense. He felt for Penny and Cyril - Katie dead, would they ever get over it? He thought of his mother's breakdown and suicide after being stalked, now more stalkers had followed Katie and Sarah - and Katie was dead.

Hall out of the frame now - Baz being hunted by the police. His own situation seemed paltry by comparison. What if Sarah had walked out of the club with Baz? His stomach lurched at the thought. He slammed the glass on the bar.

Kydd brought him back to the present. 'Easy, Matt. So what are you going to do now?'

He phrased the question in a calm manner. Proctor knew where Kydd was coming from, trying to temper his anger. Yet the fury raging inside Proctor wanted out. He knew that was what Ron's question was about, to help him to spill out his bile, his rage. He took several deep breaths and reached over and put his hand on Ron's arm. 'Thanks.'

Ron smiled, 'Getting home time, Matt?'

'Yeah, you're right.'

Ron dropped Proctor off at about midnight. Sarah's bedroom curtains were closed so he guessed she would be fast asleep. He put the key in the lock and stepped inside. His heart lurched when he saw a smear of blood on the carpet. Barney wasn't lying on his rug. He rushed through to the kitchen, fell on his knees and groaned. He put his arm around Barney, stared at the dog's tongue protruding from its mouth, touched the deep gash around the dog's throat.

'No, no.' He leaped to his feet and rushed upstairs, burst into Sarah's room. She lay fast asleep, her breathing slow and rhythmical, her hand resting on an open book on top of the duvet. Proctor slumped against her bed. She woke up and in a drowsy voice said, 'Dad, hello.'

'You all right?' he asked.

She went to sit up, he said, 'It's okay, I just wanted to check on you.'

'I was dead tired when I got back. Came straight upstairs to bed.'

'You were out? When did you get back?'

'Not long.' She struggled to keep her eyes open, 'Chris and Millie asked me over to their place, haven't been there. Nice, I think Millie's teaching Chris housework.'

'Chris and Millie well?'

'Yes, yes, getting on like a house on fire, those two. We all needed to talk, dad, together, you know?' She yawned and Proctor held back about Barney.

'Yes, yes, I know. Good, good, go back to sleep then. See you in the morning.'

She turned on her side and pulled the duvet up over her shoulders. He stood by the bedroom door watching the gentle movement of her body as she went back to sleep, thinking what if... what if she'd stayed in, hadn't got back home late.

He wiped the back of his hand across his eyes as he went to the still, cold body of Barney. He lifted the dog and carried it to the garage and threw a dustsheet across the body.

Chapter 45

Chris Proctor's fingers danced across the computer keyboard as he drilled down into the heart of the operating system, unmasking programme files that Matt Proctor never knew existed. He worked non-stop for a couple of hours while Proctor supplied a stream of coffee.

Sarah watched in silence, flicking through a magazine but not taking any of it in. Proctor leaned over Chris's shoulder. He said, 'How's it going?'

'Nearly there, look.'

The screen displayed tightly packed groups of word and symbols that made no sense to Proctor. Chris pointed to a couple of lines.

'See that string,' he said.

Proctor got closer, a name screamed out at him. 'Dutson'.

He shouted the name and Sarah looked up. Looking across at her, Chris said, 'The Nightwatchmen'; I've broken into the clan's identity register. Phil Dutson is one of their members, it'll take a few more hours but I think I can get all their identities. There are four of them.'

Proctor pointed to a section of text. 'What's kuru?'

'I remember coming across it when doing A level biology.' He hesitated then said, 'It's not nice, dad. Grisly stuff.'

'Let's hear it.'

Chris glanced over at Sarah, 'I'm thinking of what happened to Katie.'

Sarah threw her magazine on the floor and stormed over to look at the computer screen. She said, 'I want to know.'

Proctor recalled how he'd carried Barney's body to the car and drove off to the vets. Her tears were silent then and she had said little for nearly twenty four hours. He felt her anger now.

'Okay,' Chris said. 'Earlier I checked some of this stuff out on the internet. Got more detail than what I remembered. Basically - kuru is a Papua New Guinea natives' word. They practiced cannibalism. Result was they got fits of trembling, kuru means tremble.' He paused and said, 'Their brains rotted, became like sponges filled with holes.'

'Like CJD,' Sarah asked.

'Yes - or BSE in cows. Brains break up - become riddled.'

'Why would that stuff be on here?'

Chris was uncertain, 'Not sure. But there are stories of tribes - from all corners of the world - who believed that eating the brains of your enemies meant you absorbed their intelligence, increased your tribe's abilities in battle through superior thinking.'

Sarah gasped and put her hands over her mouth. She rushed upstairs and Proctor listened as she gagged in the toilet. 'Shit, he said.

'I told you it was grisly, dad.'

'So - the clan were following those rituals?'

'I think so - they scooped the brains from their victims...'

'Eating human brains.' Proctor covered his face in his hands. 'Poor Katie. Mad bastards.'

'Literally,' Chris said. 'I guess Martin researched this stuff - like kuru - but thought that healthy, bright people would have sound brains.'

'That's what happened to Dominic Masters.'

'The guy killed in Victoria Square, right?'

'Yes. Police kept details under wraps, about the hole drilled in his head. You know how the sensationalist press run stories like that. Would have scared the wits out of people.'

Chris frowned and was quiet for a time. He said, 'So the clan got to Masters and killed him - in the same way they killed Katie. Did he play Hollowcost?'

'I'll bet he did. And if those websites he'd got listed had been allocated proper computer forensics, we might have got to the bastards before Katie...'

'Dad, mind your language. You're not setting your son a good example.' He tried to smile but it was a forced smile that soon vanished. He tapped the keyboard, 'I need to get to into their hard disks.' Proctor saw symbols appear on the screen that were gobbledegook to him. 'l33t'; Snark; 'lolspeak'. Proctor frowned.

'Webspeak, dad, need to work through several computers.'

Proctor said, 'Webspeak? Bloody Geekspeak I think.'

'There,' Chris said. He entered, 'Dominic Masters.'

He looked up, bobbing his head, 'He played Hollowcost - he was part of a clan that played out of the university.'

Proctor patted Chris on the shoulder, looked at the screen, 'You've done well. Can you save or copy this stuff? I'll need to show it to Azzra Mukherjee.'

'Been seeing her a lot, haven't you?' Chris gave Proctor another slight smile and carried on tapping the keyboard.'

'Mind yourself, young man.'

'Sound just like Cloughie in the film.'

Proctor said, 'I'm going to have a beer, fancy one?'

'Yes, please.' He stood up, 'I need one, dad.'

Proctor called up to Sarah, asked if she was all right. She said she'd be down soon.

He poured the beers, thought about what Chris had unearthed. He couldn't get the image of Katie lying in a puddle in Broad Street with a hole dug into her head out of his mind.

He also remembered Barney. He looked to the rug where the dog loved to lie; he placed both hands on the kitchen worktop to support himself. That was it. Enough's enough.

He called through to Chris, 'With what you've got there, Chris, can you make contact with them.'

'What - well, yes.'

'Tell Dutson I want to meet him. Anywhere, any time.'

'Is that wise, dad?'

'Probably not. But I need to stop him, whatever I have to do.'

Chapter 46

Twenty four hours later Chris, Sarah and Millie sat around the kitchen table in Proctor's house drinking coffee. Sarah's eyes were still red-rimmed and for minutes at a time she went into a kind of daze. Barney had been her dog, brought home by Proctor on her tenth birthday. Millie pushed her coffee cup towards her, 'Drink your coffee, Sarah, do you want to watch a DVD later.'

Sarah made an effort to smile. She said, 'Where'd dad say he was going?'

Chris exchanged a glance with Millie, 'Out, meeting someone.'

'You both spent an eternity on that computer last night.'

Millie snorted, 'Sometimes think he'd rather be tucked up in bed with that thing than me,' she stared with mock aggression at him.

'Don't think so, Mill...though cyber shagging's catching on. I could have an avatar and...

'Don't even go there, Chris Proctor!'

'Where is dad, Chris?' Sarah said.

'Like I say - he...went to meet someone.'

Sarah looked him straight in the eye. 'You're hiding something, aren't you?'

Millie followed her lead, 'Course he is, you can tell,' she leaned over putting her face inches away from his. 'It's a girl thing - we can tell!'

Chris pushed back his chair and went to the tap, drew off a glass of water and drank it down in a long swallow.

'Give,' Millie said.

He leaned against the worktop, exhaled loudly and said. 'Dutson, he's gone to meet Phil Dutson.'

'What! Why?' Sarah jumped to her feet.

Chris held up his hands. 'When we were on the computer last night I hacked in to several websites - and password controlled email addresses.'

Millie gasped, 'You can do that sort of stuff.'

He shrugged. 'Anyway,' he looked at Sarah, 'Phil Dutson is one of The Nightwatchmen'.

'A what?' Millie screamed.

Sarah said, 'It's a...clan, a computer gaming clan. Katie and me - we played them in this game. They got mega pissed off with us beating them.'

'Beating them - in a computer game. They killed Katie for beating them in a bloody computer game - they mad or something?'

Chris said, 'Probably.'

'Have you told anyone - about this meet?' Sarah asked.

Chris shook his head. 'He wanted to - Sarah, he's had enough!'

'Dad's lost it, all this worry.' She thought for several seconds, 'We need to tell someone - you know where this meet is?'

'Yes,' Chris said.

'Where then?' she yelled.

'Place above Ron Kydd's offices - old disused workshop in the Jewellery Quarter.

'Right, I'll call 999.'

'No, wait.' He pulled out his mobile and opened the contacts list. 'He...he gave me a number, said only use it if there's an emergency.'

'Oh, shit.' Sarah grabbed the phone. 'Who?'

'Azzra - Azzra Mukherjee.'

She pressed the call button and listened to the dialling tone ring out.

Chapter 47

The four figures approached the building at ten pm. The street was quiet, dark; down one side was a line of cars, displaying resident only permits, parked nose to tail. Two hundred yards away, a car emerged from one of the few remaining drinking pubs, turned away from where the group stood, its engine note faded in the distance.

The lead figure held one hand up. Gestured to the others to follow. He pointed to his head. All four pulled balaclavas over their faces. The front figure moved towards a tall ground floor window in the building. He reached up, inserted a tool and a minute later, they all crawled through the window into the building. The last person in passed over a heavy oblong box; slid the window shut behind him.

They moved fast as a unit up the concrete stairs, along a corridor making brief stops while the front man shone a heavy duty torch ahead. He held up his hand, located a cupboard that he opened, shone the torch inside, threw on the old mains switch. The sharp click echoed down the bare brick walled corridor. They waited; moved forward again.

They reached a closed door, the first man inserted a key, turned the lock. The lead man stretched his arm inside, searched for a light switch and turned it on. A single bulb lit up.

Proctor sat alone at a bare table in the centre of a large workshop, both his hands resting on the table surface. Old scarred workbenches stood against the walls, obsolete angle lamps hovered like crooked claws over the benches, where discarded tools and bits of metal lay. Cracks and flaking grey paint marred the concrete floor. A smell of damp and mildew hung in the air.

Proctor wore a jacket and an open-necked black shirt. Black stubble darkened his face. The four figures stopped in their tracks for a moment when they saw him.

He studied them, in their balaclavas, camouflage jackets, combat boots. Of the four, three were well built, burly; one was of a slight build - Skinny.

'What kept you?' he said. 'Thought you'd come mob-handed as a reception party?' Proctor studied them in silence for a time. 'Which of you bastards is Dutson, then?'

One of the group padded over to Proctor, stood over him from across the table. 'You shouldn't have played the game.'

Proctor stared at him, 'I don't play games - that's a no-brainer, Dutson.'

He expected the smack on the mouth, leaned away as it came. Caught it. He spat blood.

'There is no Dutson! I am The Man. We are the Nightwatchmen. Warriors of the Cyberworld.' He slammed his torch down on the table. 'You are one mad bastard, Proctor.' He gestured around the empty building. 'Got a death wish - like little Katie, like The Knifethrowers? Losers! Your daughter Sarah's next. After you.'

Proctor shot to his feet and flung out a fist. The two burly men hurled themselves at him, grabbed his arms and pinned them back, smashing his head down against the table.

'That's it - sort him,' The Man shouted. He turned to the fourth man, 'Skinny', 'Do it - now.'

The tall, thin man scurried to open the plastic toolbox and got out a roll of ducting tape. The others bundled Proctor back into the chair; the slight man wound the tape around Proctor's body, arms and legs until he was strait-jacketed.

'You should not have got involved,' The Man spoke quietly, but the rage in his voice betrayed his attempt at calm. 'You thought you could defeat the best soldiers, the best warriors.'

'Soldiers, warriors. Men of honour, eh? Meet me alone, you said - Dutson.'

The Man pushed his head close to Proctor, spoke in a tight whisper, 'We won - we always win,' He placed a gloved hand on Proctor's head, ran his fingers over it in a caressing movement. 'Now we take the prize. I'll bet you have something really juicy inside there.'

He snatched his hand back and looked at the others, pointed to the toolbox and said, 'We do it now.' He faced Proctor, 'Now, you will find out what happens in the game. Ever wondered what it's like to have your brains sucked out - while you're still alive?' He gave a high pitched laugh. 'A first for us too.' Another high-pitched laugh on the verge of hysteria.

Proctor felt his resolve fade. Where the hell was Ron Kydd? He'd told him ten o'clock at latest. Had Ron been unable to stir the West Midlands police's finest into action - had they thought him some kind of eccentric nutter rabbiting on about brain eating computer maniacs?

Skinny' removed a set of electric mains leads from the toolbox, stepped in slow strides to Proctor and hesitated.

'Do it, do it - now. This was what you wanted, do it!' Dutton screamed and behind his balaclava his eyes bulged. He reached into his jacket and pulled out a pistol, pointed it at his accomplice. 'Do it, do it. Now!'

'Skinny's' head jerked up at the sound of The Man's raging voice. He dropped the leads and grabbed Proctor's trousers and shorts, ripped them down. He picked up the leads and pinched the crocodile clips over each of Proctor's balls. Proctor shouted as the clips bit in.

'Skinny' trailed the leads across the floor to a wall socket, inserted the plug. He held his hand over the socket switch.

'Do it, fucking do it.' The Man waved the gun.

Proctor closed his eyes, braced himself and felt tears well. Big mistake, big time mistake. He clenched his hands. The tape crushed his chest, he wanted to explode his breath, smash off the bindings. He closed his eyes tighter as he waited for the pain. Wanted to welcome it.

A mobile phone text message signal went off; The Man froze, opened the phone and looked at the text message, he read it several times, his mouth opening and shutting. He said, 'So, your Sarah, she wants to play the game then, one last battle?' He leaned over Proctor, his voice was shrill as he said, 'Dear little Sarah wants to play - with her dear dad as her fellow warrior, isn't that sweet of her?' He tapped a reply, sent it. Closed the phone, pointed the gun at Proctor. 'Sure, we'll play. Then we drain you of power; next we suck your daughter dry.' His laugh sounded more hysterical than ever, even crazy.

Proctor's heart went into overdrive, he gasped.

The Man swung his gun at Skinny. 'Open the Internet, free his hands.'

Skinny struggled to undo the tapes around Proctor. The Man's eyes bulged; he shoved Skinny away and grabbed the tape, ripped it off Proctor's arms and legs, who yelled in pain. The Man tapped a number a number into the phone, breathed in quick bursts as he waited for the call to be answered. His hand shook as he gripped the mobile. Shouted into it, 'Bitch. Your old man's about to play the game - get ready? Then we fry his balls.'

Skinny placed the laptop on the table. He opened the tool box and removed a terminal/monitor and game controller joystick that he connected with a cable to the laptop, pushed the controller in front of Proctor.

The Man sat in front of the screen opposite Proctor, signalled Skinny alongside. He nodded his head several times, 'Now - we play.' He pointed the gun across at Proctor, 'Then we eat your brain, and your clever daughter's - we learn all the secrets of the game, become masters of Hollowcost.'

Proctor shouted, 'All the secrets. I'll show you all the secrets.' He grabbed the monitor with both hands and drove the edge across the table smack into The Man's head. He heard bone crack and brought his hand down in a karate chop against The Man's gun holding wrist. He roared with pain and anger, the laptop fell across his thighs, he spilled his gun. The Man dived over the table at Proctor; knocked him flat, fell on top of him. Proctor glimpsed Skinny who had retrieved the laptop and held it close to his chest like a mother protecting her child. Proctor piled a fist into The Man's face and pushed him over, looked for the gun; gone. He ran to Skinny, grabbed the laptop as the other two goons stirred. The Man launched himself again; Proctor swung the laptop at him, heard the crunch as it struck his head. The Man fell to the floor. The laptop split in two. Proctor spotted the gun, scrambled after it and grabbing it, retreated to the warehouse door. He turned to face all four, pointed the gun at them.

The police ram hit the door like a bomb going off. Helmeted officers hurtled into the workshop, a voice shouted, 'Police, police, on the floor, on the floor.' Two officers threw themselves at the Nightwatchmen heavies, a third hit Skinny across the shoulders with a riot stick, he crumpled to the floor. The Man took off across the workshop into unlit recesses at the far end.

Azzra Mukherjee ran to Proctor. She looked at him for several seconds, he saw the tense smile behind her visor. She called an officer over, 'Cover him up, someone please.' She glanced at tape still adhering to his legs, 'And cut that off.'

The policeman reached into his clip belt and took out a small knife. She said, 'Try not to cut anything else off.'

Proctor listened to The Man's shouts and screams echo down the workshop. He suspected he was offering resistance - and he guessed the police were more than happy about that. The longer the resistance the more time to dole out a hammering. Azzra looked at the three apprehended men, then down the building; looked away again. She spoke into her intercom. 'Control'.

Ron Kydd walked up to Proctor.

'Took your time, Ron, didn't you?'

'My delay caused me considerable frustration, dear friend.'

'Right. Nearly got me bloody electrocuted.'

Kydd said, 'Look who's here.' Sarah emerged through the doorway. 'You owe her a big thank you.'

'Sarah!' Proctor flung out his arms and hugged his daughter. 'You bought me time. I was a goner there. Thanks.'

'She made contact with Azzra - I was getting nowhere.' Ron pointed to Proctor's groin, 'Can you put those away, old chap, not for public consumption, what? Frighten the life out of your daughter.' Sarah suppressed a smile, looked away.

Proctor pulled up his pants. He watched the police remove the balaclavas from their captors - he didn't recognise two of them. The man with the toolbox he did know - it was Martin, Chris's uni buddy. Skinny Martin - the Geek. He watched as The Man was dragged into the light, balaclava removed - a well battered Phil Dutson's face exposed.

Chapter 48

Detective Chief Superintendent Emma O'Rourke sat at her desk when Proctor and Azzra entered her office. She shot up from her chair and came around her desk; she shook both their hands.

'Please, Matt, Azzra, take a seat.' She gave Proctor a tight little smile and returned behind her desk.

'Now then first things first - well, I'm not the best at apologising, but Matt, I'm sorry.' She glanced at a family photograph on her desk, 'Your niece's murder has shocked us all. Our deepest sympathies, Matt.'

Proctor acknowledged her apology, accepted her condolences, resisted the temptation to comment. He thought maybe at last he was learning.

O'Rourke said, 'Right, then. I think Azzra has kept you fairly up to date.'

'Yes, I'm grateful for that.'

O'Rourke's office had been redecorated, Proctor thought it seemed softer, more feminine. He studied Emma's appearance. She had changed her hairstyle and her face looked gentler, more relaxed. More made up too, he thought. On her desk was a photograph; he studied it more closely. Two young women in graduation gowns, and Emma with a man. The photograph was new. He said, 'Your daughters, Emma? You must be proud of them.'

'Yes, yes, both got their studies behind them now, both working in fact. My police salary might go further in future.' She watched Proctor and Azzra study the framed picture.

'And that's Philip.' She didn't add anything further, neither Azzra nor Proctor said anything, kept their faces still.

'So,' Emma clapped her hands together. 'A brief recap - and then we want to see you back in harness, Matt.' She pulled her lips together, gave a small shake of her head. 'You've had a hard time of late, Matt. ACC Merritt will confirm it's all over after this meeting.'

'Sounds good to me, Emma,' Proctor said.

Azzra shifted in her chair.

'First, Dutson. He's in custody, was extremely truculent at the start - but quieter now. Azzra, would you like to say more?'

'He was an undisciplined soldier. Word is he killed a superior officer in action but nothing could be proved. Not too careful either when it came to Iraqi civilians. Anyway, when he came out he met up with a couple of other disaffected soldiers. Probably traumatised too. They were all good technicians - got into computers through a retraining programme but took to game playing instead of work.' She paused, 'And fantasising.'

Proctor asked, 'How'd they meet the Geek?'

'Through the Internet, they realised he was especially good at this Hollowcost thing. They recruited him into their clan.'

O'Rourke said, 'I know I said all this was fanciful - but why would Martin join up with a bunch of tough ex-soldiers?'

'He needed to feel a "man".' Azzra looked at Proctor, 'Chris identified that. Said Martin had military books, memorabilia, he wasn't happy to be just a computer nerd - he needed more.'

'This brain stuff - where on earth did that come from?' Emma turned up her face in disgust.

Azzra said, 'Again we got this from Chris. It appears that as well as being an expert on military memorabilia, Martin read about anthropology. Ancient tribes, ritualistic stuff.' She became thoughtful, 'Sad in some ways, once we got him talking about that his eyes lit up - like a zealot - he believed that stuff about improving your intellect and strength by consuming others' brains. The clan didn't need much convincing; they were already desensitised.'

'Dutson seemed just a thug, hardly into anthropology,' O'Rourke said.

'I know - we pressed him.' She looked at both in turn. 'He did it before - on a fellow soldier.'

'Ugh,' O'Rourke said.

'So,' Proctor said, 'he was already a convert - Martin's words must have come like an affirmation of faith.'

O'Rourke sat up straight. 'Enough of this sick mind business. More straightforward policing stuff, please.'

She outlined how forensic evidence showed Martin's DNA traces on the wire that garrotted Katie. From CCTV footage outside the gent's toilet and on Broad Street, they had developed a scenario.

When Martin saw Katie leave the club with Baz, he went to the toilet, then exited the club by the emergency rear exit door that he left open. Once he reached Katie, she was on her own. He strangled her with the wire garrotte, then ran back into the club via the same door.

'No harm done by Baz then?' Proctor said.

'No, odd thing that, camera shows Baz buggering off leaving Katie alone in the street.'

'That's what Karen saw as well,' Azzra said.

O'Rourke said, 'She's unreliable - was well pissed.'

'Something - or someone - frightened Baz off,' Proctor said.

O'Rourke said, 'So, to his friends' knowledge sat inside the club, Martin had only been away at the toilet - not outside.'

'But he must have come back soaking wet? And got caught outside on CCTV video like Baz?' Proctor said.

Azzra said, 'No. There was an outage - the damned weather that night. CCTV stayed down after the outage. He did have a big brain, did Martin. Carried a rucksack everywhere he went. Change of clothes - and...'

Proctor looked at the floor, 'And a drill.'

'And a drill.'

O'Rourke was quiet for a while. She said, 'When Martin returned back into the club, that was when Sarah reappeared and asked about Katie's whereabouts.'

Azzra listened. She chipped in, her voice low. 'Martin wept telling us about it. He said...' She spoke in a concentrated way recalling his exact words, 'I wanted to be a clan member, to prove myself to them, to...prove I was a real soldier too.'

Proctor said, 'So they delegated to Martin the Geek the prize of killing Katie - his 'rites of passage' clan initiation. As all soldiers must go through.' He smiled a sweet smile at O'Rourke.

O'Rourke glanced at her watch, held her hands up, 'And you already know about Hall, fraud charges being brought.' She glared at Proctor then softened her appearance, coughed, 'We still haven't found that little toerag, Baz Manning yet.'

Proctor looked up quickly, 'What's he got to do with anything?'

'He left the club with Katie, last person to see her alive.'

'No, he wasn't. Martin was.'

Again she held up her arms.

O'Rourke's phone rang. She listened, 'ACC Merritt can see us now,' she said. 'I think the Chief wants to look in as well.' She glanced at Proctor, a warning glint in her eye.

She looked through the window, 'We can walk over to Police H/Q, only take five minutes, fresh air will do us good.' She stood up and patted her stomach, Proctor thought she looked like she had lost a stone in weight. He exchanged a smile with Azzra.

Inside ACC Merritt's office, the formalities were exchanged. Merritt walked around his desk, devoid of paper as usual, sat down to control the meeting.

'So, why was I stitched up?' Proctor stared at ACC Merritt.

A silence dropped. Merritt held the silence then sighed.

'Listen, we're all friends here, so this is in strictest confidence. I mean that.' He waited for each to register assent before he continued, 'We had to get you out of the way. You were the elephant in the room.'

'Elephants have long memories.'

Merritt pointed a finger, 'Don't rile me.'

Merritt got up and walked to the window. 'We have a lot of villains out there. One, we must find the evidence; two, arrest the culprits; three, bring them to court.' He faced his three colleagues, 'Not rocket science, is it? No, it's not. But sometimes - often - we have other matters to consider.'

'Like politics,' Proctor said.

Merritt shot him a sharp glance, 'That's true. But something else as well. Sometimes we have to make sure the right hand does not know what the left hand is doing.' He paused, 'The anti corruption team were on to Romney and Carpenter. When Romney came with his 'allegations' against you, we knew what he was up to, Matt. You see, those two weren't the only ones in the frame.'

Proctor gave a short laugh. 'Right,' he said.

'You whistle blowing would have scuppered twelve months of undercover work.' He spread his hands, 'It was a tough call, Matt

- they had to believe they weren't rumbled. They were part of a network. Sorry.'

Two apologies in a day from the hierarchy. Proctor looked around for the flying pigs. 'And the politics?' he said.

Merritt shrugged, 'That's always there. But with a by-election imminent; shit flying is the last thing wanted. You had to go off the radar.' He rose from his chair and walked round the desk, sat on the edge of it close to Proctor. 'We want police officers like you in the service, Matt, you know that?'

Proctor got up and went to the window, stood there for a few seconds then returned and sat down.

'Romney and Cartwright?'

'For the high jump.'

'Not Belfast, then.'

Merritt smiled, 'They've got enough problems over there.' He took a deep breath, 'So, maybe we can get you back into circulation, right?'

Proctor said, 'I'm looking forward to that.'

Merritt looked at O'Rourke and Azzra, 'You've all done a good job here. Congratulations.'

'One thing, Jon,' Proctor said.

'What's that?'

'Baz Manning and Ranjit Hassan.'

'What about them?'

Emma O'Rourke jumped in, 'We can pull in Hassan any time, Manning's proving more elusive, sir.'

'Emma, Baz Manning is a small time druggie.' Proctor went on, 'He needs a break - he did a runner on Broad Street because a crew were after him. He owed them stuff and cash. They would have cut him. He scarpered and left Katie alone.'

Azzra and O'Rourke stared at him.

'What - how do you know that?' Azzra stammered.

Proctor hesitated, 'Through good police work.'

Azzra tightened her mouth, 'Bloody Stevie Cole, wait till I...'

Merrit held up his hand, 'So, Matt, what do you have in mind?'

'No charges brought against Hassan or Baz. I want Hassan as a snout - with what we can get from him, we can clean up the city much better than an election address will. And we give Baz a fresh start. You need his evidence anyway to nail Romney and the rest.'

'I want that little sod Manning charged,' O'Rourke hissed, 'He put us to a lot of unnecessary trouble.'

Azzra looked away and bit her lip.

Merritt said, 'No way, Matt, the law must take its course.'

Proctor said, 'Be a shame if a corrupt cops and drugs bribes story somehow leaked to the press before the chairman's election...sir?'

O'Rourke and Azzra looked aghast.

Merritt froze, 'Are you threatening me? I can have your guts for garters.'

Proctor shrugged, 'So be it'.

Merritt shoved his face close up against Proctor's, 'Sometimes I think you have a death wish, Matt.'

Proctor held his eye. 'You're not the first person who's said that to me.'

Merritt opened and shut his mouth a couple of times, 'Stay here,' he fumed. He slammed his door behind him; O'Rourke and Azzra looked stunned.

Proctor started humming to the tune from The Wizard of Oz film.

O'Rourke said, 'Matt, you had better apologise - and fast.'

Proctor stopped humming and began to sing words to the same tune, 'We're off to see the chief cop, the wonderful chief cop of police'. He whistled the tune as he stared out the window at the busy city scene below.

Merritt returned; he was calmer, he wore a thin smile. He addressed Proctor 'Did you know I'm going to be Deputy Chief?'

'No, sir, congratulations. It was always likely. Well done.'

He pulled his chest up, 'Yes, the Chief's just confirmed it to me. Press release going out,' he looked at his watch, 'right now in fact.'

'DCC Jolly's had a good innings, we'll all be sorry to see old Bill go.'

'That's true. Do you know something else, Matt?'

'What's that, Jon?'

'I don't like being blackmailed.'

'A lot of things people don't like. Blackmail, gardening leave…political suicide. Sir?'

'I won't forget this!' He pointed at Proctor, 'My arms are long; I'll have my eyes on you, sunshine'. He squeezed out his next words, 'The Chief agrees with your thoughts on Hassan and Baz.' He dismissed all three with a wave of his hand.

Merritt's newly promoted PA Julie Anderson shook her head staring down all the time at her desk as Proctor left the office, in the wake of O'Rourke and Azzra. She switched off an intercom and looked up, whispered, 'You aren't half a chancer, Matt Proctor.' She held his gaze as she said, 'You do know how much we felt for you - for your poor niece Katie when…' her voice trailed away.

'Thanks, Julie.'

Chapter 49

Azzra walked into Proctor's new office. She pointed to a chair, 'Do you mind?' she said.

He smiled as she sat down; she looked gaunt and there were shadows under her eyes. 'Feel I've been on a rollercoaster, Matt. Don't know if I can take much more of this.'

Proctor walked around his desk. He hunkered down in front of her and held both her hands. 'You can, Azzra, you can. We both can.'

Her smile came slowly; she squeezed his hands, 'Yes. Yes.'

Look out for the next Matt Proctor novel…
visit tombrysonwriter.co.uk for details.

IN IT FOR THE MONEY

Chapter 1

'H -are you all right? What is it?'

A sinking feeling hit Chief Inspector Matt Proctor's stomach.

'What?'

Harry 'H' McGeady couldn't speak. His mouth dropped open. What little colour was left in his face drained away leaving a corpse like pallor. His hands trembled and travelled to his face as he looked over Proctor's shoulder. Proctor turned his head to follow bookmaker Harry McGeady's eye line.

Only two minutes earlier Chief Inspector Matt Proctor had approached Harry McGeady's betting shop in the city centre with a spring in his step. It was late afternoon in October but felt like a summer's day. A golden sun sparkled in the blue sky and even Birmingham's city centre motorists were conceding road space to fellow travellers and driving with smiles on their faces. He couldn't hear a single horn hoot.

Life was good - he'd just driven from across town after a great day's cricket, scored with a winning bet on the horses and his daughter Sarah had phoned on her mobile to tell him she'd at last got rid of that spacewaster of a boyfriend. He fished around in his jacket pocket and retrieved a crumpled betting slip. He mentally rubbed his hands together. Time to collect!

Proctor wrinkled his nose and held his breath as he negotiated his way past two smokers standing by the bookmaker's entrance; as an ex-smoker he didn't want the temptation of a blast of nicotine re-igniting his habit. He stepped inside, blew out his cheeks and glanced up at the large television screen; a meeting at Worcester was on and the next race about to start. A loud commentator's voice ran through the runners and the latest odds watched by several grey faced punters, 'Jolly Fiddler is strongly fancied following a recent return to form and a victory at Lingfield last week. A lot of money following this popular horse, certainly the housewife's favourite.' In the background a tinny speaker competed with the television relaying live information from the course.

Proctor ambled up to the betting clerk's hatch and presented his winning slip, an unusual smile playing on his lips. Why, even his boss Chief Superintendent Emma O'Rourke looked pleased with herself these days - amazing what the new man in her life had done. Last time he saw her in the office she positively glowed and he guessed she'd dropped a few pounds. Mind you, plenty left to shed.

'Harry around?' he asked the bored looking teller who glanced up, nodded his head towards the back office, resumed staring down at his records. Proctor waited and pulled up his tan leather windcheater jacket zip an inch or so, he flicked a loose thread from his cream chinos. The teller yawned. Proctor leaned forward, stuck his chin out, 'Call him, tell him I want to say hello. Like now.'

The clerk's head came up, he looked startled, 'H - someone to see you,' he shouted, his voice high-pitched.

A muffled reply came from a side door. Harry McGeady, bookmaker, scallywag and the best snout Proctor had ever used emerged from his warren. He had proved invaluable to Proctor over the years, given him leads in a lot of tough cases. Although Chief

Superintendent O'Rourke wasn't that amused when she saw Proctor's expenses claims for McGeady's services. She believed that snouts, along with bookmakers, were only a shade above villains in the population respectability stakes - he wondered if she ever considered how police work and crime solving could cope without them.

Proctor went rigid and the corners of his mouth fell as he took in McGeady's appearance; his pasty complexion, haggard face and baggy eyes. He frowned and held out his hand and said, 'H, what's the matter, you look like shite.'

McGeady stared at Proctor through listless eyes, 'Yeah, bad times, Guv, bad times.' His handshake was as damp and limp as a wet rag. Even his normally pristine comb-over was dishevelled displaying his pale bald skull. He appeared to have shrunk six inches.

That was when McGeady looked over Proctor's shoulder; when Proctor turned around.

About the Author

Tom Bryson was born and grew up in Northern Ireland in the historic city of Derry - Londonderry aptly coined 'Stroke City'. He lives in the West Midlands of England and worked in engineering, local government and public transport. His specialisms are HR, training consultancy and writing/editing.

Tom now resides and writes in the attractive village of Kinver in south Staffordshire. He writes novels, plays and short stories. He is developing an e-Book/POD publishing venture and a website with the support and encouragement of his wife Jane and offspring expertise. His short stories have been included in anthologies with some broadcasts and plays professionally directed and performed in West Midlands theatres/arts venues.

His latest novel is nearing completion; once more featuring DCI Matt Proctor whose murder investigations take him into the deadly world of sport's spot fixing gambling syndicates.

Extracts from the novels and a selection of short stories and plays can be read or downloaded from his website.

www.tombrysonwriter.co.uk